ONLY THE LONELY

A Death Gate Grim Reapers Thriller Book One

AMANDA M. LEE

Copyright © 2018 by Amanda M. Lee

All rights reserved.

No part of this book may be reproduced in any form or by any electronic or mechanical means, including information storage and retrieval systems, without written permission from the author, except for the use of brief quotations in a book review.

❀ Created with Vellum

Prologue
TWENTY YEARS AGO

Belle Isle.
Belle Isle.
To me, it sounded like a fantasy land where magic things could happen. When I heard my parents talk about the island, though, they seemed ... less excited. I didn't know how else to phrase it.

Even now, as they worked next to the shimmering gate that led to what I thought of as other worlds, they made fun of the island and its lack of offerings.

"I just want a good cup of coffee," Mom supplied, as she wrinkled her nose and sipped from the mug Dad had handed her moments before. "I don't think that's too much to ask. If they expect us to work here, we most definitely should be able to get good coffee."

"Perhaps they're considering making caffeine a banned substance," Dad offered as he moved behind me, slowing his pace to monitor what I was doing. "If that happens, dear, you'll have to register as an addict."

"Screw that." Mom wasn't paying attention to Dad's gaze so she didn't notice it was focused on me. "I'll do what everyone else does and hide my addiction. I think that works best for everyone ... including our blood-sucking friends."

"Uh-huh." Absently, Dad knit his eyebrows and knelt to look at my drawing pad. "What are you doing, Izzy?"

I shifted my eyes to him, his tone making me wary. I was only seven, but my parents said I was "wise beyond my years." I recognized when it was time to be careful about what I said. "Just drawing."

"I see. And what is that?"

I wasn't sure how to answer the question. "It's just ... something I saw in my head."

The gate's shimmer ratcheted up a notch, but my father didn't react, so I figured he was expecting it. His full attention seemed to be focused on me, which made me uncomfortable and happy at the same time. "You saw this in your head?"

My lips parted as I shifted on the cool floor, grabbing my stuffed dog for comfort as I nodded. The dog, a present from Santa the previous Christmas, was the one thing I toted with me wherever I went. The drawing pad, a gift from my mother, was a close second on my "favorite items" list. I liked to practice, drawing what I saw in person and dreams. My mother said I had a gift for it. "Did I do something wrong?"

"No, baby." Dad stroked the back of my head and forced a wan smile. He was trying to soothe me, but I didn't miss the look he shot Mom.

Finally, as if coming out of a trance, Mom dragged herself away from the computer she was focused on and joined us. The quizzical expression on her face immediately shifted to something else as she bent over and snatched the sheet of paper from my father. "Are you kidding me?"

Dad ignored Mom's outburst. "Izzy, what's in the picture?"

I didn't know how to answer. "It's just something I saw."

"But ... you had to see it somewhere. This isn't something you saw while playing outside. I need to know where you first saw it."

"I don't know where." I fought back tears as I clutched the dog to my chest. "I don't know where I saw it."

Dad licked his lips as he waged an internal war to maintain his temper. I recognized the expression on his face ... and I didn't like it. "Sweetheart, Daddy isn't mad at you. Not even a little. This picture, though, it's important. You had to see this somewhere. You're not in trouble. I need to know where you saw it."

"In my head."

Dad threw his hands in the air and made a disgusted sound in the back of his throat as he locked gazes with my mother. "I can't even ... ."

Mom, calmer, shoved him out of the way to move closer to me. "Sweetie, do you see things like this in your head often?"

I nodded. "All the time, especially at night ... and when I'm here."

Confusion was evident as she wrinkled her forehead. "Did you see this in your dreams?"

I shook my head. "One of the voices told me about that."

"What voices?"

I pointed at the shimmering death gate, the door my parents were supposed to guard. That was their only job. They made sure souls crossed over to the other side and nothing ever came back through the opening. I didn't pretend to understand what they did, but as I grew older things became clearer. It was almost magical how I was beginning to understand things.

"You hear voices from the gate?" This time Mom looked panicked when she glanced back at Dad. "Did you know that was possible?"

Dad shook his head as he rested his meaty hand on my shoulder. "I didn't. Maybe she's confused. Maybe ... she's not hearing what she thinks she's hearing."

"Well, I can guarantee she hears what you're saying now," Mom said dryly. "Don't talk about her as if she isn't here."

"Fine." Dad's eyes fired before he shifted them to me. "Izzy, what do the voices say?"

I shrugged, making sure the dog remained on my lap so I wouldn't accidentally lose him. I was well aware that he was my responsibility and, if he went missing, it would be my fault. My parents were big on personal responsibility.

"You don't know what they say?"

"They say different things," I replied finally. "They ask what I'm doing and who I am. They ask if I want to visit them. They want to know if they can visit me."

"Do you answer them?"

"Not really. I don't think they can hear me."

"Why do you think that?"

The question felt too complicated to answer. "I don't know. It's just something I feel. I ... I don't know." Frustration bubbled up.

Dad held up his hands in mock surrender as he forced a smile that was more of a grimace. "Okay. There's no reason to get worked up. It was a simple question."

"We were just curious is all," Mom added, her head jerking toward the gate when it made a crackling sound. "What was that?"

"I have no idea." Dad was instantly alert as he stood. "I've never heard it make that noise before."

"You don't have to worry," I offered, feeling the need to soothe. "It's going to be okay. It's just the voices. They say he's coming."

"Who is coming?"

I shrugged. "Whoever they're sending to see me."

"They're sending something to see you?" Mom's voice jumped an octave as the gate crackled again. "Izzy, why would they send someone to see you?"

"Because they think I can help them. I told them I couldn't, but they don't believe me. Maybe they'll believe me when he finally gets here. I'm tired of telling them I can't help and having them yell at me."

"They yell at you?" My father's panic was palpable when the gate crackled again. "What do they say?"

"I already told you."

Apparently my answer wasn't enough to appease my father, because he grabbed me around the waist and hauled me up. I managed to keep the dog clutched tight, but the drawings I'd worked on so painstakingly were left behind.

"We're leaving," Dad announced, striding toward the door.

"Shouldn't we call the home office?" Mom sounded nervous as she trailed behind.

"We'll call from the house. We're getting out of here right now."

I tilted my head when the whispering grew louder. "He's almost here."

Dad didn't wait to figure out who "he" was. "That way! Right now!"

He scurried toward the door, sparing a final glance for the flickering gate. He didn't wait around to see what came through.

That was probably a good thing. He'd seen the picture. That was enough.

One
PRESENT DAY

Two decades after my parents died, I returned home.
I'd spent more time off Belle Isle than on over the course of my life, but I still thought of it that way. *Home.* It felt weird to return, yet the excitement coursing through me was almost debilitating.

"So, you're Isabella, right?"

The cab driver taking me over MacArthur Bridge kept flicking his eyes to the rearview mirror to watch my reaction as we closed in on the isolated piece of land that split the Detroit River. He hadn't said much since picking me up at the airport — the cab was arranged for me by my new employers — but I had a feeling he was more than what he pretended to be. What that "more" was, though, wasn't easy to determine.

"Izzy," I corrected automatically, keeping my eyes out the window to stare at the water. It wasn't exactly blue, as you'd expect of ocean waves or certain lakes, but the slate gray greeting me matched the worry cascading through the pit of my stomach. My mood was gray, so it somehow made sense that the river matched.

"Izzy." The driver bobbed his head, as if mulling over the word. "I'm sorry. The paperwork I received said your name is Isabella."

"It is. I simply choose to go by Izzy."

"Not Bella?" Mirth flitted through the man's eyes. "I would think, given why you're here, it would make sense to go by the name Bella."

I grasped exactly what he was getting at and managed to hold on to my temper ... although just barely. "I prefer Izzy."

"I guess that makes sense."

Thankfully, the chatty driver must have picked up on my mood because he kept his mouth shut for the duration of the drive. Once the end of the bridge came into view, I found myself leaning forward, eyes straining to take in the island I hadn't seen since I was a child.

It had been so long between visits that I couldn't decide if the things I remembered were fact or fiction, so I had read up about the island to reacquaint myself. Those facts flooded my mind now.

Located in the Detroit River between Michigan and Ontario ... one and a half miles ... museum ... golf course ... lighthouse ... boathouse ... yacht club ... aquarium ... nature center ... casino. I didn't technically remember most of those things. The ones that seared themselves in my memory were the lighthouse, beach house and aquarium ... and a little cottage long since gone. I figured the rest would eventually work its way back to me.

The driver took me straight to the beach house, which wasn't what I wanted, but I was so eager to get rid of him I didn't argue.

"Thank you." I fumbled in my pocket for a tip, which he waved off.

"Your employers have already taken care of it."

I stared at him for a long beat. "Well, consider it a bonus." I pressed the twenty into his hand and took my suitcase handle from him. "Thank you for the ride."

The cabbie, who looked to be in his late forties or early fifties, appeared amused at my abrupt goodbye. "Good luck in your new position."

"Thank you."

I kept my suitcase close as I slung my leather carry-on bag over my shoulder and directed my attention to the large boathouse. The main floor, used for weddings and other events, had become something of a social gathering hall. The house I had lived in as a child had been destroyed, so I would occupy one of the second-floor rooms. I was warned it would be loud on weekends when the weather was fair, but to basically suck it up. I was eager to return to the island, so I readily agreed to all their demands and ignored the warnings. Now was not the time to be persnickety. That was for later.

The boathouse appeared empty when I walked through the front door. I cocked my head to the side as I searched for the telltale sounds that someone was inside. When that didn't happen, I turned my attention to the front desk. A slip of paper waited for me there, and as I approached I realized it contained instructions. It was basically an invitation to show myself to the second floor and unpack. It also explained that a golf cart awaited me outside the side door. That's it. No signature, and I wasn't sure the building was empty. Of course, I didn't really care. The boathouse wasn't my biggest concern. That was still to come.

I took the elevator to the second floor and found my bedroom relatively easily. I briefly searched my new abode — it was about the size of a hotel suite with a bedroom, living area and bathroom. There would be plenty of time to explore later. For now, I had more important things to do.

I found the golf cart, and while it started on the first turn of the key, I didn't pull out of the parking lot. Sadly, I couldn't remember the exact layout of the island, which meant I had to Google a map to find my way to the correct location. The aquarium was to the west — something I remembered well — but the exact roads remained a mystery. The island was small, so I knew the layout would come back to me within a few days. Still, my heart skipped a beat as I sped along Riverbank Drive until I found the road I was looking for. It didn't take long for the aquarium to swing into view ... and it was breathtaking.

To be fair, the aquarium wasn't overly large. It wasn't the sort of facility you might find on the east and west coasts, where money is poured into the operations budget because it's a huge tourist draw. The Belle Isle Aquarium was much smaller, basically housing some tropical fish and reptiles, along with specimens from the region, but the building itself was old and glorious.

I parked in the designated employee section. I was listed as part of the aquarium's upper management team, but I would have nothing to do with the day-to-day operations of the facility. That was for other people. Normal people. My title was a front because my real job lay behind the aquarium walls, where the gate was housed.

It was the gate that called me home, after all. It was the gate I needed to see now.

"Isabella Sage?"

I jerked my head to the left as I entered the aquarium lobby, forcing a smile for the young woman standing behind the counter. She seemed to be expecting me — at least that's what her bright eyes and sunny smile reflected — and the grin she lobbed in my direction was earnest enough to be grating. I didn't do earnest. I was a realist.

"Izzy," I automatically corrected. "Call me Izzy."

"Okay, Izzy." The woman was unfazed. "I'm Tara Middleton. I'm supposed to show you around."

I pursed my lips as I shifted my eyes to the main floor of the facility. "Who is going to watch this place if you're giving me a tour?"

Tara didn't seem concerned with the question. "It's March."

"I know."

"It's March in Michigan." Tara's smile never wavered. "We don't get a lot of visitors in the winter because the bridge isn't exactly fun to traverse during icy conditions. We won't see many visitors for at least another month — more like six weeks — and then we'll be slammed the entire summer season ... and early fall."

That made sense. I remembered snow from my childhood, of course, and I saw it on the national weather reports. After the incident, though, I had moved to New Orleans to live with my paternal grandfather, even though my maternal aunt was a local and wanted me to stay with her. My grandfather put his foot down and insisted I go with him ... and I wasn't sorry. I grew to love New Orleans and embraced the culture there — especially the Bruja women with their magical ideals and strong personalities — but my mind always wandered to this place and what I'd left behind. I figured there had to be a reason, and I had every intention of finding out what that reason entailed.

"I forgot about the cold." I offered her a rueful smile as I smoothed my onyx hair. It was long and straight — exactly as I liked it — and when I caught a glimpse of my reflection in the mirror behind the counter I couldn't help but marvel at the way the lighting made it gleam. "Things here must be pretty seasonal, huh?"

"Definitely." Tara graced me with an appraising look. "I love that belt. Is that ... snakeskin?"

I glanced down to the item in question and nodded. "Copperhead. I bought it from a store in the French Quarter. They don't kill the snakes just for the belts — if you're worried about that — but sometimes the snakes die when being milked for venom. That's when they make the belts. They're supposed to be powerful."

Tara blinked several times in rapid succession, her green eyes clouding with confusion. "Powerful? How are they powerful?"

Hmm. I hadn't really considered the possibility that the person waiting to greet me wouldn't be magical. I thought for sure that she would be in the know and able to explain a few things regarding my new reality. It looked as if that wasn't the case.

"It's simply part of New Orleans mysticism," I offered lamely. "Don't worry about it."

"Okay." Tara's expression never changed. "I'm supposed to give you the big tour of the aquarium and a brief look at what's on the other side of the door. Your first day isn't until tomorrow, though, so most of the staff is off doing other things."

I fell into step with her as she moved through the high archway that led to the animals. I wanted to press Tara further about the "other side," but my grandfather always preached patience being a virtue. I tried to embrace that now.

"I'm sure you'll catch on in no time," Tara said brightly.

Hmm. I really hated being trapped in an informational void, especially since I was technically going to be in charge of this operation ... once I got caught up on everything, of course. "How many people work here?"

"Six during the off season and fifteen when summer hits."

I had no idea if that was a big or small number. "And who does what?"

Tara's lips curved as she led me through the animal displays. "The majority of the staff works in the aquarium. We have to keep the tanks clean, feed the animals, and handle the tourists. But even during peak tourism times, we're rarely inundated to the point we can't handle the influx of visitors."

"That's good."

"It's ... simply how things are." Tara cast me a sidelong look that was unreadable. "Your staff is much smaller. You have two other people working directly under you right now — you won't meet them until tomorrow because they had to lend their services to a reaper family in Grosse Pointe — but that number grows by two in the summer. Still, your staff is smaller than the aquarium staff."

Well, that answered that question. "Reaper family?"

"You will be working in conjunction with various reaper families," Tara explained. "We have at least eight in southeastern Michigan. The souls they collect are transported here, which is when they become your responsibility."

I understood the demands of my job, which made Tara's tone grating. "I know what I'm supposed to do."

"I know you know." Tara's smile never wavered as she gestured toward a set of locked doors at the back of the facility. A card reader was affixed to the wall on the right side, and she pulled a plastic rectangle from her pocket and opened the doors with a smooth swipe. "Your security pass will be here tomorrow morning. We had a bit of an ... incident ... today. That's why the people who were supposed to meet you are not where you expected them to be. I'm sorry about that."

Curiosity got the better of me. "Where are they?"

"Apparently one of the Grimlocks — they're our most prominent reaper family — stumbled across a nest of wraiths. It was a big thing because the family decided to take out the wraiths, which put them behind on collecting their souls. They needed help."

I wasn't as familiar with the reaper end of things as Tara apparently believed, although that was something I was loath to admit. To get the job, I had to work a series of clerical positions in various home offices. That meant moving around the country, even though my dream was to return here. The good thing for me was that Detroit wasn't considered a prime placement and very few people put in for the Belle Isle location as their first choice. When I finally procured the experience I needed to be considered a gatekeeper, I was the only one who requested Detroit and I won by default. I was certain that had some people waggling their eyebrows, which I expected.

"Is that normal for here?" I asked. "I mean ... the part about the reapers needing help. I've only interned in the field collecting souls. I thought the operation was supposed to be much smoother than that."

"I wouldn't worry about going into the field," Tara offered, her eyes focused straight ahead as she led me down a dark hallway. "That's a rarity. The Grimlocks do tend to find trouble — I don't think they can help themselves — but they get themselves out of it quite often. They're down a man — er, woman, to be more precise — because the daughter is pregnant."

"A pregnant reaper?" The thought had never occurred to me. "I didn't think the souls were dangerous."

"They're not, but she's *very* pregnant. According to office scuttlebutt, she's due to give birth any day now. She's the one who tends to stumble over wraiths left and right, so her father wants her out of the field. She found the wraith nest today, and if the emails flying fast and furious are to be believed she won't be returning to the field anytime soon."

"And what does that mean for my staff?"

"Nothing. The Grimlocks have a plan in place to cover during her maternity leave. Today was just one of those weird things. When you find that many wraiths in one place, it's best to wipe them out so they can't spread."

The words niggled at the back of my brain. "I've read some of the reports from the area. You have a larger than normal wraith population."

"We do." Tara nodded. "Before you ask the obvious next question, I'm not sure why. There has to be a reason, but I don't know what it is. I don't get involved in reaper politics."

That made sense, although it did beg another obvious question. "And what do you do here?"

"I'm a facilitator." Tara was matter-of-fact. "I'm something of a liaison between the real world and this one. I don't have a foot firmly planted in either world, although I can answer questions on both sides."

"So ... basically you're saying it's the best of both worlds."

"I'm saying that I know a little bit about everything," Tara clarified, her earlier smile all but invisible as she opened the door at the end of the narrow hallway and hit the light switch on the wall, flooding the cavernous room to the point I had to blink several times to adjust. "This is your territory. You're in charge of this ... and I don't envy you."

I jerked my eyes to the one thing I'd been dying to see since I'd returned. Oh, who am I kidding? I'd been dying to see it since I was a kid, since that one brief glimpse I got at another world. It had shaped me. The death of my parents was only part of it. The whispers on the other side, the voices, they were what constantly called to me.

This is why I was back. The death gate. The portal to the other side.

"Wow!" My voice came out in a breathy whisper as I took in the shimmering surface of the portal. "That is ... exactly as I remember it."

Tara was less than impressed. "Yes. It's pretty. It's also dangerous."

I barely registered her words. "How is it dangerous? Has there been a breach? If so, that wasn't included in my packet."

Tara involuntarily shuddered at the implication. "There has never been a breach, at least as long as I've been here. I don't know why you would say that. A breach isn't funny. It's not a joke."

I arched an eyebrow as I regarded her. "I know it's not a joke. It's just ... you said it was dangerous. That's naturally where my mind jumped. It was a question, not a suggestion."

"Yes, well, I don't like it as a suggestion either." Tara was clearly uncomfortable as she shifted from one foot to the other. "Nobody wants a breach. That could be disastrous."

I didn't disagree. Tara, however, seemed chilled to the bone at the very thought. "I'm here to make sure there's not a breach," I offered softly.

"Yes, well, I hope you're good at your job." Tara turned prim as she tugged on her polo shirt to smooth it. "I'll leave you to look around. Like I said, the rest of your staff will be here tomorrow. I'm sorry about the delay."

I wasn't. The idea of looking around on my own was a dream I thought impossible to realize. I was happy for the few moments of quiet. "Don't worry about it. I don't plan to stay long. I simply want to look around, get my bearings, and then tomorrow is another day."

"It is indeed."

Tara offered a half-wave before shuffling toward the door. It didn't escape my attention that she worked overtime not to stare at the gate. To me, it was a magical portal to another world ... one where my parents were being kept comfortable until I could join them on the other side. To her it was obviously something else.

"I'll see you tomorrow," I offered quietly.

"Yeah. Tomorrow." Tara didn't so much as glance over her shoulder as she disappeared through the door.

I watched her go, a mixture of trepidation and curiosity flooding me. She was an odd one and I looked forward to learning more about her. For now, I had other things on my mind.

I focused my full attention on the gate opening and smiled when the telltale sound of whispers reached my ears. This is what I remembered from my childhood, the voices and the feeling of warmth emanating from the opening.

This is why I came back.

This is what I searched for since I was seven and had lost everything.

This is ... home.

I had no intention of losing it a second time.

Two

I didn't sleep well.

It could've been the fact that I was in new surroundings. The island was eerily quiet, something I would have to get used to. I'd spent the better portion of my life in the French Quarter, which always bustled with activity. Belle Isle seemed almost desolate in comparison.

Anxiety over my new job fueled me, too. I was technically the boss here. I was in charge of the gate. If something happened, it would be on me. I didn't shy from responsibility, but I was still getting used to the idea of being the big boss.

Of course I had no idea what sort of boss I wanted to be. I figured that would come with time. At least I hoped it would come with time.

I arrived fifteen minutes early. My security cards had been delivered while I slept, slid under my door. I tried to keep my hands from shaking as I let myself into the aquarium. It was early, so Tara wasn't behind the front desk. That was probably for the best.

I glanced at the tanks as I shuffled through the building and headed toward the door that led to the facility's inner sanctum. My shoes echoed on the marble floor, creating a spooky environment, as if I were trapped in a horror movie and about to be attacked. I pushed those thoughts out of my head — they weren't helpful — and used my new card to enter the back hallway.

I was almost to the room that housed the gate when I finally heard voices, which caused me to slow my pace as I listened to what sounded like a rather robust conversation.

"I'm not saying that I want to be a prostitute," a woman insisted, her voice young and strong. "I'm merely saying that I don't understand why prostitution is illegal."

"It's illegal because people are puritans," a male voice responded. "People want to tell others how to live their lives, and sex is an easy gateway for that."

"I wish people would spend more time worrying about themselves and less about what others are doing."

"That goes against human nature."

"What do you know about human nature?"

"More than you might realize."

I could've remained in the hallway eavesdropping. Part of me wanted to. It was an excellent way to get to know my new co-workers. But if they caught me it would reflect badly. That wasn't the reputation I wanted to garner.

Instead, I pushed open the door and pasted a bright smile on my face. It felt unnatural, forced, but I didn't want to appear unfriendly.

The two people in the room looked up when they heard my shoes on the floor and my senses kicked into overdrive when I felt a spasm of power clench. I couldn't decide if it was due to an involuntary reaction from me or a little something special offered by the two strangers staring at me with unveiled interest.

"Hi," I offered lamely, internally cursing myself. "I'm Isabella Sage. Call me Izzy. I don't really respond to Isabella. I definitely don't respond to Bella —you know, the whole *Twilight* thing — but if you call me Izzy I'll always answer."

I was babbling, which made me feel even goofier than normal.

The man, who looked to be in his early thirties, with brown hair and eyes, smirked as he met my gaze. "We know who you are. The home office supplied us with a photograph so we wouldn't accidentally invite the wrong person behind the safety doors."

"That would be bad," the red-headed woman offered, her grin pleasant and inviting. "Can you imagine some poor soul visiting the snakes and instead getting a gander at the gate? That wouldn't go over well."

"Definitely not," I agreed, struggling to remain calm. I still didn't have names to go with their faces, and because the home office hadn't supplied me with personnel records (saying I could simply look over whatever files I needed when I arrived), I felt out of place. "And you are?"

"Oh, I'm sorry." The man wiped his hand on his hip and extended it in my direction. "I'm Oliver Samuelson. This is Renee DuBois. I guess you could say we're your team, but we have seasonal helpers once May rolls around, too."

"They're usually from the local reaper academy," Renee volunteered helpfully. "They're fun because they have a lot of energy and we can give them the crappy shifts."

"Oh, well, that sounds fun." I accepted Oliver's hand, furrowing my brow at its coldness. "We don't get a lot of heat back here, huh? I should remember to bring a hoodie next time."

"Definitely," Oliver agreed, a small smile playing at the corners of his mouth. He was unbelievably handsome, ridiculously so, but I didn't get a sexual vibe from him. He was essentially an emotionless void, which was a unique experience. "Fingerless gloves might come in handy, too. It's not bad in the summer — actually it's nice in the summer because we can cool off down here — but it gets uncomfortable in the winter."

"I'll make a mental note of it."

"There's plenty of shopping in the area," Renee supplied. "Although I'd recommend heading to Royal Oak if you want to do it right."

"I'm familiar with Royal Oak."

"You are?"

"I grew up in the area." I licked my lips as I flicked my eyes to the whispering gate. I heard the voices even clearer today, and instead of giving me chills as it would normal people, I enjoyed the sound. "I spent several years here as a child, in fact."

"Oh, right." Realization dawned on Oliver's face. "Your parents were killed during the incident twenty years ago. That was a breach, right?"

I never really considered it a breach, so I bristled at the word. "I don't know if that is how I would describe it."

"How else could you describe it?"

"I ... ." I trailed off, uncertain how to answer. In truth, I had no idea how to refer to it.

"We were always told that something managed to escape from the other side, and that's what killed your parents," Renee explained. "Somehow you managed to escape, although that part of the tale is hazy."

It was hazy in more ways than one. I didn't remember much about the incident. I simply remembered a dark shadow appearing out of nowhere, the certainty that I was going to die taking over, and then the screaming. I had no idea why the creature screamed the way it did, but I could never forget that sound. After that, I woke in the hospital and knew my life would never be the same.

I shook my head to dislodge the memory. I didn't like dwelling on it. My grandfather was big on focusing on things I could change and letting go of what I couldn't. The gaps from back then were profound. The puzzle was missing far too many pieces to compile a complete picture.

"I don't really remember." I felt uncomfortable given the woman's scrutiny. "I was young."

"Of course you were." Oliver made a sympathetic sound with his tongue and I didn't miss the warning look he shot Renee. "But now you're back. How was your first night on the island?"

"It was ... quiet," I hedged. "I'm not used to things being so quiet."

"That will change once the weather improves."

"I don't mind the quiet," I added hurriedly. "I'm just not used to it."

"You'll come to relish the quiet," Renee said as she sat at a nearby computer and typed something into the running program. "The Grimlocks just sent eight souls at once. I wish they would stop doing that."

Distracted, Oliver moved to stand behind Renee and study the computer screen. "Those are probably the souls they forgot to send last night. We need to check them against the list." He grabbed a clipboard from the top of the filing cabinet pressed against the wall and focused. "Read them off to me."

"Mark Lincoln. Emily Vanderbilt. Marla Porter."

"That's them." Oliver started checking off names as my curiosity got the better of me and I shuffled closer. "All eight are accounted for. That means we won't have to fill out paperwork. I'm glad we waited before sounding the alarm last night."

I was confused. "I don't understand," I said finally. "I thought the reapers had to send their souls on the day the orders were issued. Are you saying this family ... these Grimlocks ... aren't doing it in a timely fashion?"

"Oh, well ... ." Oliver shifted from one foot to the other as he looked at Renee for backup. "The thing is, the Grimlocks aren't always on time."

"And why is that?"

"They've had a lot going on the last couple years."

That sounded like an excuse. "So they have permission to send their souls late?"

"No." Oliver dragged a restless hand through his dark hair, the vein on his forehead standing out before his bangs dropped to cover it. "They don't often send souls late. But it does happen occasionally. My understanding is that they took out a nest of wraiths yesterday. They probably got distracted by that."

"Their main job is to collect souls," I persisted, refusing to back down. "How could they forget the most important part of their job? If they don't send the souls to us, they're trapped in limbo. Last time I checked, that's not a good thing."

Renee wrinkled her nose as she stared down at her rather impressive cleavage. I could practically see her mind working. "The thing is ... we kind of cover for one another out here. This is a different environment from what you're probably used to."

That definitely sounded like an excuse. "If they're not doing their jobs that reflects poorly on all of us."

"They do their jobs."

"You just said they didn't."

"That's not what I said," Oliver countered. "The Grimlocks are the best reaping family we have. They're simply ... distracted ... on a regular basis."

I had no idea what that meant. "Distracted how?"

"It's the wraiths." Oliver was clearly choosing his words carefully because he seemed to be struggling. "We have more wraiths in this area than almost anywhere else in the country. Although, to be fair, I think you had your fair share in New Orleans, too, after Katrina. The difference is when the people returned to New Orleans, the wraiths fled."

I remembered the time of the wraith population explosion well. My grandfather, a respected Bruja in the area, was careful to keep me close even though I was a teenager at the time. At first I chafed under his constant vigilance, but after witnessing a brutal attack on a classmate that resulted in her death I came around to his way of thinking.

"I guess I'm going to need more information," I said finally, unsure. "What's the deal with the wraiths in this area? Why is it so much worse here than in other areas?"

"For several reasons," Oliver replied without hesitation. "It started because of the abandoned buildings. Do you have any idea how many abandoned buildings there are in Detroit?"

"No."

"Neither do I, but it's a lot. They're working on the problem, but the abandoned buildings make great hiding places for wraiths."

I stroked my chin as I considered the information. "That makes sense. I'm guessing the population in a lot of these areas is poor, too, which makes for good hunting grounds."

Oliver nodded. "Exactly. But that's only part of the problem. We also had an uprising of sorts that lasted for several months. I don't know all the details, but there was a mystic faction gathering the wraiths to use as an army. That faction was wiped out, but it's been like playing whack-a-mole to take out the remaining wraiths ever since."

"They're hunkering down, digging in," Renee explained. "So when the Grimlocks found the nest yesterday, it was important they take it out without delay. Right now we're trying to dismantle the wraith population."

My mind was busy. "No one mentioned any of this when I applied for the position."

"That was probably on purpose," Oliver supplied. "The last two people who held your title left as soon as their contracts expired. This isn't a coveted area."

"I know. That's why I thought there was a chance I could snag the position despite my age. I was excited when everything came together. Now ... ."

"Now you're not so sure," Oliver finished. "I get it."

"I'm still happy to be here," I said hurriedly, realizing how ungrateful I sounded. I didn't want to come across as petulant or hard to deal with. "I simply wish I had been given all the information when I applied."

"I don't blame you there." Oliver's smile was back. "The thing is, I get that you want to follow the rules, but it's not always possible in this environment. The Grimlocks are unbelievably strong. They're hard workers."

"All the boys are hot like the sun, too," Renee offered enthusiastically. "They're pretty, pretty boys."

I wasn't in the market for a romance, so I merely nodded. "Well, that's important."

Oliver snickered. "Don't mind her. She likes to pant after the Grimlocks. As far as I can tell, every woman who has ever met them feels that way."

"I don't think I'll have to worry about that."

Oliver's gaze turned appraising. "Really? Are you playing for the other team? If so, I know a few women in Ferndale who might be interested in a night out."

"I'm not interested in that either. I'm here to do a job. I'm not concerned with dating."

Renee snickered. "Famous last words."

"I mean them."

"Fair enough." She held up her hands. "You might change your mind when you see them."

"I doubt it." I turned my attention to the computer. "I guess the first order of business is to learn your filing system. I guess I'll let the

21

Grimlocks' lack of attention to detail slide for now. If problems continue, though, I'll handle them later."

"I would love to handle them." Renee's expression turned wistful. "I'm not even picky about which one I want to handle."

Oliver pursed his lips as he shook his head. "Your Grimlock love is getting old. You know that, right?"

"Hey, they're hot." Renee patted the open seat next to her and shifted her eyes to me. "Come on. The computer system is easy. In fact, this entire gig is easy. Nothing ever happens here. I think you're going to be disappointed if you're looking for action."

I took the seat and swiveled to watch the screen as her fingers deftly moved over the keyboard. "You just told me this place is crawling with wraiths. That doesn't sound boring."

"Yes, well, I wouldn't hope for a wraith encounter if I were you. They've taken to running in packs."

"Packs?" I'd never heard of that. "Why?"

"They were organized by a militant faction," Oliver answered for Renee. "They learned they could get more done as a group. They're reluctant to leave the packs now. I wasn't joking about them being dangerous."

"I'll keep that in mind." Something occurred to me. "Do they come out here?"

Renee and Oliver exchanged a weighted look.

"They do," Oliver said after a moment's contemplation. "In fact, we've been seeing a lot of them lately. We're not sure why, but the gate might be drawing them. It's up for debate at the home office."

I didn't like the sound of that. "Have they made it into the building?"

"A few times."

"What do they do?"

"They try to get back here. As long as the door latches, it's fine. They haven't been able to get back here yet. I have no idea what they would do if they managed to cross the threshold."

"Right, well ... ." Something occurred to me. "The door latches automatically, doesn't it?"

Realization dawned on Oliver's face as he slowly swiveled. "Sometimes you have to give it a little tug." He strode toward the door, purposeful. "I'll check."

As if on cue, the swinging doors flew open with enough force to slam against the wall and a tall figure appeared in the entrance. I was familiar with wraiths — I had crossed paths with at least five during my time in New Orleans — but the menacing creature standing before me now was straight out of my nightmares.

"What the ... ?"

"Omigod!" Renee tripped as she scrambled out of her seat, terror washing over her features as she hustled to put distance between herself and the creature.

I didn't remember standing, but my shaky legs told me that running wasn't an option. Instead, I stared at the wraith with unfathomable fear as the creature grabbed Oliver around the neck and tossed him across the room as if he were a doll.

"Oliver!" My first instinct was to help, but the wraith stood between me and my new co-worker. My second instinct was to flee. There was nowhere to go, though, so I remained rooted to my spot.

The wraith stalked in my direction, causing my heart to skip a beat. Its hissing was so high-pitched it caused me to cringe. It was almost upon me when I finally gathered my wits and turned to my right.

Instead of grabbing me, the wraith lashed out and shoved so I was no longer in its path. The contact was brief, but I felt my energy waning. It seemed focused on one thing, and one thing only: the gate.

My mouth dropped open so I could issue a warning, but it was already too late. The wraith blew past Renee and threw itself at the shimmering opening.

The gate emitted a sound like a giant suction cup breaking free from glass as the wraith crossed over from our world and disappeared into the next, leaving the three of us breathless as we tried to grasp what had happened. I was the first to discover my voice.

"What the heck was that?"

Three

I didn't know the security procedures as well as Renee so I left her to call for help while I checked on Oliver. He seemed shaken but otherwise okay, which was a relief. I helped him to a chair and grabbed a bottle of water from the vending machine against the far wall. When I offered it to him, he politely declined.

"Is help coming?" I asked Renee when she joined us.

"Yeah. The home office said they had someone in the area. He should be here within the next fifteen minutes." Lines of concern crowded Renee's eyes as she knelt next to Oliver. "Are you okay?"

"I'm fine." Oliver's smile was wan. "I'll be fine once I settle. It simply caught me off guard."

That was an understatement. "Yeah." I straightened and focused on the gate. "I don't understand why that happened." I looked to Oliver for answers. "Why would a wraith purposely want to cross over? The whole reason it turned into a wraith in the first place is because it didn't want to die. Racing to the other side is essentially dying, right?"

Oliver opened his mouth to answer and then snapped it shut, holding his hands palms out as he shrugged. "I have no idea. It might be different for wraiths. I'm not sure what to make of it."

I spent the next ten minutes circling the gate. Nothing came out.

Nothing went in. It was simply a gate, although the whispering increased tenfold right after the wraith jumped through the opening. It was back to normal relatively quickly ... until a new player emerged on the scene and then the whispering began again in earnest.

It was the whispering that caused me to snap my head toward the door, and I narrowed my eyes when I saw the man standing there. He seemed sure of himself, as if he belonged, but he didn't announce his arrival.

"How did you get in without a keycard?"

He didn't immediately answer, his eyes instead drifting toward the gate. He looked to be about thirty, broad shoulders on full display in a fitted black T-shirt. He wore simple jeans and black boots, his black hair gleaming thanks to the gate's shimmering light display. His most striking features were his eyes — a violent shade of purple — but they didn't as much as shift in my direction.

His refusal to answer my question grated.

"How did you get in here?" I repeated, taking a purposeful step toward him. "You need a security card to enter."

"I have a card." The man finally dragged his attention to me. He seemed surprised by what he saw. My fashion choices reflected the French Quarter, but those were the clothes I was most comfortable in and there had been no time to adjust my wardrobe for the colder Michigan weather. "Who are you? You're not Cyrus."

I drew a blank. "Cyrus?"

"He was the guy who had your position before you," Oliver answered. "He couldn't get out of here fast enough when he heard there was an opening in Des Moines."

The newcomer let loose with a derisive snort. "Yes, that shows great taste. What's in Des Moines?"

"Fewer wraiths."

The man nodded. "Good point. Tell me what happened."

Oliver made to do just that, but I cut him off.

"Excuse me, but ... who are you?" I tried to keep the recrimination from my tone, but it was difficult. "I have no idea who you are."

"Oh, I'm sorry." Renee found her voice as she scurried across the floor, taking up position between the newcomer and me. "This is

25

Braden Grimlock. He's a member of the family we were telling you about. Braden, this is Isabella Sage. She's the new gatekeeper."

"Izzy," I automatically corrected. "Call me Izzy."

Braden arched an eyebrow. "Okay, Izzy, tell me what happened."

I wasn't in the mood to acquiesce to his demands. After all, I was in charge here. He was simply ... well, I had no idea what he was doing here. "I'm sorry — and forgive me if this comes off as rude — but my understanding is that you're a reaper. Why would the home office call a reaper to act as an expert for the gate?"

"I don't believe I said I was an expert," Braden countered. "I was called as backup because a wraith attacked. I have a bit of experience with wraith attacks."

"Braden's family are kind of wraith experts," Renee explained, earning a flirty wink from Braden that caused her cheeks to flood with color. "In fact, they're revered wraith fighters."

"I wouldn't go that far," Braden cautioned. "We have dealt with a lot of wraiths. That's why I need to know what happened."

It was a reasonable enough request, but that didn't mean I was ready to cede my authority. "Well, what's your security clearance level?"

Braden snorted. "Seriously?"

I nodded.

"Level three."

"I'm level four. I'm not sure how much information I'm supposed to share with you."

"Well, my father is level seven," Braden said. "We have special security clearance in our house. I'm sure it will be fine."

"And what if it's not?"

"It will be fine," Oliver interjected quickly. "I know you're new to the area and the hierarchy here, Izzy, but the Grimlocks will know everything by the end of the day regardless. You're saving everyone a bit of work by simply telling him."

I didn't care about saving people from work. I did, however, care about getting answers. Apparently Braden Grimlock was my best shot at getting those answers. "Fine." I told the story from start to finish. It didn't take long because there wasn't much to tell. When I was finished, Braden looked as confused as I felt.

"Huh."

I waited a beat. "Is that all you have to say?"

"For the moment." He looked back to the gate and shook his head. "I don't know what to make of that. Has it ever happened before?"

"Not that I know of," Oliver replied, moving to stand next to the broad-shouldered reaper. They made quite the sight. If they were in a bar women would be throwing themselves at the two of them as drool flew fast and furious. "It definitely has never happened here. And I've never heard of it happening elsewhere."

"It doesn't make much sense," Braden admitted, his hand stroking his chin. "Why would a wraith want to cross over? Without a soul … ."

"I thought wraiths had fragmented souls," I countered. "Part of the soul remains, but it's been shattered into pieces so it's not a true soul."

"I don't know that we have definitive answers on that," Braden countered. "We have learned quite a bit about wraiths in the last year or so. My brother is heading up the research."

"This comes back to that whole soul walkers thing we were briefed about, right?" Renee pressed. "I saw the memo, but I didn't read it from start to finish. I didn't think it would be important given where we were stationed."

"I don't know that you missed all that much," Braden said. "Basically, wraiths are a byproduct of humans trying to soul walk. People were trying to live forever, but the process they chose caused the souls to fragment. That's how wraiths were born, and it wasn't the end result the soul walkers expected."

"How do you know all that?" I asked the question before I thought better of it. I wasn't trying to be rude — no, really — but he didn't seem the bookish sort to me.

As if reading my mind, Braden's lips curved. "My brother is the scholarly type."

"And he laid all this out for you?"

For a split second Braden's expression shifted into something profoundly sad. He collected himself quickly, though, and covered. "We had a little inside information. It was eight months ago. My brother has continued digging deep since. He's the sort of guy who wants answers."

"He's also the sort of guy who looks like a movie star," Renee enthused. "He has long hair — like Kylo Ren hair — and he's ridiculously hot."

Braden made a face. "I'm way hotter than him."

"But he's got movie star hair," Renee countered. "You're cowboy hot. He's action hero hot. Both are great."

Braden didn't look convinced. "We look alike other than the hair. Do you have any idea how long he spends primping that hair? It's ridiculous. My hair is hot and practical."

I'd had enough. "I'm sorry, but ... why are we talking about hair when a wraith managed to breach our security and jump through the gate? Shouldn't we be focused on that? We can discuss haircare products when we have answers."

The statement came out shriller than I expected, but it was too late to back down, so I merely folded my arms over my chest and waited for Renee and Braden to show some embarrassment. Neither bothered.

"I'm awesome at multi-tasking," Braden drawled, shaking his head as he returned his odd-colored eyes to the gate. "I don't know what to tell you. How did the wraith even get into this part of the building?"

My cheeks flamed as karma caught up with me. I wanted him to be embarrassed, but I was the one feeling the burn. "That was my fault."

"It was nobody's fault," Oliver interjected. "That door is funky. You have to tug on it to make sure it latches. It's Izzy's first day. She couldn't have known."

Instead of reacting with sympathy Braden turned smug. "Oh, so you did this."

I wanted to smack him. Hard. He wasn't wrong, though. "Yes. I understand you have to report it to the home office. It's on me. I take full responsibility."

"It was an accident," Oliver repeated hurriedly. "She couldn't have known. They didn't tell her anything before shipping her here. She didn't even know about the explosion in our wraith population."

Surprise evident, Braden drew his eyebrows together. "Why would they send you out here without telling you what's going on?"

I shrugged, noncommittal. "I'm sure they had their reasons."

"I'm sure they did, too." Braden was thoughtful as he snagged gazes with Oliver. "You've been around for a long time. What were their reasons?"

"No one wants to stay in this post long term," Oliver answered automatically. "It's not one of the prime positions. Izzy volunteered to take it, but the job description was severely lacking when it was posted. Despite that, she was the only one who applied so ... here she is."

"Uh-huh." Braden rolled his neck until it cracked, causing the whispering from the other side of the gate to increase. His expression didn't change, reinforcing the idea that I was the only one who could hear it. I knew that from childhood, but somehow I thought that might have changed. Apparently I was wrong.

"It's still my fault." I was big on personal responsibility, so I refused to back down. "I expect to be reprimanded for my actions."

Braden's eyes lit with mirth. "Somehow I think you'll be okay. If the home office puts up with Grimlock shenanigans, a genuine accident won't cause a stir. It sounds to me as if anyone could've made the mistake, although it does make me wonder if a wraith was hiding in the shadows to take advantage of the door situation or something. How else could it know?"

That hadn't even occurred to me. "But ... how would it get into the aquarium?"

"That is a very good question." He ran his tongue over his lips as he stared hard at the gate. "I've never seen it before. Does it always look like this?"

"As opposed to what?"

"I don't know. I guess I expected more shiny stuff, like glitter. We were taught about the gate at a young age. I expected something fancier."

I was offended on behalf of the gate. "Well, we'll try to teach it some tricks for your next visit."

Instead of being offended, he snickered. "You're funny. I hope you're not wound this tight on a normal day. I get that this is your first day and pretty much the worst thing possible happened, but this is not the end of the world."

His tone grated. "Oh, really? What's the worst thing that could possibly happen?"

His eyes flashed with sadness before he caught himself. "There are definitely worse things. Let's just leave it at that."

I considered pressing him further, but the look Oliver pinned me with caused me to change course. "So, what do we do? I mean ... do we ignore it? Do we try to lure the wraith back out? Do we try to send something to the other side to find it?"

"All excellent questions," Braden mused. "I don't have any answers for you."

"Then why are you here?"

"Because I'm an excellent conversationalist." This time Braden's ready wink was aimed at me. "You need to chill. I don't have answers. That doesn't mean we can't figure it out. It simply means we need a place to start."

"No offense, man, but you're a lot more chill than I remember," Oliver noted. "You used to be the one who was wound tight in your family. What happened?"

"Life happened." Braden reached a tentative finger toward the gate surface. "I wasn't wound tight, no matter what you think. That was my sister."

"And you," Oliver pressed. "But it's not important now."

"Definitely not."

Braden's finger continued moving toward the gate surface and instinctively I took three long strides forward and grabbed his hand before he could touch the magical ripples.

"Don't," I ordered, shaking my head. "The barrier isn't meant to be crossed. You could hurt yourself."

Braden wrinkled his nose. "Will it hurt?"

"It will sting," Renee answered. "You really shouldn't touch it, dude. It's frowned upon."

"Well, I hate doing things that are frowned upon." Braden's smile was easy and light but I didn't miss the darkness that fleetingly lurked behind those fascinating eyes. "As for the wraith ... ."

Before he could finish speaking the gate gave a hiccup of sorts. My memories of the gate were clouded by childhood — and one big event

— but the slight spasm jarred my memory. For a brief moment I was back in time. It was the night my parents died and my world irrevocably changed. The gate did the same thing ... and then something was there in the room with us, giving chase. I couldn't remember what it was. The harder I tried to remember, the more elusive the images became.

That was probably a good thing, because thoughts of the past fled in an instant when the gate surface sparked again.

"What is that?" Braden asked, casting me a sidelong look. "Is it malfunctioning?"

"It's not a computer system," I growled, my instincts taking over as I grabbed his arm and gave it a good tug. "I mean ... we have a computer system that works in conjunction with it, but it's not a program or anything."

"That's not really what I asked," Braden said dryly, refusing to budge. "Why is it making that noise?" When I didn't immediately answer — I couldn't because my heart was threatening to pound out of my chest — he flicked his eyes to Oliver. "What's going on?"

"I'm not sure." Oliver's face was sheet white. "I don't know what this is. I ... ."

A hand, almost transparent except for the red fingernails, emerged from the gate. My instincts kicked into overdrive and I tugged as hard as I could to get Braden out of the line of fire.

"Step back!" I instructed.

Confused, Braden did as he was told. That was good, because at that exact moment a creature emerged from the gate and stepped into the real world. It was impossible. There was no way to cross over, yet something had. I recognized the figure right away, although somehow it was different.

"That's the wraith." I was breathless as I tried to control my feelings. "That's the same wraith that crossed over."

If he doubted me, Braden didn't show it. Instead he brushed my hand off his arm and reached inside his coat, coming back with a wicked-looking silver dagger. The wraith seemed dazed, as if the trip had somehow altered its thinking. Still, it recognized the dagger and took a loping and unsteady step away from the threatening reaper.

"Kill it," Renee demanded. "Kill it before it touches us."

Braden didn't have to be told twice. He strode directly toward the creature, a little added swagger in his step, but he stopped before he could close the distance when the creature screamed ... and then practically bowled him over as it ran toward the door.

Braden looked as if he was going to fight, but thought better of it and wisely stepped out of its way as it slammed through the double doors and disappeared down the corridor. Its hissing scream sent chills down my spine.

Braden found his voice first.

"Well, that was different."

I felt sick to my stomach. "What was your first clue?"

Four

I wasn't having the best first day. So far I'd inadvertently allowed a wraith that may or may not have been stalking the facility to cross over to the other side – which was unheard of – but I'd also allowed it to escape upon return. I wasn't sure, but that probably had to go down at the top of the list in the annals of bad days everywhere.

"He's here," Renee announced excitedly an hour later, rubbing her hands together as she scurried from her spot at the door where she'd been holding watch for what felt like forever. "He's here and he's not alone."

I had no idea what that was supposed to mean. "Who is here?" I jerked my gaze from the computer screen, where I'd been watching footage of the wraith arriving and leaving on a continuous loop, and focused on the door. "I don't understand what's going on."

"The home office sent someone to take over the investigation," Renee explained. "He's practically famous in certain circles."

"Yes, he's famous," Braden drawled, straightening when a middle-aged man who happened to look exactly like him strolled through the door with three other men who shared his eyes and coloring. "He'll never let you forget it either." His smile was rueful as he met the older man's gaze. "Dad."

"Braden." The man's eyes bounced around the room, lingering on the gate before landing on me. "You must be Isabella Sage."

"Izzy." The need to constantly clarify my name was getting old, but it was something of a reflex. "You may call me Izzy."

"Right now I'm simply going to call you Ms. Sage," he replied, his expression hard to read. "I'd rather not make things personal at present."

Something about his tone grated. "I don't think you have to worry about that. I don't even know your name. No one informed me that you were coming."

"I don't believe I have to inform you of my actions. I am in charge."

His pompous attitude threw me for a loop. "Excuse me?"

Braden cleared his throat to keep things from flying further off the rails, stepping between his father and me but focusing on the man who clearly served as a source of the entire family's looks. "Give her a break, Dad," he instructed, his voice strong and clear. "She's had a lot to deal with for a first day, and it's not even ten yet."

The man didn't appear happy with the suggestion. "And what exactly did happen here?"

That seemed an important question. I had another one. "Wait." I held up my hand to still Braden before he answered. "I'm not trying to be a pain — at least I'm not trying to be a big one — but I have no idea who you are. I don't know the pecking order of this particular office. I feel out of my depth ... and kind of like you're trying to intimidate me. I could be way off on that. It wouldn't be the first time, but I feel it so I'm going to say it."

Instead of immediately responding, all five Grimlock men merely stared in my direction. Finally, the one with the long hair commented.

"Oh, she's going to make me laugh."

His tone told me that was an insult. "I'm merely trying to do my job."

"Of course you are," Braden said smoothly, his lips twitching. He appeared ready to burst into gregarious guffaws. "In the interests of saving time, I will make the introductions."

He extended a finger. "That is my father, Cormack Grimlock. He's second in command at the Detroit office so ... don't get him going."

Second in command? Uh-oh. That meant the imposing figure was even higher in the food chain than I realized. "Nice to meet you, sir." I extended my hand, a lame gesture that Cormack clearly found amusing. He shook it, though, which was something.

"The one in the back who looks as if he's about to give himself a conniption fit laughing is Redmond," Braden continued. "The one who looks like he belongs in a band is Cillian. The quiet one is Aidan. We also have a sister, but she's clearly not here."

"I ordered your sister to stay home," Cormack interjected, his eyes firing. "In fact, she's done working until she gives birth. I don't want her out on assignments until her maternity leave is over. She's due any day, and if she's trapped on a job when it happens … ." He trailed off, but his aura quickly shifted from a logical tan to a fiery red at mention of the missing Grimlock. "So, from here on out your sister is officially on leave … and if anyone thinks they're going to placate her by breaking the rules, think again. I will dock your pay."

The mini-diatribe confused me. "Aren't we supposed to be focusing on the wraith?"

"We are indeed," a new voice said from the doorway, catching me off guard as I peered around Cormack and found an odd sight. "Let's talk about the wraith, not my pregnancy."

"What the … ?" Braden spun toward the door, surprise evident. "Aisling!"

I didn't need Braden to shout the woman's name to recognize her. Like her brothers, she boasted black hair (although hers was offset with white streaks) and lavender eyes. She wasn't overly tall and appeared to be thin … except for her expansive stomach, which looked as if she was about to give birth to a watermelon.

"I thought you were on maternity leave," Cillian blurted out, his aura momentarily shifting from green to the same red his father boasted. "You shouldn't be wandering around without someone watching you."

For her part, the lone Grimlock female didn't look happy. "I'm an adult. I don't need someone watching me."

"You're pregnant," Cormack countered, grabbing his daughter's arm and directing her toward the chair where Oliver sat. "Get up!" He kicked at the chair to get Oliver to move, causing me to bite the inside of my cheek to keep from laughing. "My daughter needs to sit down."

Oliver did as instructed, not uttering a word of complaint. If he was bothered about being bossed around he didn't show it.

"I don't need to sit down," Aisling argued. "I'm kickass. I'm always going to be kickass. This doesn't change that." She gestured toward her huge stomach.

"Aisling, you're going to give birth to my first grandchild any day." Cormack was firm as he pushed Aisling into the chair. "You're done being kickass until you're back from maternity leave."

The face Aisling made was one for the record books. "I hate all of you."

"We know." Cormack absently patted her shoulder. "You'll feel better when I surprise you with an ice cream bar for dinner."

Aisling brightened considerably. "Sprinkles?"

"And gummy sharks."

"Sold."

I furrowed my brow as I tried to absorb the family dynamics. "How is it a surprise if you tell her what's happening?" I asked finally, earning an annoyed look from Cormack and an amused smirk from Aisling. "That seems the opposite of a surprise."

"My father isn't above bribing," Braden supplied, his eyes thoughtful as they landed on his sister, who looked about as uncomfortable as one person could look as she shifted in the chair. "He's also a nervous wreck on Aisling's behalf. He can't help himself. Don't take it personally."

Redmond, the Grimlock with the blue aura, moved closer to his sister and knelt. "What are you doing here? We purposely left you at home."

"With a chaperone, no less," Cillian interjected. "You didn't hit Maya over the head and lock her in the closet, did you?"

"Maya is perfectly fine," Aisling countered, lifting her legs so she could glare at her swollen feet. "They look like sausages ... and they hurt, for the record. If I didn't need to run after you guys because you cut me out of the action, they wouldn't hurt."

"Yes, this is all our fault," Aidan said dryly. He moved closer to his sister, his abstract tan aura making for a sharp contrast with his sister's magenta coloring. Magenta was rare in the aura world — although I'd seen it a time or two before — and Aisling's personality was so strong the magenta practically rolled off her in waves. "You were supposed to stay home and rest. I thought Maya had some foot soak to make your feet feel better."

"She was getting it when I fled," Aisling supplied. "I waited until I was sure she wasn't watching, and then I ran for it because I'm mad at all of you."

"Oh, well, good." Redmond smoothed his sister's hair, which looked as if she'd been trapped in a wind tunnel. "It's not a proper workday if you're not angry with us."

Watching the scene was difficult. As an only child, I was happy to have my grandfather's full attention. Once my parents were gone, he was all I had left. He was a strict man, but he knew how to enjoy himself. The idea of sharing his attention with others didn't sit well.

The Grimlocks, on the other hand, clearly shared their father's attention. The sister seemed to be getting the bulk of it at present, but that was to be expected. The way the brothers doted on her was surprising, though. It was almost as if they formed a protective wall around her.

The entire family dynamic was interesting, but we had other things to worry about.

"So ... the wraith?" I prodded, hoping to get everybody back on track.

"I still don't know what happened with the wraith," Cormack said.

I launched into the tale, describing everything in a calm and rational manner. When I was done, the Grimlocks exploded into pandemonium.

"How is that even possible?" Aisling asked.

"I don't understand how the wraith got inside," Redmond said.

"Did the wraith touch anyone?" Aidan asked.

"How did the wraith look when it crossed back over?" Cillian queried.

"Why didn't you kill it, Braden?" Cormack challenged.

I raised my eyebrows at the chaos. "Um ... ."

Braden took the onus of the conversation off me. "I was going to kill it, but I wasn't quick enough. Plus, well, it was bigger."

"Bigger than what?" Cillian asked.

"I don't know how to explain it," Braden replied, gesturing toward the computer. "We have video if you'd like to see."

The male Grimlocks moved toward the computer, leaving Aisling to struggle to stand without the benefit of family aid. Instinctively, I went to her and offered a hand. She took it and groaned as she attempted to find her footing. Ultimately she gave up and waved off my efforts to help.

"It's useless," she muttered, dragging a hand through her hair. "I'll have to live here now."

I didn't want to laugh. She seemed so downtrodden and grim it felt wrong to mess with her. She was funny, though. There was something about her that I liked, but I couldn't say why. She seemed spunky ... and close to the edge at the same time. It was an interesting dichotomy. "When are you due?" I offered a smile as I knelt. "Not soon enough to make you happy, I'm sure."

"Four days," Aisling replied, her fingers roaming her belly. "But my father thinks I'll go past my due date. Apparently my mother did with all of us."

"Is she around to help you?"

Aisling shook her head. "She died."

"I'm sorry." I meant it. "Being surrounded by men, you could probably use her about now."

"They're not so bad." Aisling turned an affectionate eye to the men watching the footage on the computer. "They're just overprotective."

"That's not always a bad thing."

"No," Aisling agreed. "But I don't like being treated like a baby." She made a face as she shifted again. "Especially when the baby kicks so much I'm sure he or she is going to be a karate champ."

I smirked. "Well ... ." Instinctively I reached out a hand but stopped short of touching her. "May I?"

Aisling nodded, unwary. "Everyone touches my stomach. Most people don't ask."

I rested my fingertips on her huge abdomen, a foot instantaneously making contact with my right palm. "Wow! Someone is feisty in there, huh?"

Aisling wearily nodded. "I think it's a girl."

"You didn't want to find out?"

"I did, but my husband didn't."

My eyes went unbidden to her naked ring finger. "Is he a reaper, too?"

"No. He's a cop. When my fingers got too swollen, he locked my ring in the family safe. We haven't been married very long so I put up a fight, but he was insistent."

"You'll be able to wear it again soon." I moved my hands and frowned. "Yellow."

"Yellow what?"

"Aura. The baby's aura is yellow." I realized after the fact that I'd spoken out loud. I risked a glance at Aisling and found her watching me with overt interest rather than laughing. Most people, especially in the reaper world, didn't spend much time worrying about auras. "I mean … um … ."

"You can read auras," Aisling mused, knitting her eyebrows. "Is that something you had to train to do or were you born with the ability?"

"I was born with it. I didn't realize I saw the world in a different way until I was about seven or so. Then my parents warned me to keep it to myself. I should've remembered that and not blurted out what I said."

Aisling shrugged. "What color is my aura?"

"Magenta."

"What does that mean?"

"Basically that you're a nonconformist and you make your own rules."

Aisling's lips curved. "That's true. What about my father and brothers?"

I ran through the list for her because she seemed to be enjoying herself. When I finished, she couldn't stop laughing.

"That fits all of them," she agreed. "I kind of want to bring my best friend Jerry to you. I'm dying to know what color he is."

"I'm sure we can make it happen."

"Good. Although ... ." Aisling trailed off, causing my eyes to narrow.

"What?" I prodded.

"You didn't mention Braden."

"Oh. I guess I didn't. He's orange."

"And what does that mean?"

"That he's a thrill-seeker and doesn't believe in limitations."

For a split second I thought I saw a hint of worry flit through Aisling's eyes before she shuttered her emotions and forced a smile. "What color aura does a pain in the ass have?"

"That's not an aura color. Everyone has that ability."

"Yes, well, Braden has it in spades." Aisling's lips curved down. "He's not just orange. You said Aidan was blue because he lives from his heart. Braden is blue, too."

That seemed to be an important distinction to her, so I merely nodded. "Okay."

"It's possible to be two colors, right?" Aisling turned earnest. "He's not just a daredevil, is he?"

"I'm sure he's not." I didn't understand her need to clarify things. "He's probably mostly orange right now because of the adrenaline coursing through him. The wraith took us all by surprise."

"Yeah. I'm a little worried," Aisling admitted. "The wraiths have been out of control since ... a few months ago."

Whatever she was going to say, she changed course halfway through. I didn't press her on it. "We'll figure it out. Perhaps there's a way we can cross to the other side and figure out what the wraith did while it was there."

"We can't do that," Cormack argued, shaking his head as he focused on us. His gaze was thoughtful as it bounced between faces. "Anyone who crosses the threshold will die."

"How do you know that?" Aisling challenged. "I didn't even know the gate looked like this or that you could cross over. How can you be sure that someone will die if they try?"

"People have tried before," Cormack replied grimly.

"I've never heard about that," Cillian said. "When did that happen?"

"A long time ago." Cormack shook his head. "Crossing over is not an option. I'm not even sure how the wraith managed it. We have to find out. That's our first order of business."

"And how do we do that?" I asked. "Where do we find those particular answers?"

"I'm not sure, but I have an idea." Cormack rolled his neck until he was looking at Braden. "You know who I have in mind, right?"

Braden looked resigned. "Yeah. I'm not sure it's a good idea, but I know who you're talking about."

"Good, because I want you to head over and see if you can get some answers."

"What are you going to do?" Braden asked.

"I'm taking your sister home if we can get her out of that chair and then I'm sitting down to conduct some research with Cillian," he replied. "Redmond and Aidan need to finish the soul rounds. We don't have a long list today, but we can't fall behind. That leaves you to handle the heavy lifting on this one."

"Okay."

I was determined to be a team player, but the fact that I was being cut out of everything annoyed me to the very tips of my toes. "I think I should be involved in this, too," I interjected.

Cormack slid me a sidelong look. "I thought that because you were just starting you would need some time to adjust to all of this."

I refused to break eye contact. "You thought wrong."

"All right." Cormack didn't act as if he was annoyed by my insistent nature. "You may go with Braden."

I was unsure what that entailed, but I had no intention of backing down. "Great. I can't wait."

"You say that now, but you'll change your mind after spending twenty minutes with my brother," Aisling offered. "I've found that if you want him to shut up it's best to hit him over the head with a shoe or something. Or, maybe stop at the mall so you can buy a gag. That couldn't possibly hurt."

Braden burned holes in his sister with his glare, and Cormack merely rolled his eyes.

"I'll keep that in mind." I smiled at her. "Bring your friend Jerry by when you're ready. I would love to meet him."

"Those are famous last words," Braden muttered.

"I heard that!" Aisling's annoyance was on full display. "I'm going to tell Jerry what you said and you'll be sorry when I do."

Braden made a derisive snort. "Bring it on."

Five

"Where are we going?"

Braden opted to drive. I didn't have a vehicle, so that was convenient. The fact that he drove a BMW X5 caused me to raise an eyebrow, but I didn't comment on the expensive vehicle. I had no idea reapers were paid so much.

"There's a woman we know," Braden replied, his gaze focused on traffic. "Pick a lane, lady!"

I pursed my lips as he flipped the finger at a woman who had to be in her sixties and zoomed around her. "She's pretty knowledgeable and she's helped in the past."

The way he phrased the statement caused me to wonder if he was hiding something. "What aren't you saying?"

"What makes you think I'm hiding something?"

"I didn't say you were hiding anything," I clarified. "I simply believe you're leaving something out of the telling. There's a difference."

"Right." His grip on the steering wheel tightened to the point his knuckles whitened. "She's an old family friend, but she's secretive."

That wasn't much of an explanation. "And?"

"And I'll let you form your own opinion when you meet her," Braden replied. "I don't want to gossip about her."

Obviously something else was going on beside an aversion to gossip, but I decided to let it pass. "Your family is interesting."

Braden's handsome face brightened at mention of the Grimlock brood. "Yes, we should have our own reality show. Of course, Aisling would be the star, but she might allow all of us a few minutes of screen time each week."

He didn't sound bitter, more amused than anything else. "Are you excited to be an uncle?"

"I am. That will be the most spoiled kid in the universe. I'm sure there will be competitions to see who her favorite uncle is. Jerry thinks he has the post locked up, but the rest of us aren't going to make it that easy for him."

"I thought Jerry was your sister's best friend."

"And Aidan's fiancé. They're getting married in a few months."

"Oh." I found the tidbit fascinating. "So ... your sister's best friend is your brother's future husband. How did that happen?"

"Jerry says it was fate."

"What do you say?"

Braden shrugged, his lips curving. "I think Jerry has always been a member of our family, so it really doesn't matter. When he and Aidan got together, it was a surprise to everyone. Aisling melted down a bit because she felt she was being displaced, but she got over it. Now we're all one big happy family."

"With a new member on the way."

"Yes." Braden bobbed his head as he hit his turn signal and pulled off the highway. The exit sign said we were heading toward Royal Oak. I recognized the name, and it triggered a sense of unease. "I saw you talking to my sister. What did she say? I hope you tried to dissuade her from following us until she pops out that kid."

I tamped down the brewing agitation and focused on him. "She doesn't want to be left out of the action. She's afraid a new baby will dislodge her from her place in the family. She'll get over it."

Braden made a face. "Did she tell you that?"

I kept my gaze out the window and didn't answer.

"She didn't tell you that," Braden scoffed after a beat. "She doesn't even know you. There's no way she would've told you that."

"She didn't have to tell me. It's written all over her face. Why do you think she insisted on following your father and brothers even though her feet are so swollen she's in actual pain?"

"I don't know." Braden's gaze turned thoughtful. "I thought she was exaggerating about her feet."

"Have you looked at them?"

"Yeah. They look like canoes without the openings."

"Well, she's in pain." More than that, I silently added, she's terrified. She didn't want her brothers to know that, so I kept it to myself. "You should be nice to her. She's about to change all your lives."

"What makes you think I'm not nice to her?"

"I get the feeling that all of you enjoy a rousing game of 'annoy your siblings' whenever the mood strikes. You might want to give her a pass for a little bit. She's growing a human being, after all."

"I take it you're sticking up for her because you're a woman. I've noticed Maya doing that, too."

"And who is Maya?"

"Cillian's girlfriend. They moved in together a few months ago, but she's been hanging around Grimlock Manor because she wants to make sure Aisling is being taken care of. She doesn't think a house full of men is what Aisling needs, even though my sister has turned every man in the house into an errand boy."

The words could've come across as bitter, yet Braden was relaxed. "Are you an errand boy, too?"

"Yup. As you said, she's about to create a human being out of thin air. My father is going to be a grandfather and he's so giddy he's practically floating. We're all doing our best to take care of her. You don't have to worry about that."

"I'm not worried."

We made the rest of the trip in relative silence, my gaze focused out the window and Braden's attention on the heavy traffic. When he finally parked, I was surprised to find we were in the middle of a retail area and the building he pointed me toward looked to be something out of a movie.

"What is this place?" I pulled up short and tilted my head back to read the sign.

"Tea & Tarot. It's a magic store, with a little voodoo thrown in for good measure. The woman who runs it knows a little bit about everything. I'm hoping she can help us."

I licked my lips, my mouth running dry. "The woman who runs it. What is her name?"

Braden ignored the question and gestured for me to follow. "You'll meet her in a second. Don't worry. She's perfectly harmless ... at least a good seventy-five percent of the time."

"Wait."

He didn't wait. He was already at the front door. I had a choice; I could follow or turn on my heel and run away. I was certain I could find a cab. I wasn't ready to face what was inside, but there was no way Braden could recognize that.

"What are you doing?" All traces of patience disappearing, Braden fixed me with a pointed look. "You wanted to be part of the team. This is what our part of the team is doing. Stop screwing around. We don't have all day."

My temper lashed out fast enough that Braden was knocked back on his heels thanks to the magic I kept pent up inside. Thankfully, he didn't recognize the source of the shift. Instead, he merely shook his head as he regained his footing.

"Windy, huh?" He rubbed the back of his neck. "That was weird."

I covered quickly. "It's still winter in Michigan." I gripped my coat tighter around my torso. "Of course it's windy."

"Well, come on." Braden held open the door so I could skirt inside ahead of him. "Let's get this over with."

THE STORE WAS different from my memories of it. Of course, my memories of the space were from a much smaller vantage point. I remembered it being bigger ... and darker. The woman standing behind the counter was a different story. She looked exactly the same ... and it made my stomach flip.

"Thank you and come again." She smiled at the customer shuffling away from the counter and waited until he disappeared through the front door before turning her full attention to Braden and me. The look on her face momentarily reflected shock, and then her features eased. "Well, I didn't expect this."

"Hello, Madame Maxine." Braden was grim as he shoved his hands into his pockets and regarded the woman slowly making her way in our direction. "Long time no see."

"Yes, it's been months, Braden." She never moved her eyes from my face. "I see you have a friend."

"Oh, right." He recovered his manners quickly. "This is Izzy Sage. Izzy, this is Madame Maxine. She's a bit of a legend around these parts."

"A legend?" I swallowed hard. "I always knew you thought of yourself as a legend, but I had no idea you'd managed to convince others of it."

"Yes, well, I'm the queen Bruja around these parts, so it had to happen." Maxine stopped in front of me and extended her hand to brush against my aura, a test of sorts. "You look like your mother."

"And you look exactly as I remember you, Aunt Max. You haven't changed a bit."

"It's been two years. I've changed a little." To my utter surprise, she pulled me in for a tight hug. "I'm glad to see you. I thought it would be a few days before we had a chance to sit down."

"That was the plan." I awkwardly patted her back. We weren't strangers, but it had been so long since I'd seen her that it felt that way. "But something came up."

Maxine's eyes were glassy when she pulled back. "I figured that out when you brought this ruffian to darken my doorstep. The Grimlocks only show up when something bad is about to happen."

"It's great to see you, too, Madame Maxine," Braden gritted out, his eyes shifting to me. "Is there something you want to tell me?"

His tone was so accusatory it set my teeth on edge. "Maxine is my aunt. I believe that catches you up."

Not placated in the least, he made an exaggerated face. "Oh, really? I'm shocked."

"Leave her alone, Braden." Maxine cuffed the back of his head before pointing toward the table in the corner of the room. "I think we should sit down and have a conversation."

"That sounds just great," Braden drawled, scuffing the bottoms of his shoes against the ceramic tile as he marched toward the table. "I can't wait to hear this story."

I exchanged a look with my aunt behind his back, baffled. Maxine merely shook her head and made a dismissive motion with her hand.

"Don't worry about him," she said, her voice low. "He has a lot of unresolved feelings he's working through. His anger isn't directed at you. It's me he hates."

"But ... why?"

"It's a long story."

"Maybe I should hear it all the same."

"Not now." The sadness that washed over my aunt's features was enough to have me snapping my mouth shut. "We can catch up on our personal stuff later. I'm guessing you're here for a different purpose."

"We definitely are," Braden agreed as he took a chair, stretching his long legs out in front of him as he leaned back and linked his fingers on his stomach. "I have to say, I didn't see this coming. You didn't mention we were coming to visit your aunt, Izzy."

"I didn't know where we were heading," I reminded him, barely managing to keep my temper in check. I didn't understand the anger he directed toward my aunt. It seemed unnecessary given the woman I knew. Of course, I wasn't up to date on her life. Perhaps I was missing something. "I didn't realize who you were visiting until I saw the name of the store. I haven't seen this place since I was a kid."

"Right." He furrowed his brow. "I didn't even know you had a niece, Madame Maxine. I don't think my father has ever mentioned it. Does he know?"

"I don't know." Maxine refused to react to Braden's bitter tone, instead shoving a cup of tea in front of him before delivering the same to me and herself. "I didn't get to see Izzy much when she was growing up. She lived with her grandfather in New Orleans. We did talk regularly."

"Her grandfather? Isn't that your father?"

I sipped and shook my head. "No. My paternal grandfather. Aunt Max was my mother's sister."

"Well ... okay." Braden's attitude reflected profound unease. I wasn't sure how to fix the situation. In truth, I wasn't certain I wanted to ease his burden. He was something of a jerk, though I was convinced he didn't see that. "We need information on a wraith attack on Belle Isle, Madame Maxine. I wouldn't have come if it wasn't necessary. You know that."

The conversational shift was jarring, but I was thankful for it. "It was definitely weird," I agreed. "I wasn't expecting it."

Maxine gripped my hand tightly. "You were attacked by a wraith?"

"Not exactly," I hedged. I told her the story, opening my mind enough that she could pick up the surface images I offered and get a picture of what had happened. We shared a magical link — one I'd been sure to keep from my employers because I didn't want to draw unnecessary attention — but it came in handy now.

"That's quite the story," Maxine said when I'd finished.

I waited for her to continue, but she didn't. "That's all you have to say?"

Braden snorted. "Get used to that. I told you she was secretive."

Maxine, always hard to read, was an open book as she pinned Braden with a serious gaze. "Is there something you want to say, Braden?"

Most people would've withered under the look, but Braden Grimlock refused to back down. "Why would I possibly have something to say to you?"

I was at a loss. "What am I missing here?"

"Nothing," Maxine and Braden barked at the same time.

"Well, great." I sipped my tea and regrouped. "I'm glad I'm current on the status of your relationship."

Braden narrowed his eyes to dangerous slits before purposely relaxing his facial muscles. I could see the effort he exerted thanks to the change in his aura, but he managed to rein in his temper and focus on the here and now. "Do you have any idea why a wraith would cross over and then come back? We can't figure it out. You seem to know things that no one else does, so I thought maybe there was a chance you could help us."

Instead of replying in kind, with an edge to her voice, Maxine let loose a weary sigh. "There's only one reason I can think of that a wraith would want to visit the other side. They wouldn't be welcome there. The sentries would hunt them down and eradicate them, so that's why the trip was probably so short. The wraith knew what it wanted, where it was going, and had to race back to avoid being destroyed."

"What sentries?" I asked.

"Even Heaven and Hell have security," Maxine replied. "They would've been alerted the minute the wraith crossed the gate threshold."

"How do you know all this?" Braden challenged. "We're not taught any of this when we go through training."

"That's because your training deals with this side. What happens on the other side is none of your concern."

"I still feel we should know that."

"Take it up with your bosses. It's not my fault you don't have all the information you'd like."

"There's plenty else that's your fault," Braden grumbled under his breath.

Maxine opened her mouth, I'm sure a sharp retort on the tip of her tongue. She didn't lash out, though, instead focusing on me. "My best guess is that the wraith got an influx of vitality on the other side. That's what it wanted. Once it succeeded, it raced for the gate to flee the sentries."

"Vitality." I rubbed my forehead, racking my brain. "How does that work?"

"Wraiths feed off the souls of others to survive."

"I know that."

"Vitality is different," Maxine explained. "Vitality is what survives on the other side. If a wraith got enough vitality, it would grow in strength to the point it would become something else entirely."

"What?" Braden asked, instantly alert. "What would it become?"

Maxine held out her hands and shrugged. "I don't know. Until now, it's only been a hunch. It's the soul walkers who first hypothesized it would be a solution to their problem. As you well remember, they made a lot of mistakes."

"I remember," Braden growled, straightening in his chair. "If what you're saying is true, you're insinuating that wraith supercharged itself. Does that mean it will be harder to kill?"

"I've never seen or heard of a wraith actually accomplishing this," Maxine cautioned. "We've talked about it in different circles, worried about it even a few months ago given what was going on. But it didn't happen, so we chose to forget it."

"Well, it's happened now." Braden didn't look happy. I couldn't blame him. "We need to figure out how to fix this. Any ideas on how to track down the wraith in question?"

"No. I'm not sure what to tell you."

"Then I guess this was a wasted trip."

I felt otherwise but didn't give voice to my feelings. "We need to think outside the box," I suggested. "Where do the wraiths in this area go? They're creatures of habit. We need to figure out this particular wraith's habits."

"That's easier said than done," Braden argued. "It's not as if the wraiths confide in us."

"So, what do you suggest?"

"I don't know. I need time to think."

"Great. You think." Maxine lobbed an indulgent smile in his direction. "While you do that, I'm going to catch up with my niece. Is that okay with you?"

"Would it matter if I wasn't okay with it?"

"No."

"Then I'm fine with it."

Maxine's smugness came out to play. "I thought you would be."

Six

"He's intense."

We left Braden to stew at the table, Maxine leading me to a set of comfortable overstuffed chairs on the other side of the store. I couldn't stop myself from watching him despite the pall he cast. He was clearly struggling.

"He's the most intense of that clan," Maxine agreed, pouring me a fresh cup of tea. "The girl was intense for a long time, too. Actually, I thought there was a chance the girl would grow up to be unbearable due to her intensity. Her father spoiled her to the point I often wanted to slap her around. But she outgrew it."

"Aisling?"

Maxine's eyebrow lifted. "You've met her?"

"A few hours ago."

"That was quick."

"She didn't want to be left behind."

My aunt's chuckle was warm. "That sounds like her. She'll be giving birth soon. That will change the Grimlock dynamic. I'm hoping in a good way."

"You seem to know them well."

"I know *some* of them well," she clarified. "Redmond and Cormack

I know best. Cillian stops by for research material occasionally, but he's more focused on books than people. Aidan stops by when he's looking for something specific. I haven't seen Aisling in several months, not since the last big battle they faced."

"I thought they faced constant battles. That's what Renee and Oliver said. They're the people I'm working with, by the way. They seem nice enough."

"I know Oliver." Maxine's smile was mischievous. "Once you get to know him you'll like him a great deal. I'm not familiar with Renee. I'm sure you'll fit in ... eventually."

"But I'm the boss. I'm supposed to be in charge."

"And you don't feel in charge because the Grimlocks swooped in and took over your first day," she surmised. "I get that. The Grimlocks know what they're doing when it comes to wraiths. Let Cormack do his thing ... at least for now."

She sounded practical. That didn't mean the idea sat well with me. "What's going on with you and Braden? He seems to hate you. You've been careful not to say too much, but I know something happened between the two of you. He was in a much better mood before he saw you, despite everything that happened."

Maxine's gaze was thoughtful as it landed on Braden. "That's not my story to tell," she said finally. "Suffice it to say, life has been difficult for the Grimlocks at various points. They're a gregarious bunch, loyal to a fault, but Braden has always been the most serious of the lot."

"That wasn't really an answer."

"It's the only answer I can give you. I mean ... think about it. Do you want me spreading our family business all over town, telling the Grimlocks the secrets we hold dear?"

"Of course not."

"Then I can't tell you the Grimlock secrets," Maxine said. "They're entitled to their privacy. The good thing for you is that they're bad at keeping secrets, even their own, so you'll probably find someone who will open his or her mouth if you're really that interested. I would aim for Aisling."

"Because she has a big mouth?"

"They all have big mouths. She definitely does. She's also bored and feels left out."

"How do you know that?" I was officially intrigued. "I felt the same thing when I was with her earlier. Her emotions are right on the surface, but she didn't actually come out and say that. I thought you said you hadn't seen her in a bit."

"I've been keeping an eye on her ... from afar. I've developed an interest of sorts. She's an intriguing little thing, full of sarcastic comments and a need to speak before she thinks. She's matured a lot in the last two years, but she can't change her nature."

"Well, I don't want to gossip out of turn," I hedged. "I kind of liked her. I didn't get to spend much time with her, but she's interesting. The whole family is interesting. I appear to be working for them, but that's not the job I signed up for. It makes me nervous."

"Don't kid yourself. You signed up to watch the gate because of what happened to your parents. You might be able to fool others, but you can't fool me."

"I can't remember all of it," I admitted. "I see bits and pieces. I can't make out the whole picture."

"Is that why you came back?"

I shrugged, noncommittal. "I came back because this is home and something inside was urging me to come home. I can't explain it."

"You'll figure it out." Her hand rested lightly on mine. "You always figure things out, Izzy. That's one of your strengths."

"I don't feel particularly strong right now. I'm out of my element and I've already lost control."

"You'll find your balance." Maxine sounded sure of herself as Braden finally stood and shifted his eyes to me. "He will eventually, too. His anger with me isn't directed at you, so don't take it personally."

"That's easier said than done."

"He doesn't mean it. He's a Grimlock. Thinking before speaking is an alien concept."

I chuckled dryly. "I'll keep that in mind."

"I believe he wants you to go with him now. He must have an idea."

"Why do I think it's a bad idea?"

"Because you're a good judge of character."

"WHAT IS THIS PLACE?"

I cringed as Braden parked in front of an abandoned warehouse thirty minutes later. When he pointed us toward what could only be described as a rough neighborhood, I had my doubts. Now that we were parked and stood out like pickles in a carrot patch, I was downright against whatever idea he planned to force upon me.

I still didn't know what his genius idea entailed.

"This is a former wraith nest," Braden replied as he strode to the back of his vehicle and opened the hatchback. "We cleaned it out about three weeks ago."

"If you cleaned it out, why are we here?" I watched as he rummaged in a black duffel bag and came back with a bejeweled dagger, which he wordlessly handed to me.

"This was an absolutely huge nest and it was a lot of work to wipe it out. It took hours. We even had to get my brother-in-law involved because we needed extra hands, which didn't sit well with my sister."

"She mentioned her husband was a police officer." I slid the dagger inside my coat as I fell into step with him. "There must be an interesting story associated with their relationship. I thought we were supposed to keep the true nature of our jobs hidden from outsiders."

"Yeah, well, Aisling never met a rule she didn't want to break. As for Griffin, he walked in on her killing a wraith before they even hooked up. It was an accident ... and he managed to accept everything in our world without putting up too much of a fuss. Surprisingly, he fit right in."

"And now he helps you?"

"Not usually. He has a job to do. We needed help with this nest, though. Usually we would've taken Aisling, but she's far too big and my father has somehow turned into a mother hen where she's concerned. He's always been careful to keep her protected, but now that she's pregnant he's stopped just short of following her around with pillows to make sure she doesn't get jostled."

"That's kind of cute."

"Not really." Braden nudged the warehouse's front door with his toe and cautiously peered inside. "It looks the same as when we left it. I don't know that we'll find anything here. I don't know where else to look. My father and brother are conducting research. That's not exactly my forte."

"What is your 'forte'?"

This time the smile that ghosted Braden's lips was genuine. "I'm an excellent pool player and no one can beat me at basketball."

"That wasn't really what I meant."

"It's what I've got to offer."

"Fair enough." My nerves were beginning to fray thanks to the dim lighting and acrid scent. "It smells like someone died in here."

"A lot of wraiths died in here."

"Yeah, but ... it smells like a person died in here."

The look Braden shot me dripped with curiosity. "Tell me about yourself," he said after a beat. "Were you born into a reaper family?"

"Not exactly."

Braden slipped into the room in front of us and stared at every corner before arching an eyebrow. "Would you care to expound on that?"

This was the part of the conversation I'd been dreading. I'd pushed Maxine to reveal Braden's secrets, but wasn't interested in sharing mine. I recognized that was unfair, but I barely knew him ... and I was a total busybody. Sometimes life simply doesn't balance out.

"My father was a reaper," I said finally. "My mother wasn't. She worked for the home office, but we didn't go out in the field."

"Okay." Braden lifted his phone to use as a flashlight as we hit another room. "What did you do?"

"We ran the gate."

"Really?" Intrigue flitted across Braden's face. "Did you grow up on Belle Isle?"

"Only until I was seven."

"Were you transferred after that?"

"In a way." I sucked in a calming breath. I would eventually have to answer questions. Delaying the inevitable would help nobody. "My parents were killed on the island. I was spared, but I obviously couldn't stay there. Maxine wanted me, but my grandfather pulled rank. He took me to New Orleans."

"Wow!" Braden's dumbfounded expression said it all. "I'm sorry that happened. I ... that's awful. If you don't mind me asking, how did your parents die?"

"I don't really remember."

The answer clearly wasn't what Braden was expecting. "Were you there?"

"They say I was." The flashes I saw in my dreams told me I was there, but I didn't feel comfortable enough with him to admit that. "I'm not sure what happened. The police came. There was a lot of blood. I remember some screaming ... although I don't know if it was my mother or me. I simply can't remember."

Braden's face was ghost white as he turned to face me. "I'm really sorry. I shouldn't have asked you about it."

"It's okay. Someone eventually would've asked. I need to get comfortable talking about it now that I'm back."

"I guess." He slowly swiveled so we could pick our way through the building. It was devoid of furniture, but it was clear local teens had thrown a party or two, given all the discarded beer cans and trash. "My mother died, too."

His voice was so quiet when he made the admission I almost missed it. "Your sister mentioned something about that, but she didn't go into detail. I can't remember exactly how it came up, but she seemed reticent to mention it."

"Yeah, well, we're all reticent where my mother is concerned."

"I understand. Trust me. If anyone understands, I do. Of course, I can't remember my parents all that well. I mean ... I have memories, but they're kind of cloudy. How old were you when your mother died?"

"Twenty."

"So, you were older."

"Older than you, that's for sure," Braden agreed. "It was still a shock."

"How did she die?" It was an invasive question, but I couldn't stop myself from asking.

"It was a fire. She was collecting a soul. It's a really long and convoluted story."

"And you don't want to talk about it," I noted.

"Not really. It's hard to talk about. It's ... things happened after the fact that make all of us uncomfortable. We don't talk about it much. My father is a big proponent of looking forward rather than back, so that's what we're doing."

"With your sister's baby?"

"Aisling likes to think that she's the center of our world — and my father has done nothing to dissuade her from that thought — but our family is more than just Aisling. Cillian recently moved in with Maya, and they're looking toward the future. I guarantee they'll get engaged soon.

"Aidan and Jerry should have been married months ago, but Jerry is insisting on the biggest and best wedding in the world," he continued, his lips curving. "They've already started filling out paperwork in anticipation of adopting a child. Aisling, of course, wants to pick the kid, but they've shut that down."

"And you?"

"I'm still trying to figure out exactly what I want," Braden admitted, cocking his head to the side. I watched him, curious. It was almost as if he'd heard something. I had supersensitive hearing, but I was convinced I hadn't heard a thing.

"Is something wrong?"

Braden lifted a finger to his lips before quietly sliding into the room at his back. Inadvertently, my heart started beating at an accelerated pace and I found my palms sweaty. I rubbed them over my jeans, determined to make sure I could safely grip the dagger Braden had supplied me with earlier.

I watched the strong lines of Braden's body as he carefully searched the room, squinting into the darkness as I tried to make out his movements. I was so intent on him, my hand sliding inside my coat to retrieve the dagger, that I didn't hear the sound of rustling fabric until it was directly behind me.

I turned quickly, my senses kicking into overdrive, and gaped at the wraith sliding from what looked to be a closet into the hallway. "Son of a troll!" The words escaped before I realized how ridiculous they sounded. It was impossible to yank them back, so I opted to ignore them.

"Izzy!" I couldn't see Braden, but I heard him scrambling in the next room. He wasn't my focus. He couldn't be. The creature reaching out an ethereal hand was my worry.

"Kanpe." I fell back on my grandfather's creole without thinking. The simple word wasn't enough to stop the creature, though.

The wraith ignored Braden's impending arrival and focused on me, its fingers wrapping around my neck as I struggled to grip the dagger. I'd read about wraith attacks plenty of times. I'd even seen company-approved videos. This was something else entirely.

I wasn't the type to panic, yet I felt as if my ears weren't working correctly and my heart was about to burst.

"Izzy!" Braden was still behind me, and because his barriers were down I felt the terror washing over him. He was convinced I would die, right here and now, and there was nothing he could do to stop it.

"Kanpe," I rasped out, finally managing to free the dagger.

The wraith ignored my order. I knew I had no choice but to act. I gripped the handle of the dagger and slammed the sharp end against the wraith's chest. The creature barely shifted, which told me I hadn't hit my intended target.

I drew it back again and called on the magic inside. I needed help, and the magic was all I had. This time when I lashed out something ripped free from inside and propelled the dagger into the creature's chest with enough force that I swear I felt the blade breaking bone.

The wraith released my neck almost immediately, causing me to reel back. I dropped to my knees despite my best efforts to remain on my feet.

Braden moved in beside me, catching me before I hit the ground. Something fluttered against my face. At first, I thought it was tears … or maybe the fabric from the wraith's cloak. Then I realized it was ash.

"What's this?" I was dazed as I caught some of the ash on my fingertips. I didn't understand what was happening. "I … don't feel so well."

"Oh, do you think?" Braden's face was animated as he struggled to lift me. "That's because you just went toe to toe with a wraith and it put its hands on you. Never let a wraith put its hands on you!"

"Good to know." I felt detached, as if I was living someone else's life. "I think I'm going to fall asleep soon. Could you wake me before school? I can't be late for school."

Braden's expression twisted into puzzlement. "I ... you're going to be okay. Do you hear me? You're going to be okay."

"I hear you. I will be okay." Somehow I knew that, which was why I didn't fight the inclination to let go. "I'll see you in the morning."

"Wait. Don't pass out!"

It was too late. The last thing I heard was a muttered curse, and then I was floating in the darkness. It wasn't such a bad place to be.

Seven

The next thirty minutes flew by in a blur. Braden managed to get me out of the warehouse — I was fairly certain he carried me, but I was too much of a feminist to admit that I readily allowed it — and into his BMW. I recognized we were on a freeway, although I had no idea where we were going. My mind was a jumble of images, my body cold. In fact, the chill pervading me was so intense Braden cranked up the heat and directed as many dashboard vents as he could in my direction.

Still I shivered. He was sweating by the time we pulled inside a gated enclosure and parked in front of what was either the biggest house I'd ever seen or a train station.

"Are we leaving town?" I felt stupid. My head refused to work the way the goddess intended. "Are we going somewhere?"

"Just inside." He grunted as he helped me from the BMW, using his strength to keep me upright as he pinned me to his side and used his free hand to open the door.

The first thing I saw was a gleaming marble floor in what appeared to be a foyer of some sort, gorgeous mahogany staircases leading upward on either side. Even though I was detached, somehow separate from my body, I couldn't stop myself from goggling.

"Is this a castle?"

Braden chuckled as he dragged me to the right. "My sister and Jerry used to pretend it was."

"It feels like a castle."

"Yeah, well, I'll give you the grand tour if you snap out of this. I'm not big on bribes, but I feel confident offering that one."

"I'll consider it. Oomph." I tripped over my feet and pitched forward. Braden had a firm hold on me. He gripped my waist and kept me from careening into the wall. "I do my own stunts. Can you tell?"

He barked out a laugh. "At least your spirits are up." He stopped in front of an ornate door and pushed it open without knocking, dragging me inside as several dark heads snapped to attention. I recognized all three of them — although I was too confused to remember names — and continued to shiver as Braden lowered me to a couch.

"Stoke up the fire, Cillian," Braden ordered as he dragged a blanket from the back of the couch and threw it over me.

Cillian. The name was familiar. For some reason, when Braden said his name all I could picture was books.

"What happened to her?" A woman, one who looked as if she'd swallowed a beach ball, grunted as she knelt next to me. "Her skin is cold."

"Wraith," Braden explained, tucking the blanket in at my sides. "We went to that warehouse we cleaned out a few weeks ago because I thought one or two of the ones that escaped might have returned."

"You shouldn't have gone alone," the older man chided, his eyes filling with annoyance. "You could've been hurt."

"I'm fine," I offered lamely. "I do my own stunts."

I thought I sounded fine, but the face the woman made said otherwise.

"Her teeth are chattering," she said. "She needs to be warmed up."

"What do you think I'm doing, Aisling?"

Aisling. That's right. I remembered the name. It was unique ... like her.

"You're not doing it fast enough," Aisling admonished. "The quickest way to shake wraith shivers is body heat."

"I can't believe you gave it a name," Cillian snickered, shaking his head. "That's so you."

"Well, out of everyone here, who has been attacked by wraiths the most?"

"Kid, I'm not a fan of you bringing that up," the older man said as he rested his hand on his daughter's shoulder. "You're right, though. We need to warm her up. That means body heat or a bath."

The idea of these people trying to strip me naked so they could shove me in boiling water loosened my tongue. "No bath." I struggled to a sitting position, determined to prove I was in control of my destiny. "I'm fine."

The dark-haired foursome ignored me.

"It has to be body heat," Aisling said pragmatically. "She doesn't want to be undressed. I don't blame her. She doesn't know us. We could be perverts for all she knows."

"Body heat it is." The older man — for the life of me I couldn't remember his name — planted his hands on his hips and gave Braden an expectant look.

"Why me?" Braden whined, essentially slamming his elbow into my ego.

"Because you didn't take care of her when you should have," the father replied without hesitation. "If you'd watched her this wouldn't have happened."

"Besides, Dad is too old and Cillian has a girlfriend," Aisling added. "You're the only single one. It's your duty to warm her up."

"Oh, whatever." Braden made a face as he stripped out of his coat and kicked off his shoes. "I want you to know that I'm doing this under protest."

"I'll make a notation in my report," the older man said dryly. "Now ... do it."

"Fine." Braden offered me a sheepish smile as he lifted the blanket and slid in behind me. He dropped the heavy afghan over both of us before pressing his chest against my back and wrapping his arm around my waist. The second he touched me, some of the cold disappeared. "Um ... is this right?"

"You just need to warm her up," Aisling replied, a hint of mischief flitting through her eyes. "You don't need to be graded on your prowess or anything. If you need reinforcement, I'm sure she'll be up for it later."

"Oh, very funny," Braden growled. "If you weren't pregnant, I would totally slap you around."

"Don't threaten your sister," the father ordered, eliciting a smug look from his daughter. "Your only job is to warm that girl up and tell us what happened."

"I already told you what happened."

"Well, I want to hear the story again. Start from the beginning, and don't leave anything out."

I MEANT TO STAY AWAKE. For some reason, I thought it was important. I wanted to hear Braden relate the tale and then launch into what I was sure they would find a brilliant plan once he was done.

Instead, I slept.

There was something about the crackling fire and the warmth of Braden's body against mine that caused my eyelids to droop. I was out within minutes. I had no idea how long I'd slept, but when I woke it was to gregarious voices.

"There's the love of my life."

I cracked an eye but remained still to get my bearings. The first thing I saw was a handsome man — this one boasting brown hair and eyes — strolling across the office and planting a smacking kiss on Aisling's mouth.

"Oh, you're the love of my life, too," Aisling said. "I especially feel that when you rub my feet." She wiggled her toes for emphasis, causing the man to snicker as he lifted her legs so he could sit next to her and wrap his fingers around her swollen feet.

"Oh, I knew there was a reason I married you." Aisling threw her head back and let ecstasy take over as she made a series of moans that caused my cheeks to flood with heat.

"Whatever you're doing to cause her to make those noises, stop it right now." The father — his name was Cormack, I remembered now

— strolled into the room and gave the man with Aisling a pointed look. "Those noises are obscene, Griffin."

Griffin. It was a nice name. I couldn't remember if Aisling mentioned it earlier, but it fit the man rubbing her feet without complaint after a long day of work.

"You're telling me," Griffin teased his father-in-law, amusement evident. "I have to live with her. She used to make those noises for another reason. Now I'm relegated to foot patrol."

"That is not amusing." Cormack extended a warning finger. "You used to fear me. Do you remember? What happened to those days? I miss them."

"You turned into a big marshmallow and spoiled Aisling to the point of no return," Griffin replied, not missing a beat. "You're not exactly terrifying when you're arranging ice cream bars every week to keep your daughter happy."

"I could still be terrifying."

"Yeah, yeah." Griffin waved off Cormack's bold words and let his eyes drift to the couch where I rested, forcing me to keep very still. "Who is that?"

"Braden's new girlfriend," Aisling answered, wriggling her feet to make sure Griffin remembered she needed attention. "I like her a great deal. In fact, I want to trade her for Braden."

"How did Braden get a new girlfriend so quickly? Last thing I knew, he was playing the field. That's what he told me when he scheduled two dates for the same night last week."

"What a pig," Aisling complained, shaking her head. I couldn't help but agree with her assessment. The man in question remained behind me, his heavy breathing causing me to believe he was asleep, so I couldn't exactly make my opinion known.

"That's the new gatekeeper," Cormack supplied. "We had an incident today."

"Oh, you know I love it when you guys have incidents." Griffin did something with his hands that made Aisling practically purr as she flexed her toes. "I don't understand what a gatekeeper is. I've never heard that term."

"She handles the gate between the veils," Aisling volunteered.

"After we're done collecting the souls, they get transported to her so they can move through the gate."

"The gate to Heaven?" Griffin looked confused.

"Not Heaven," Cormack countered. "Think of it more as a waiting room of sorts. The souls have to be sorted before moving on to their final resting places."

Griffin remained confused. "And that's what's on the other side of this gate?"

"Essentially," Cormack confirmed. "Earlier today a wraith managed to breach security and jumped through the gate. We thought it might be a suicide mission of sorts — I mean ... what else would it be? — so I dispatched Braden. He wasn't there very long before the wraith reappeared through the same opening, but this time it was altered, and it disappeared before Braden could kill it."

The look on Griffin's face told me he was officially dumbfounded. "I don't think I understand," he said finally. "How was it altered?"

"It was bigger," Aisling replied. "They wouldn't let me see the video because I was stuck in a chair, but my understanding is that it was big and scary."

"Wait." Griffin held up a hand to still his wife. "Why were you close to a wraith?"

"I wasn't close to a wraith."

"You're supposed to be done with work." He turned a set of accusatory eyes to Cormack. "You said you were putting her on maternity leave early because it was the best thing for her. We agreed."

"I did put her on maternity leave," Cormack shot back. "She tricked Maya and snuck out. It's not my fault she refuses to follow orders."

"You're her boss," Griffin grumbled, digging his thumbs into the soles of Aisling's feet. "You're supposed to find a way to make her do your bidding."

"Nothing happened to me," Aisling pointed out as she squirmed. "That feels really good."

"I should let you suffer for sneaking out of the house."

"We both know you're not going to do that," Aisling countered. "My feet are like sausages ... and they hurt."

The simple statement was enough to make me snap my eyes open. I wasn't surprised to find Cormack watching me with unbridled curiosity. He clearly realized I was awake before I finally decided to stop pretending.

"Hello, Izzy." The smile he offered was genuine. "I'm glad to see you're feeling better."

"Yeah, well ... ." I trailed off, dragging a hand through my hair as I struggled to a sitting position. Braden didn't stir, instead continuing to snore lightly as I faced my embarrassment without backup. "Thank you for taking care of me."

"We didn't really take care of you." Cormack gestured toward the chair across from his desk. "We simply kept you safe while your body did the rest."

I sat in the chair he indicated, offering Aisling a thin-lipped smile as she watched. Her husband merely smiled as he continued rubbing her feet, which were so swollen they looked as if an explosion was imminent.

"Braden told us about what happened at the warehouse," Cormack supplied. "He shouldn't have taken you there. I'm sorry you were injured."

His stilted apology caused the hair on the back of my neck to stand on end. "It wasn't his fault. Neither of us paid attention to the closet. It looked empty. It was a fluke."

"You don't work in the field, though."

"So?"

"I shouldn't have allowed you to go with Braden from the start," Cormack replied. "You haven't been trained for this sort of excursion. That's on me."

By all appearances, he was trying to make me feel better. His words had the opposite effect. "I'm not delicate."

"I didn't say you were."

"You're acting like it."

Cormack's eyes momentarily darkened. "I'm trying to take responsibility for my mistake."

"Well, it's not necessary." I was in no mood to play victim. "I knew what I was getting into. I'm not sorry I went. The gate is my responsibility. I should be involved in the investigation surrounding the breach."

"Yes, but ... ."

"Ignore him," Aisling interjected, making a dismissive gesture that caught my attention. "He's not trying to be a pain. Er, well, he does sometimes enjoy that. That's not what he's doing here, though. He feels bad about what happened, and his guilt manifests in sexism."

Cormack balked. "I'm not sexist!"

"You most certainly are," Aisling shot back. "You're totally sexist ... and then some. When I was a kid I had a different set of rules from the boys."

"Name one rule you had the boys didn't."

"I wasn't allowed to swim shirtless at the lake."

Cormack rolled his eyes. "It's not my fault that there are different sets of rules for boys and girls when it comes to swimming etiquette. Take it up with Miss Manners ... or whoever made that rule. I didn't impose that rule on you; society did."

"How about when the boys were allowed to stay out all night for their proms but I had to be back by two in the morning?"

"That was for your own safety," Cormack replied without hesitation. "Teenagers — especially boys — are horn dogs. I was keeping you safe, and I'm not sorry for it."

"You didn't keep the boys safe," Aisling shot back.

"Maybe that's because you're my favorite and I didn't care if they came back," Cormack suggested. "Have you ever considered that?"

Aisling was clearly in too much pain to argue. Discomfort was etched all over her face, something I couldn't take any longer.

"Good grief. How can you people torture her like this?" I rolled out of my chair and dropped to my knees in front of Aisling, giving her husband a wary look as I held up my hands. "May I?"

"May you what?" Griffin asked, refusing to release his wife's feet. "What are you going to do to her?"

"Make her feel better." I had only one goal with my next maneuver, and that was to alleviate the occasional whimpering I heard inside Aisling's head when her barriers weakened. "She's not just complaining to complain — although I know that's what you think. She's in serious pain."

Griffin narrowed his eyes. "I never said she was complaining to complain."

"No, but you thought it."

Griffin opened his mouth to argue, but no sound came out.

"How do you know what he was thinking?" Aisling asked.

"It's a little ability I have."

"You're psychic?"

"I'm ... sensitive," I clarified. "I can sometimes feel emotions, see inside people's heads and even dream about things I have no business knowing about."

"That's not a reaper ability, right?" Griffin queried.

Cormack shook his head. "No. It's a witch ability."

"Bruja," I corrected. "I'm not a witch. My mother was a Bruja."

Griffin wasn't ready to accept my claims about being able to help his wife. "What's a Bruja?"

"A fancy witch," Aisling replied. "Can you really stop my feet from hurting?"

"I can ease some of the issues."

"Then go for it. I can't take much more of this."

"Wait a second." Griffin kept his hands protectively over Aisling's feet. "How do I know you won't hurt her?"

"Why would I hurt her?"

"It happens all the time. I think it has something to do with her mouth."

"Well, that's not who I am." I worked hard to corral my temper. "I have no interest in hurting her. In fact, it's the pain she's struggling with – something that's so loud in her head I hear it echoing in my head – that I want to ease. She's already in pain."

Griffin cast his wife a sidelong look. "I'm sticking close for this."

Aisling didn't seem surprised by the statement. "Great. Awesome. Knock yourself out." She focused on me. "What do you need me to do?"

I smiled at her ability to throw caution to the wind. "Do you have any Epsom salts?"

Eight

Braden was awake by the time Cormack gathered the supplies I'd asked for. I requested a bucket be filled with warm water and placed at Aisling's feet before I dumped some Epsom salts in and motioned for her to lower her feet into the liquid.

Whether she trusted me or not — my guess was she was on the fence — Aisling was in so much discomfort she did as I asked without hesitation. Griffin remained close, keeping at his wife's side as he watched me rest my hands on the edges of the bucket.

"What are you going to do?" Braden's curiosity got the better of him as he joined us. "This won't hurt her, will it?"

"She'll be fine." I smiled at Aisling as I flexed my fingers. "I can't fix everything because this is nature at work, but I can ease some of the discomfort."

"Because you're a Bruja?" Aisling was intrigued by the process. "Just for the record, we've crossed paths with a witch or two and it didn't end well. There were a lot of evil shenanigans going on, and I only like my shenanigans mildly evil, not fully evil."

"I'm not that kind of Bruja. I'm more of a traditionalist, female empowerment and the like. My grandfather owns a magic store in New

Orleans. I learned a lot from him, although he was technically born a reaper."

"Is he still there?" Cormack asked as he lowered himself into a nearby chair to watch.

I nodded. "He is. He wasn't keen on me returning to Detroit. He wanted me to stay with him."

"He raised you after your parents died, right?" Braden asked.

"He did."

"Even though Madame Maxine wanted you to stay with her."

Aisling's eyes flashed with surprise. "What?"

"Oh, did I forget to mention that?" Braden rubbed his hand over the back of his sleep-mussed hair. "Izzy is Madame Maxine's niece. I found that out this afternoon during our visit."

"That would've been helpful information," Cormack chided, shaking his head. "I knew Maxine had a niece — and I'm vaguely aware of the incident that claimed her sister's life — but I had no idea that Izzy was the woman in question."

"Well, now you know." I forced myself to remain chipper as I worked my fingers over the water. "Now, be quiet for a second. I need to concentrate."

I didn't miss the amused look Braden shared with his father, but they remained silent as I pulsed magic from the ends of my fingertips. I'd learned the healing spell from an elderly Bruja in the French Quarter. Louise was a good friend of my grandfather's — I often wondered if they were more than friends — and she taught me her whole bag of tricks before I departed. I was thankful for the lessons, although the studied way the Grimlocks watched me now made me question the intelligence associated with volunteering my talents.

"Just relax, Aisling," I instructed. "The water is going to bubble. That's normal."

"I don't care if the water starts talking," Aisling murmured as she leaned back on the couch, her eyes closed. "That feels amazing."

I risked a glance at Griffin and found him smiling as he watched his wife enjoy her foot bath. He was hard to get a read on, a bit of wariness tinged his blue aura, but it was clear he would do whatever it took to make Aisling feel better. Sure, he was convinced she was milking her ailment to get attention, but he honestly didn't care. He was willing to dote on her until the end of time, which was apparently what she wanted.

"Is she sleeping?" Braden asked suddenly, leaning forward. "She sounds like she's snoring."

"She snores a lot louder than that," Griffin countered. "But she is sleeping. She went heavy against my side. In fact, I don't think she's slept this hard in weeks."

"She's uncomfortable," I explained, the magic continuing to pulse in short bursts from my fingers. The Grimlocks couldn't see what I was doing. They simply recognized that I was helping Aisling and opted to let me go about my business without intervening. "She's a thin woman. The only weight she's carrying is in her chest and stomach. That makes matters worse because her back and feet are screaming twenty-four hours a day."

Griffin jerked his head in my direction. "I thought she was just bucking for massages when she said her back hurt."

"Really?" I cocked a challenging eyebrow. "Can you imagine carrying this much extra weight in one spot? How would your back feel?"

"She's got you there, Griffin," Braden teased. "Although, to be fair, I thought she was whining simply to whine, too. Are you telling me she's been in pain all this time?"

"Not pain," I clarified. "I wasn't around for the beginning of her pregnancy. I can't tell you what she was feeling then. She's close to the end. Her discomfort will only magnify. It's not helped by the fact that she's terrified of giving birth."

Cormack shifted on his chair and drew my attention. "She's terrified? How do you know that?"

"She's an open book as far as emotions go. She probably can't shade her emotions right now, which is why they're so easy to read. That's common in women before their time."

"But ... Aisling isn't afraid of anything," Braden argued. "Why would she be afraid of this?"

"Is it the birth itself?" Griffin asked worriedly. "We had to go to this class where they showed us video of an actual birth. She was fine before that, upbeat even. That video was scary. Neither one of us slept that night."

I offered him a heartfelt smile. "She is terrified of the pain, but she knows that it's temporary. She's more afraid of being displaced than anything else."

"Displaced?" Cormack rubbed his hands together. "Why would she be displaced?"

I shrugged. I wasn't a mind reader. I couldn't know everything that went through the woman's head. "I don't know. I can't answer that for you."

"It's because she's used to being the center of attention," Braden interjected. "That has to be it. Once the baby comes, everyone will be focused on it rather than her."

"Well, we simply won't let that happen." Cormack was matter-of-fact. "We'll spoil her just as much as we normally do. We'll make a point of it."

"You mean that you'll spoil her as much as you normally do," Griffin corrected. "You're the one who goes out of your way to make sure she's the center of everyone's universe."

"Oh, please." Cormack refused to let Griffin paint him into a corner. "You spoil her just as much as I do. In fact, I'll wager you spoil her more than I do."

"That's not possible."

"And I don't think it matters," I interjected, my tone forceful. "She can't help her fear. We all know she has nothing to worry about. I barely know you people and I recognize that. It's normal for expectant mothers to feel fear. That's all this is."

"What should we do?" Griffin pressed. "I want her to feel safe and secure."

"I don't know." That was the truth. "You know her best. Figure it out."

THEY INVITED ME FOR DINNER.

I was uncomfortable at the thought — the Grimlocks were a close-knit family, after all — but I didn't have a way back to Belle Isle because Braden had driven. I could've tried for an Uber, but ultimately I agreed to stay because a rejuvenated Aisling informed me they were having prime rib and an ice cream bar. She was so enthusiastic I acquiesced.

Now, looking at the huge spread in the dining room, I could understand why Aisling spent half the afternoon talking about the prime rib. "This is ... wow!"

"Yeah, it took me a while to get used to it, too," Griffin said as I got comfortable between him and Aidan. "Now I have to work out twice as often because I eat double the calories."

I could see that. "This place is fantastic. I can't believe you live here all alone, Mr. Grimlock."

At the head of the table, a glass of bourbon in hand, Cormack arched an eyebrow. "Call me 'Cormack.' And what makes you think I live here alone?"

"Oh, well ... ." The question caught me off guard. "I was under the impression that your wife had died. I assumed you were alone. I'm sorry. That was a stupid thing to say."

"It's not stupid. I'm not married. I don't have a girlfriend or significant other."

"Yeah, last time he did that we all lost our minds a bit," Braden explained from across the table. "We prefer him single and sad."

"Don't say things like that." Aisling threw a roll across the table. Braden clearly wasn't expecting it because it bounced off his head.

"That was uncalled for," Braden snapped, making a face. "The second you pop that kid out — I mean the absolute second — I'm giving you nine months of brotherly love taps. You'd better prepare yourself."

He was all talk. I recognized that. He didn't realize it, but his concern for his sister was right on the surface when I mentioned her terror in his father's office. Apparently arguing was part of their sibling shtick.

"Oh, I'm shaking in my unswollen feet," Aisling shot back, smiling at me. "Thanks for whatever you did, by the way. I haven't felt this good in weeks. You're a miracle worker."

My cheeks burned under the praise. "It was nothing."

"That's not true." Griffin was serious. "She feels so much better than she did. I can't thank you enough."

"It wasn't a big deal."

"It was." Griffin refused to let it go. "I don't like it when she's in pain."

"Mostly because she makes the rest of us feel the pain, too," Braden grumbled.

Griffin ignored him. "Really. Thank you."

"We're all thankful," Cormack agreed. "You did a great thing, and we're all grateful."

"What are we grateful for?"

I flicked my eyes to the door when Redmond, Cillian and a woman I didn't recognize walked in. They were laughing, and didn't appear surprised to have a guest at the table.

"Izzy fixed Aisling's feet," Braden supplied. "She's a witch."

"Bruja," Aisling clarified on my behalf before I had a chance to respond. "If you haven't noticed, she doesn't like the term 'witch.'"

"I don't see a difference," Braden argued. "A Bruja by any other name is a witch."

"They're not all that similar," I argued. "There are distinctive differences."

"Like what?"

"Like mind your own business," Aisling snapped, her temper on full display. "She's allowed to feel whatever she feels ... especially after she saved my feet." As if to prove her point, she pushed back from the table and lifted her bare feet. "Do you see this? She erased five pounds of water weight from each one. I no longer feel as if I'm about to explode."

"And we're all very thankful for that, Aisling," Cormack said, shaking his head as he graced his daughter with a fond look. "I don't care how much better you're feeling, though. Feet don't belong on the table."

"Whatever." Aisling's annoyance was evident. "I wish Jerry were here. He'd understand my excitement. Where is he?" She turned to stare at Aidan. "I thought he was coming for dinner tonight."

"He got caught up with a wedding consultation," Aidan replied as he watched the cook carve the prime rib at the end of the table. "Apparently the mayor's son is marrying a state representative's son and they have big plans for the cake."

"Jerry owns a bakery in Royal Oak," Aisling offered helpfully. "It's called Get Baked and it's amazing. He's been keeping me in sugar for the past few months. I'll take you to meet him when we both have an opening in our schedules. You're going to love him."

Griffin rested his arm on the back of Aisling's chair. "How do you know she's going to love Jerry?"

"Everybody loves Jerry!"

"She's right." Aidan winked at his sister before focusing his full attention on me. "You should go with Aisling, though. I think you'll like Jerry, and I guarantee Jerry will like you. He's a big fan of people who can wear leather coats without looking like the Fonz."

Aisling snickered as I glanced at the jacket I had draped over the back of my chair.

"He likes people who look like the Fonz, too," she offered. "Don't let anybody kid you."

"Oh, well ... the coat belonged to my father. My grandfather kept it for years and gave it to me when I graduated high school. I've always worn it. I don't think anything of it now."

"Oh." Aisling looked appropriately contrite. "That's a good reason to wear it. It's awesome anyway, vintage."

"Like you know anything about clothes," Aidan countered, shaking his head. "You've spent the last two months in sweat pants and T-shirts. You haven't even bothered wearing a bra unless you were certain you were going to run into Dad."

Cormack slapped his hand to his forehead. "Must you bring this up?"

"I was simply making a point," Aidan shot back. "Aisling has no room to judge anyone when it comes to fashion."

"I wore a bra to work," Aisling offered, although the furtive look she shot Aidan told me that wasn't necessarily true. There was a lot of warning sewn up in her glare. "I didn't want to frighten the souls, so I always wore a bra at work. Isn't that right, Griffin?"

Her husband suddenly found something interesting on his empty plate. "Who else is looking forward to spring? I know I am. I absolutely hate winter. The best thing about winter is cuddling in front of a fire, and given Aisling's hot flashes, that hasn't been nearly as much fun this year."

I pressed my lips together to keep from laughing at the murderous look on Aisling's face.

"I think that means Aisling hasn't been wearing a bra to work," Braden noted. "I'm shocked she did something that wasn't professional. I mean ... shocked! She's always been the picture of reaper fashion elegance until this point."

"Knock it off, Braden," Griffin warned, resting his hand on top of the table. "I'm a big fan when she doesn't wear a bra."

"I think we've heard just about enough from you, Griffin," Cormack warned, making a tsking sound with his tongue as he stared at his brandy. "What is taking so long with the roast?"

The man cutting the meat didn't answer, instead remaining intent on his task.

I felt the need to ease the tension — which was probably a byproduct of me being an outsider — so I said the first thing that came to my mind. "You know, Aisling is probably better off not wearing a bra. With her back problems, a bra could make her feel worse ... and I know everyone here wants her to feel okay. Wearing a bra isn't a big deal unless you make it a big deal."

The table fell silent and I pressed the tip of my tongue against the back of my teeth as I slid a sidelong look to Cormack, who was watching me with unreadable eyes.

"I mean, I'm not a doctor or anything," I babbled. "I don't pretend to be a doctor. I've seen a lot of doctors on television. I've also witnessed a lot of back pain associated with bras, and Aisling is preparing to bring a human being into the world — something you guys know nothing about. I'd think you'd cut her a little slack."

Aisling was the first to break the silence as she chuckled. "Oh, I like you. I like you so much I'm going to make you my sidekick."

"Jerry won't like that," Aidan noted. "He'll take it as an affront to his best friend status."

Aisling didn't look remotely worried. "He's going to love Izzy. Just wait."

I wasn't sure what to say regarding her enthusiasm, so I merely smiled. "Um ... thanks."

"You're welcome."

"Is your father still staring at me?"

"Yeah, but you'll get used to it. I'll say something inappropriate in a few minutes and he'll forget all about the bra conversation."

"That's a relief."

"Only if I pick a safe topic to cover next, which isn't a given."

"Let me know which way you're leaning."

"You'll be the first to know."

Nine

Braden was chatty when he dropped me at the boathouse. He promised to be in touch when they had more information. I was exhausted, so I fell face first on my bed, down for the count.

I woke late the next morning because I forgot to set my alarm. I had time to shower and then race down the stairs. Someone had returned my golf cart to its parking spot — something I hadn't even considered when I took off the previous afternoon — and I was grateful because I didn't want to be late on my second day.

Oliver and Renee were already at their stations when I arrived, and I felt a momentary twinge of guilt for not checking in with them after departing the previous afternoon. I was ready to issue an apology, but Renee was so bubbly I didn't get the chance.

"How was your day with Braden? Did you get along? People say he's the surliest Grimlock, but I don't know a lot about him. Did you find the wraith?"

Since I was a babbler of the wackiest variety, I couldn't help but take pity on Renee. She spoke before she thought. I could relate to that.

"He wasn't surly." I thought about his reaction to Maxine. "He wasn't especially surly," I corrected quickly. "We ran into a wraith while out searching and there was an incident, but it wasn't the wraith we were looking for."

"What happened?" Oliver asked, his eyes keen as they roamed my face. "Are you okay?"

"I'm fine."

"You look ... drained."

The way he phrased the simple statement gave me pause. "What do you mean?"

"You look tired," he corrected. "Maybe a little run down. Did something happen?"

"A wraith got its hands on me, but I killed it. I'm fine. I slept hard last night. In fact, I overslept because I forgot to set my alarm."

"Are you sure that's all?"

"I'm sure."

"Well, okay." Oliver shifted his eyes back to his computer screen. "We're back on schedule after the delays yesterday. The home office is sending additional security to check every access point in the building, including the door that doesn't latch properly. They promise that will be fixed by the end of the day."

"That's good news." I fought to keep a chipper demeanor. "I'm sorry about taking off yesterday. I should have kept you guys informed. I lost track of a few things after the wraith attack."

"It's fine." Renee made a dismissive motion with her hand. "We had things under control here. Obviously the wraith crossing the barrier is our biggest concern. That's what we need to focus on."

"I still should've made contact."

"Cormack Grimlock informed us when you arrived at his house," Oliver supplied. "We knew you were working and didn't have time to place a call. This couldn't have happened at a worse time. We're all trying to get to know one another because we're essentially strangers. Don't worry. Things will work themselves out."

I could only hope he was right.

I SPENT THE MORNING learning the system. It was something that should've happened the previous day but didn't for obvious reasons. Oliver and Renee were patient as they ran me through the day-to-day schedule. I knew the basics from the classes I'd taken during my apprenticeship, but there was nothing better than hands-on experience.

I enjoyed the environment. Other than the occasional conversations I shared with my co-workers, it was quiet. The whispering remained, of course, but that was somehow soothing. I remembered it from childhood and realized that the whispering was one of the things that drew me back. I supposed the whispering was something that occurred at all the gates, but this one was the one I cared most about, so that's where I focused my energy.

"What do you think it's like on the other side?" I asked Oliver as he navigated the filing system while I watched. "I mean ... Cormack described it as a waiting room of sorts last night. I never thought of it that way. Do you think that's what it's like?"

"I don't know." Oliver's eyes were curious when they locked with mine. "I've never given it much thought."

"You've never given the magical gate that leads to the other side much thought?" I was dubious. "Why don't I believe that?"

"I don't know what to tell you." Oliver shrugged. "Death isn't something that plagues me."

"I'm not plagued by death either."

"You've been touched by it," he pointed out. "You saw your parents die when you were a kid and the memory has shaped your life."

He was an intuitive soul, that was obvious, but I had trouble catching even a stray glimpse of a surface thought when we were close. That was unusual. "I don't remember the night my parents died."

"You've said that."

I cocked a challenging eyebrow. "And you don't believe me?"

"I don't know what I believe," Oliver countered. "I don't think you're lying, if that's what you're worried about. I think it's far more likely you buried your memories. They're probably accessible, but I'm not sure you want to know what happened."

"Why wouldn't I want to know?"

"That's the question of the day."

I tilted my head, considering. "I want to know."

"Okay."

"No, really," I persisted. "I want to know what happened that night. I can't, though. I've tried."

"You were young."

"I was old enough to form memories. You would think this one particularly held enough interest for me to cling to it."

"Perhaps you did but your subconscious doesn't believe you're ready to embrace it."

The suggestion bothered me. "I'm not some precious orchid. I can handle what happened. The truth can't be worse than the things I imagined over the years."

"Probably not," Oliver agreed, watching as I angled my head as an especially strong whisper crossed the threshold. "You hear it, don't you?"

Whatever I was expecting, that wasn't it. "Hear what?"

"The whispers."

I couldn't hide my surprise. "Do you hear them?"

Oliver shook his head, his expression thoughtful. "No, but I know others who can. You're not the first, but I don't think you're one of many."

"Who else hears them?"

"No one here. No one with our outfit, at least as far as I know. Those who hear the voices are more sensitive. Are you psychic?"

I hated that word. It was a catch-all that could be applied to far too many things. "No."

"Are you sure?"

"I'm not a psychic."

"Bruja?"

Most people used the word "witch." Only those familiar with a specific population used the word "Bruja." The previous day, Aisling quickly glommed onto my preferred word, but the rest of her family — all males, for the record — used "witch" as if the terms were interchangeable. The fact that Oliver instinctively knew to use "Bruja" was intriguing. "That's the word I would use," I said finally. "I'm sensitive but not psychic. I can't read minds."

"But you can hear the dead," Oliver pointed out, unruffled by my growing anxiety. "Your father was a reaper, right?"

"Yes."

"That means you inherited part of his gift. That means your mother was a Bruja."

"Her whole family."

"You're trained, at least partially," he mused. "You were raised with your grandfather. He was your father's father, if I'm not mistaken."

"You seem to know a lot about my family." I grew edgier by the second even though Oliver's countenance never shifted. "How is it that you know so much?"

"I make it a point to know who I'm working with. Your story isn't as secret as you would like it to be. Most people are at least aware of what happened to your parents, even if the details are sketchy."

"Do you know what happened to my parents?"

"Only that they died."

"But not how?"

"No. Do you?"

I didn't, but it was my most fervent wish to find out. That was a motivating factor in my return. I didn't want to admit that, but I had a feeling Oliver already recognized the truth. "No. I simply remember panic ... and screaming ... and then the overwhelming urge to hide. I can't remember much of anything else from that night, and I'm not sure what I remember is even true. It could be something my mind filled in the gaps for because I needed something to focus on."

"That's a possibility," Oliver agreed, turning back to his computer. "You're here now. You're back. You'll remember when you're ready."

He sounded so sure of himself I could only hope he was right. "Yes, well, here's hoping."

"Here's hoping indeed."

RENEE INVITED ME TO lunch in the aquarium's small cafe. I hadn't given the food situation on the island much thought, but I was going to have to make some arrangements. I couldn't eat out for every meal — it wasn't healthy or cost effective — but the island didn't boast a grocery store and I had no idea if I was allowed to use the kitchen in the boathouse. I would have to make a call.

"This is Collin O'Reilly." Renee beamed as she introduced me to the man standing behind the counter in the small cafe. "He runs this place and lives in the lighthouse."

"You live in the lighthouse?" I had no idea that was allowed. "I didn't know they had living quarters there."

"It's a small apartment," Collin replied, wisps of an Irish brogue causing his voice to sound almost musical. "A lot of weddings are held outside, but access to the inside of the building is limited."

"Do you live there by yourself?"

Collin's smile slipped. "No. I live there with my wife."

"Claire," Renee supplied, her eyes sparkling. "They're quite the couple."

Instead of returning Renee's smile, Collin scorched her with a dark look. "Now don't you start."

Renee adopted an air of innocence. "What did I say? I was simply being truthful."

"You were being obnoxious," Collin corrected, extending a warning finger. "Don't bring up that woman unless you want me to lick your hamburger bun."

Now it was Renee's turn to frown. "You know I don't like it when you threaten to mess with my food. That's completely disgusting and gross."

"So is my wife." Collin fixed me with a polite but no-nonsense look. "What will it be?"

I ordered a burger and fries because it seemed the easiest choice. Renee and I chose a table by the window and stared out at the cloudy skies.

"I didn't realize so many workers lived on the island," I admitted after a few moments of silence. "I thought I was the only one for some reason. I guess that's silly. I always thought my parents and I were the only ones on the island when I was growing up. I wonder why I thought that."

Renee shrugged as she sipped her soda. "I'm not sure. There're not many people who live here."

"Do you?"

"I live about five miles on the other side of the bridge."

"Do you wish you lived here?"

"There are times in the summer I'm jealous of those who don't have to leave when our shifts end," Renee admitted. "When the weather is warm and everyone is having a good time, I wish I could stay. When the weather is bad, I'm happy to have my little apartment. I prefer being close to stores and theaters, better restaurants. There's only the one food option here."

"I figured." I played with my straw wrapper as I leaned back in my chair. "Besides Collin and his wife — what's up with that, by the way? — who else lives here?"

"Oliver lives on the second floor of the casino with his boyfriend, Brett Soloman," Renee replied. "They've been together for a long time."

"What does Brett do?"

"He runs the casino."

Ah, that made sense. "Okay. Anyone else?"

"No. It's just the few. There are a handful of people who live close to the bridge, so it's not as if you're cut off from society or anything."

Even though it was only a short bridge ride to civilization, the island did feel a bit lonely, especially now when the weather kept people away. "That's good to know. I need to find a grocery store, but I'm not sure I can cook in the boathouse."

"You're allowed to use the boathouse kitchen. Don't worry about that. The previous folks who held your job all used the kitchen. It's expected."

"That's a relief."

We talked about mundane things while we waited for Collin to deliver our burgers. Inevitably, conversation turned to Claire O'Reilly and I couldn't help but ask the obvious question.

"Why does he stay with his wife if he hates her so much?"

"Claire's not so bad."

"He seems to think differently."

Renee smirked as she nodded. "Yes, well, they're merrow folk. They mate for life."

The comment was offhand, but I was understandably intrigued. "I'm sorry ... did you say merrow?"

"I did."

"You mean mermaids?"

"They don't like that term. As a Bruja, you should probably tread lightly."

That was a fair assessment, but I couldn't move past the idea. "That's what they are, right? They can grow scales and swim in the ocean."

"Basically," Renee confirmed. "It doesn't have to be the ocean. Collin says he prefers freshwater because it dries his skin less."

"Huh." I licked my lips, uncertain. "And merrows mate for life? Is that a law or something?"

"Basically. There's no path to divorce for them. He feels he was suckered into the marriage because Claire stole his hat — it's an old myth that I'm not even sure I understand — but their marriage isn't full of warm and fuzzy feelings. I've never seen a marriage like that. One that was full of fuzzy feelings, I mean."

"I saw one yesterday," I said absently. "Aisling Grimlock ... I guess her last name is Taylor. I didn't ask, although I should have. She and her husband are all over each other even though she's due to give birth any second."

"They've been married less than a year," Renee said. "They still have the shine on their relationship. Things will change. Things always change."

Renee seemed to be in a downer mood, at least on the relationship front, so I let it slide. "I didn't realize we had merrow on the island. I guess it makes sense. Michigan is surrounded on three sides by water."

"They're pretty normal," Renee offered. "Other than the constant fighting — which gets tedious, especially when the humidity is rising — they're easy to get along with. As long as they stay separate, in fact, they're both easy. It's when they get together that things turn rough."

"I would think that makes proximity in a lighthouse uncomfortable."

"They haven't killed each other yet." Renee let loose a beatific smile when she caught sight of Collin leaving the kitchen with plates in hand. "That smells delicious. I'm starving. I didn't eat dinner last night because I was so worked up about the wraith."

"Yeah, I saw it," Collin said as he handed us each a plate. "What was up with that? I couldn't believe it when I saw it. I gave it a wide berth but suggested Claire try to give it a big kiss."

My mouth dropped open, and not because of the tasteless joke. "You saw it?"

Collin nodded. "Yeah. It was making a beeline for the shore. I didn't even know wraiths could swim, but this one didn't seem worried about the water. It left an evil essence behind, almost like an oil slick. It's good the water is so cold because the essence won't linger."

A myriad of emotions ran through me. Finally, the strongest rose to the top and influenced my mouth. "The wraith had an evil essence ... and swam away? That doesn't sound good."

"It's not," Collin said evenly. "But it's not my problem. I'm here to cook and hate my wife. I excel at both."

"I need to see where the wraith entered the water. Also ... I need to make a call."

"Sure." Collin was blasé. "Hey, do you think you can get the wraith back and lock it in a room with my wife? I know you have to kill it, but five minutes won't hurt anyone."

"I'll give it some serious thought later."

"Great." Collin brightened considerably. "This day is looking up."

Ten

The wind was biting as Collin led us out of the building. I clutched my leather jacket as tightly as I could, but it did little to cut down on the chill permeating my body. For his part, Collin didn't bother to throw on a jacket and didn't appear bothered by the cold in the slightest.

It was interesting, to say the least.

"Why isn't he cold?" I fell into step with Renee, who had the world's thickest down coat zipped up to her chin and a knit cap pulled snugly over her ears. She clearly wasn't taking any chances when it came to facing the remnants of winter.

"Collin?" Renee arched an eyebrow as we followed the man in question. "I don't think the weather affects him much either way."

"So ... merrow folk are impervious to the weather?"

Renee shrugged. "That would be my guess."

I wanted to question her further but it somehow seemed rude given Collin's proximity. Ultimately, he removed the decision from my hands and took the mermaid by the tail, so to speak.

"If you have something to ask, now would be the time to do it," Collin noted as he carefully climbed a small roadway railing and held out a hand to help Renee. "I would be more comfortable if you came right out and asked rather than whispering. Just for the record, I have better hearing than most ... and you have a voice that carries."

Hmm. That would've been good to know ... five minutes ago. "Fine." I was caught. We both knew it. The only graceful way out of this was to ask respectful and thoughtful questions. "Do you have a tail?"

Whatever he was expecting, that wasn't it. Collin's eyes lit with mirth as he tugged Renee over the railing. "Not exactly."

That was a non-answer. "Do you have something other than a tail?"

"No, but my fingers and toes web in the water to make swimming easier."

"Huh." I rubbed my mitten-clad hand over my chin. He was making this easier than he had to, and I was grateful. "Why do the legends say you have a tail if you don't?"

"The females have tails."

Now we were getting somewhere. "Why don't the males have tails?"

"You'll have to ask the creator. I'm not sure why the females have tails and the men don't. I'm simply grateful for it."

"You don't want a tail?"

"Would you want one?"

That was a fair question. "If I could make it go away when I wanted I guess I wouldn't be averse to a tail. I mean ... mermaid tails are supposed to be pretty. What's wrong with having a pretty tail?"

Renee made a strangled sound in the back of her throat, something between a laugh and a warning. I kept my eyes on Collin rather than risk looking at her because I was afraid I might burst out in guffaws, and that was the wrong thing to do in this particular situation.

Collin, his teal eyes lit with an emotion I couldn't exactly identify, spent a long time looking me up and down. When he finally spoke, there was warmth in his voice ... but a touch of admonishment, too. "Merrow."

"What?"

"Merrow," he repeated. "We don't like being called mermaids."

I had to scramble to catch up. "Okay, well, I'm sorry about that. I know how annoying it is to be called something you're not. I will try to remember the correct term."

"Thank you."

"You're welcome."

We lapsed into uncomfortable silence for a long beat, our eyes never straying from each other. Finally, I couldn't take another second of it. "Do you have gills?"

Collin's lips curved as he extended a hand to help me over the frigid metal railing. "I have permeable skin that allows me to breathe under water. You would probably call the puckered skin pockets gills. I tend to refrain from calling them anything."

The railing was so cold it literally sucked the words out of me for a full thirty seconds and I couldn't unfreeze my tongue until I was on the other side. In an effort to give myself something to do while I waited for the cold to recede, I rubbed my hands over my thighs and searched my memory for anything I knew about merrow folk. Sadly, it wasn't much. Everything I knew was from books and I never thought I would have the opportunity to explore the undersea world with someone who had firsthand experience.

"Is that all?" Collin asked, his eyes twinkling.

I shook my head. "What's the deal with you and your wife?" I blurted out the question, ignoring the fact that Renee squeezed her eyes shut and made a whimpering sound to signify her distress.

Collin blinked several times in rapid succession. I was certain he was going to turn on his heel and run without saying a word, maybe even explode and tell me to mind my own business. Instead he merely sighed. "Claire is the devil."

"I figured that out myself. Why are you still with her if you hate her?"

"I don't have a choice in the matter."

"Divorce?"

"Merrow don't divorce."

"How about counseling?" I was trying to help. Honestly. The man seemed so miserable I couldn't stop myself from voicing my opinion on his predicament. "I once knew a woman who was convinced her marriage was over — her husband was cheating on her with, like, eight different women in the neighborhood — but they went to counseling and turned things around. They didn't end up divorced."

"Really?" Collin didn't look impressed. "Did the husband miraculously stop cheating?"

I pursed my lips. "Well, no," I hedged. "He just got better at hiding it, and my friend developed a drinking problem because it made ignoring the obvious easier. They didn't get divorced, though."

"That sounds like a lovely idea," Collin drawled. "I'll give it serious thought the next time my wife hurls a frying pan at my head."

I decided to change the subject. "Okay." I forced a smile. "Where did you see the wraith enter the water?"

"Right down here." Collin moved ahead of Renee and me so he could lead us to the water's edge.

When I pulled even with Renee I realized she was shaking her head as she stared. I knew what she was thinking — er, well, I had a good idea what she was thinking — so I wisely refrained from saying something that would make me look even dumber than he already suspected.

"Look here," Collin instructed, drawing my attention to the small beach area. "You can see the footprints."

I abandoned Renee to her staring and moved to Collin's side to study the ground he indicated. He was right. Footprints were clear. So was an odd yellow substance that stood out against the stark rocks and sand. "What is that?"

Collin shrugged. "I have no idea. I didn't know it was down here. I wasn't much interested in chasing the wraith."

"Right." I rolled my neck as I lifted my chin and stared at the Detroit skyline. "How far do you think that is?"

"To the city?" Collin worked his jaw as he computed. "I guess about two miles or so, if you're going at that specific angle."

"Do you think a wraith could swim that?"

"I didn't know wraiths could swim at all."

That made two of us. "Could you swim that?"

"Yes."

"Even though the water is frigid?"

"I don't feel the cold," Collin replied. "I would guess wraiths don't either, but I have no way of proving that. I've never heard of a wraith going into the water."

"This one was super-powered," Renee pointed out, moving in behind us. "Whatever that wraith did beyond the gate made it stronger. Maybe that's why it could swim."

It was as good a hypothesis as any. "I think we need to test this slimy stuff."

"The water, too," Collin said. "You probably can't smell it, but there's something foul tainting the area right here. It's so foul I wouldn't get in the water on this side of the island."

"What about the other side?"

"I haven't checked the other side."

"Well, check it." I dug into my pocket for my cell phone and debated what to do. I finally went to my contact list and found the entry I'd made the previous night. It would link me directly with Cormack Grimlock. "I'm going to get some help. I don't know what to do, and we need direction."

INSTEAD OF COMING HIMSELF, Cormack sent one of his offspring. I expected that, so when Braden parked on the side of the street and headed in our direction all I could do was offer a lame wave.

"Oh, that was kind of cute," Renee drawled, smirking as I worked overtime to ignore her curving lips. "He even waved back. I'm extremely jealous."

I wrinkled my forehead. "Why would you be jealous?"

"Because you guys like each other."

That was the most ludicrous thing I'd ever heard. "We most certainly don't like each other."

"No?" Renee didn't look convinced. "My mistake."

"We don't like each other," I repeated, keeping my voice low. "I barely know him."

"That doesn't mean you don't like him."

"Oh, whatever." I left Renee to smirk at my back and crossed to intercept Braden. "Thank you for coming ... I was sort of expecting your father."

"My father is busy serving as Aisling's keeper for the day," Braden supplied. "Griffin wants her kept under wraps, and no one else has the power to control her."

I searched my memory of the previous evening. "Your father can control her? That's not exactly what I remember."

"He has powers of persuasion," Braden said grimly, his eyes moving to the rather obvious yellow ooze on the beach. "What is that?"

"I have no idea. That's why I called."

"I've never seen anything like it." Braden crouched and gathered a small twig from behind him to poke at the substance. "It's kind of gross, huh?"

It was a struggle, but I managed to swallow my smile. "Is that your scientific opinion?"

"Pretty much. I was never much for science." He made a face as he lifted the stick and scented the substance. "It smells like ... something."

"What?"

Braden shrugged. "I don't know. Something bad."

"Rancid pickles," Collin answered, moving in from the west. I'd forgotten he was even with us until he showed his face again. He was the quiet sort, and managed to disappear without making a sound. "I found something I think you'll be interested in ... who are you?" He narrowed his eyes as Braden stood. Collin wasn't overly tall; Braden had a good four inches on him. That didn't mean Collin was about to stand down. "Are you from the home office?"

Braden nodded as he scanned the merrow's face. "Braden Grimlock." He extended his hand for Collin to shake. "Who are you?"

"Collin O'Reilly."

"He works in the restaurant," I offered lamely. "He saw the wraith flee into the water. I didn't know anyone saw anything until he told me over lunch."

"And it entered the water here?"

Collin nodded. "I avoided it for obvious reasons. It left a trail of evil behind."

"I don't know what that means." Braden looked to me for help. "I don't see a trail."

I opened my mouth to explain that Collin was a merrow, but I thought better of it. If Collin wanted to spread his secret, that was up to him. It wasn't my place to do it for him ... especially when he was standing near enough to hear. Gossip is a lot easier to share when the person being gossiped about isn't present.

"He's a merrow," Renee volunteered, taking me by surprise. She obviously wasn't worried about spreading Collin's secret. "He can see and smell things we can't."

"A merrow?" Braden's expression was straight out of a sitcom ... or *Supernatural*. Hmm. Now that I gave it some thought, he was handsome enough to be a Winchester brother. That was a scary thought because the Winchesters made me go goofy sometimes when I was in the mood to watch television for nothing but testosterone.

"Merfolk," Collin supplied.

"Mermaids?"

Uh-oh. I smoothly stepped forward and raised my hands when I saw the flash of annoyance cross Collin's face. "The correct term is merrow. Mermaids is a derogatory term, like using the N-word or the W-word."

"Or the T-word," Renee offered helpfully.

"What's the T-word?" Braden asked after a beat.

"Troll."

"Do you see many trolls in this neck of the woods?"

"No, but I wasn't always from around here."

Renee's answer was quick and without reproach, but I filed the tidbit away for later. Clearly Renee knew more than I'd initially realized.

"We need to figure out where that wraith went," I noted. "If it's out running around it could be doing a lot of damage."

"Don't you think we would've heard about that?" Renee challenged. "I mean, if it was killing people we would've heard about it on the news."

"Not necessarily," Braden countered. "The city is full of abandoned buildings and warehouses. The homeless take refuge there, especially when it's this cold. If no one reports them missing there's a decent chance the police don't know what's going on."

"So ... what do we do?" I asked.

"I don't know." Braden studied the embankment. "The wraith ran from the aquarium to here. Did you walk the entire stretch between when you headed this way?"

I shook my head. "No. We were in a golf cart."

"And what's over there?" Braden pointed toward an open field. "What is that?"

"It's a park of sorts," Renee answered. "It's small, some picnic tables and swings for the kids. There's nothing else over there."

"I want to take a look anyway." Braden started in that direction, leaving me to scramble to keep up.

"Wait."

When Braden turned he found Collin helping Renee over the railing. "Oh, sorry." He hurried to me and extended a hand. "I didn't think about how steep that embankment was."

I wanted to slap away his helping hand on principle, but I wasn't sure I could get over the railing without aid. "It's fine." I gripped his hand and fought to keep from groaning when I shifted my body over the cold metal a second time. "I could've done it myself, but thank you anyway."

Instead of being annoyed, Braden's eyes lit with amusement. "You remind me of my sister."

"I've seen you interact with your sister. That's not a compliment."

"You might be surprised." Braden gave me a moment to collect my breath before turning back to the field. This time he picked a slower pace. "My sister calls herself an acquired taste. She says that only the strongest can put up with her."

"And what do you think?"

"She's a pain in the butt."

"Ah."

"I also think she's not as bad as I convinced myself she was when we were younger," Braden added. "She's simply Aisling. She doesn't fit in a box."

That was an interesting way to put it. "She definitely doesn't. How was she feeling when you last saw her? I mean ... are her feet okay?"

"Her feet are ten times better," Braden acknowledged. "She actually walked up the stairs herself last night when it was time for bed."

"I thought she lived someplace else."

"A townhouse in Royal Oak," Braden said. "She's so close to her due date now that she's staying at Grimlock Manor."

The fact that Braden grew up in a house that had a name amused me. "I see. Why?"

"Because Aisling is terrified of going into labor when no one is around to get her to the hospital. Someone is always around at the manor, so my father suggested she and Griffin move in until she gives birth. Everyone seems more comfortable with that because we were spending half our days driving past her townhouse to make sure she was okay."

"You know, women have been giving birth for a very long time," I reminded him. "I'm sure she'll be fine."

"I'm sure she will, too. But she's our sister and we can't stop ourselves from trying to protect her. This makes it easier on Griffin. He wants to work as long as he can so he can take his leave when he can help with the baby."

"I guess that makes sense." I narrowed my eyes as we crested the small hill that led to the park. "What is that?"

"What?" Braden was distracted as he scanned the small play landscape.

"That." I jabbed my finger toward the swings. "It looks as if there's something on the ground over there."

"There is," Collin confirmed, pulling even with us. His expression was hard to read, but the way his aura shifted told me something very bad was about to happen. "It's a body."

"A body?" My voice turned squeaky. That couldn't possibly be right. "What is a body doing out here?"

"I have no idea," Braden replied, reaching into his pocket to retrieve his phone. "I'm betting whatever reason we come up with won't be good."

He wasn't the only one who felt that way. "Who are you calling?"

"Griffin."

"Why?"

"Because we have a dead body and we need the police. I would much rather he respond than someone who isn't in on the big secret."

"Good point."

Eleven

"He's definitely dead." Griffin, who showed up thirty minutes after Braden placed the call, straightened as he regarded his brother-in-law.

"Is that your expert opinion?" Braden asked dryly, mimicking my earlier tone.

"The dude is frozen to the ground," Griffin replied. "That doesn't happen if you're alive. How did you find him?"

"That guy saw the wraith we were telling you about hit the water." Braden pointed at Collin for emphasis. The merrow appeared less than thrilled to be in the presence of a law enforcement representative. "We were by the water checking it out when I realized that we should probably follow potential trails back to the aquarium."

"And that's when you found him?"

Braden nodded. "He was out in the open."

Griffin tightened his arms around his midriff to ward off the cold. "You didn't touch him, did you?"

I was agitated that he seemed to be directing all his questions to Braden, but I managed to keep from making my annoyance public.

"We didn't touch him," Braden answered, seemingly oblivious to my displeasure. "It was obvious he was dead."

"I have to call this in. I don't have a choice."

"I know."

"What do you think they're going to find in the autopsy?" Genuine worry roamed Griffin's chiseled face. "If we're working under the assumption that the wraith killed him, then how did he die?"

"I have no idea. We've never faced anything like this before."

"Okay." Griffin touched his tongue to his top lip as he dug in his pocket. "I'm calling for the medical examiner. If there's something off about the death, we'll have to deal with it. I can't make this go away."

"I didn't expect you to." Braden was solemn. "I called it in directly to you because that was my instinct. In hindsight, that was probably a mistake."

"It's not the worst mistake you've ever made," Griffin countered. "If someone asks me about it, I'll simply say you were surprised and called me because that's all you could think to do. You're my brother-in-law. It's only natural you would call me."

"I just don't want to get you into trouble."

"I won't be in trouble. I only hope that the medical examiner can find a cause of death that doesn't direct a spotlight on our family. Now is not the time to live life under a microscope, especially with your sister about to give birth."

"And you're going to be a daddy," Braden teased, genuine fondness flitting over his features. "After all the complaining you did about my father spoiling Aisling, I've got fifty bucks that says you'll do the same with your kid."

Griffin's face remained implacable. "I'll be the best father I can be. That's the only thing I can guarantee."

"I have no doubt about that."

TO KEEP US FROM GETTING hypothermia, Griffin directed us to wait for him inside. I still hadn't eaten, so I led Braden to the cafeteria. Collin set about making new burgers, leaving Braden, Renee and me to entertain ourselves. There was only one thing we all wanted to talk about.

"So, what did you guys do when you were hanging out yesterday?" Renee asked enthusiastically.

Okay, Renee was the sole rider on her own thought train.

"I already told you what we did," I snapped.

"Yes, but I want to hear it from Braden." She rested her chin on her palm and lodged her elbow on the table. "I heard you live in a castle. Is that true?"

Braden lifted an amused eyebrow and briefly met my gaze. "Is that what Izzy told you?"

"No. She didn't share any of the juicy details from her visit to your house. I've heard it from other people."

"It's just a house," Braden said. "It's a big house, but it's still a house."

"I heard it has turrets."

Braden smirked. "It does."

"Ugh. I'm so jealous." Renee made a face as she sipped her coffee. Warming up after spending a good two hours in the frigid cold was an ongoing endeavor. "I bet your sister played princess growing up there, didn't she? I always wanted to play princess with actual turrets."

"Really?" Braden's lips twitched. "What about you, Izzy? Did you want to be a princess in a castle?"

I shrugged. "Not really. Once I was with my grandfather in New Orleans, I preferred the weekends when we would head to the bayou to collect frogs and other ingredients for his shop. I guess you could say I was more of an outdoor girl."

Renee snorted. "Sounds like my worst nightmare."

"She probably thinks the same thing about your princess fantasy," Braden noted. "For the record, my sister wasn't a big fan of playing princess either. Don't get me wrong, she liked being spoiled by my father and would play the princess card all the time to get her own way, but she preferred playing games with us. Her friend Jerry, on the other hand, loved playing princess."

I pressed my lips together to keep from laughing. Everything I heard about this Jerry guy, who I had yet to meet, made me think I was going to love him as much as the Grimlock family obviously did.

"You guys simply don't play the princess game correctly," Renee complained. "I'll have to come over and teach you sometime."

"I'm sure Jerry would love that." Braden leaned back in his chair and sipped his coffee. His eyes were keen when they locked with mine. "How are you feeling after yesterday? I was a little worried that you might not bounce back, but you seem okay."

I could feel Renee's eyes crawling over me, but I refused to look in her direction, remaining calm as I warmed my fingers on my mug. "I'm fine. I slept hard, so hard that someone could've broken into my room and I wouldn't have heard them, but I feel pretty good, all things considered."

"Your body temperature is back to normal?"

"Our excursion outside notwithstanding," I confirmed. "Don't worry, you won't have to cuddle me on the couch to keep me warm again."

Renee's gasp told me I'd said the exact wrong thing. That was pretty much a normal occurrence. I struggled to keep my expression neutral as my cheeks heated and I cursed my stupidity. "What I meant was ... um ... ."

"Oh, look how cute she is when she gets flustered," Braden teased. He didn't look embarrassed in the least, which made me want to throttle him. "I didn't know cheeks could get that red."

I pretended I didn't hear the taunting. "So, what's our next move with the body?"

"We wait for Griffin," Braden replied without hesitation. "We need information from him before we can move forward."

"What information?"

"I'm guessing he means cause of death," Griffin replied as he appeared in the doorway, his cheeks ruddy with color thanks to the cold. He calmly tugged off his gloves before moving toward our table. "Are you guys eating? If so, I want in. I'm starving."

"You're staying at the manor," Braden noted as he made room for Griffin to sit. "My father keeps that place flush with food."

"Yes, but your sister has decided I can only eat when she does. I try not to eat after ten, so when she raids the refrigerator at midnight that means she's not hungry for breakfast and I'm usually asleep so I miss out on a meal. I'm always hungry for breakfast."

"She's always been a late-night snacker," Braden offered. "That will never change. Besides, you're close now. She'll be popping that kid out within the next few days and then you'll be too tired to eat."

"Don't remind me." Griffin smiled. "I'm looking forward to it."

"Why?"

"Because I have six weeks off."

"If you think a newborn isn't work, you're kidding yourself," Braden countered. "You'll be crying to go back to the job by the end of that six weeks."

"I don't believe so."

"You're deluding yourself."

As delightful as I'm sure they believed their conversation to be, I'd had enough of the baby chit-chat. "Um ... we have legitimate business to talk about. Can you guys stop talking about your family issues long enough for Griffin to give us the scoop on the body?"

I recognized the interruption was rude but refused to acknowledge it under Braden's weighted stare. Instead, I pretended as if we were having a normal lunch and I hadn't just channeled the whiniest Bruja on Dauphine Street.

"Oh, she reminds me of Aisling before all the complaints revolved around swollen feet," Griffin lamented, his smile wide.

"Hey, you're lucky to have her," I shot back, my temper getting the better of me. "Do you have any idea how much pain she was in? How uncomfortable she is? How worried she is that she's going to be a terrible mother because her mother was apparently awful?"

I wanted to haul back the words the second I uttered them, but it was far too late.

"Well, crap."

"I think I'm really going to like you," Renee offered as a way to fill the silence as Braden and Griffin stared. "You have a mouth like a freight train. There's no stopping it. Who doesn't love that?"

I could think of a few people, and two of them were sharing space with me around a small table.

"Our mother wasn't awful," Braden said finally, finding his voice. "Did Aisling tell you she was awful?"

"Braden." Griffin kept his voice low and soothing, but there was an edge to his demeanor that was impossible to miss. "Aisling doesn't think your mother was awful and you know it. She thinks that other woman was awful. You can't blame her for that."

Son of a troll! I'd really stepped into it this time. "I'm so sorry." The words rushed out. "I shouldn't have said that. It's just ... you were frustrating me. I think we need to talk about the dead guy and you guys are too busy playing 'mine is bigger than yours' and it makes me want to scream."

"Uh-huh." Griffin rubbed his cheek as he held some internal debate I wasn't privy to. He was better at shuttering than I imagined possible for a normal human. "Did Aisling tell you she was afraid of being a bad mother?"

"No." I felt disloyal for even talking about the youngest Grimlock sibling. She'd been nothing but nice to me, and here I was spilling her private business. "Her thoughts are all surface-y. I told you that last night. She can't close them off, and because I was in a weakened state, I couldn't help picking up on a few stray worries. It wasn't purposeful."

"I'm not angry." Griffin looked as if he was speaking the truth. "She's my wife. If she's upset, I want to do what I can to fix things for her."

"You can't fix things. Every mother worries she's going to be a bad mother. Sure, Aisling's fears seem a bit more intense than most, but she'll forget about them once the baby arrives. She has nothing to focus on now other than that she's been relieved of her work duties."

"I didn't even think about that." Obviously troubled, Griffin rubbed his chin as he glanced at Braden. "Maybe your father can find something for her to do at the main office. If she needs to work ... ."

"Oh, let it go." Braden's expression turned petulant. "She can't go to the main office because she'll make everyone want to kill her. She hates busywork. She's better off staying at the manor with my father. He'll indulge her the best he can. She'll be fine."

Braden's expression was hard to read as he focused on me. "My mother wasn't awful. I don't want you telling people that."

"I have no intention of telling anyone anything," I supplied, flexing my fingers to calm myself. "That wasn't my intention. Sometimes I think before I speak."

"I know all about that," Braden said. "Trust me. I suffer from that affliction, too."

"He definitely does," Griffin agreed.

"I simply don't want you to say anything negative about my mother." Braden was firm. "I'm not trying to be difficult or anything. It's just ... if you could leave her out of future conversations that would be great."

I sensed the turmoil swirling under his pleasant veneer and nodded. "I promise. I won't bring her up again."

"Thank you." He dragged a hand through his black hair as he forced himself to focus on something other than the incredibly uncomfortable conversation we were mired in. "As for the body, I think the most important thing is to figure out who he is. Someone must be searching for this guy."

"I'm not sure anyone is missing him," Griffin countered. "His clothing is fairly worn. He was layered, making me think he spent a lot of time outside. I don't necessarily think anyone is looking for him."

"He was homeless," I surmised quickly. "That's what you're saying, right?"

"I can't be certain, but that would be my guess," Griffin confirmed. "There's always a chance he lived in one of those group homes across the bridge, but it doesn't make much sense for him to head this way if that's the case. I mean, most of those guys spend their days panhandling. This is the worst possible place to panhandle at this time of year. There are no tourists out here."

"That's a good point." Braden furrowed his brow. "If he was homeless, he must have found a place on the island to serve as shelter. There are quite a few buildings out here, although most of them are secured. He's clearly not staying in the aquarium."

"There are pavilions, though," Griffin pointed out. "Maybe he broke into one of the bathrooms and has been using that as home base. We're going to have to search the island."

"Do you know how he died?" I asked, dreading the answer. I could only hope it wasn't some horrible passing that would give me nightmares.

"Not yet. He had no marks on his body. The medical examiner noted that he probably died of natural causes, but we all know that's unlikely given what happened here yesterday. I'll keep you updated when I know more, but right now, the cause of death is a mystery."

"And we don't have anywhere to look for more information," I mused distractedly. "I don't know where to look to find this thing."

"I'll keep my ear to the ground for reports," Griffin offered. "You're not necessarily looking for death reports. You're looking for unusual activity in abandoned buildings. We have a lot of homeless people taking over any decent space, but there are groups holding raves in dilapidated warehouses. It seems to me that would be a target-rich environment."

"And the people attending those parties would be less likely to report a suspicious death because they don't want to be arrested," Braden surmised. "That's what you're saying, right?"

Griffin nodded. "I'm at as much of a loss as you guys. I'll do what I can, but I don't even know how much longer I'll be on the job. As soon as Aisling goes into labor, I'm done."

"Which is exactly how it should be," I offered as something occurred to me. "I do have one question. I'm not sure if it's stupid, but I'll ask it anyway."

"Go for it," Braden prodded.

"What about the guy's soul? I mean ... you guys get lists, right? You're supposed to know when someone passes. This guy obviously didn't show up on your list."

Braden stirred, his interest piqued. "Huh. I didn't even consider that. You're absolutely right. We should've gotten notice."

"There was no soul out there, right?" Griffin queried.

Braden shook his head. "No soul. It could've wandered, I guess, but I'm almost certain that's not what happened."

"You think the wraith ate it, don't you?" I made a face as I shifted on my chair. "You think the wraith took time for a snack when it should've been escaping."

"Maybe it needed a snack to bolster its energy levels," Braden said.

"I don't know. It's an interesting question, and definitely something we need to follow up on."

"There's a lot we need to follow up on," Griffin said. "We need to share information moving forward."

"Agreed."

Griffin turned his head to the kitchen. "I need lunch first. Don't tell your sister I was eating without her either. She'll get grumpy."

"She was born grumpy," Braden argued. "How bad could she be?"

"You'll jinx us if you're not careful. Don't say things like that."

"Since when did you turn into a wuss?"

"I prefer 'concerned husband.'"

"You say tomato."

"Yeah, yeah. What's good here? I'm totally in the mood for grease."

"I think Collin will be able to help you," Renee offered. "He's an expert at grease ... and other things."

I had a feeling that was an understatement. "We all want grease. Let's order and then get to work. We need to put an end to this before things really get out of control."

Twelve

Griffin left after lunch, stopping at the bakery display long enough to buy five slices of pie. He claimed they were all for Aisling — something Braden scoffed at — but I knew better. He was trying to make his wife smile, calm her, and he honestly thought pie was the best way to accomplish that.

"Is your sister a food-oriented person?" I asked Braden as we made our way through the dark hallway that led to the gate room.

"Definitely. We all are. Why do you ask?"

"I'm simply hoping Griffin gets what he wants with the pie delivery this evening."

His face unreadable, Braden cast me a sidelong look. "How deep can you go into people's minds?"

The question made me uncomfortable. "I don't read people's minds."

"Technically, you do. You've said enough things for me to be reasonably assured that you're pretty good at reading minds."

Since Renee had excused herself to return to her duties right after lunch, I was alone with the curious Grimlock ... and it wasn't a happy occurrence. "I don't read minds."

"You read my sister's mind."

"I picked up on some stray thoughts," I corrected. "She's a bundle of nerves and emotions. She basically shoved those thoughts into my mind. I don't purposely set out to invade people's privacy and try to pick through their thoughts. I'm respectful when it comes to things like that."

"You're also defensive," Braden noted, pressing his hand to the small of my back as he ushered me through the double doors that led to the gate. "It's unnecessary. I was simply curious."

I bit back a hot retort. I couldn't blame him for asking questions. In his position, I'd do the same. That didn't change the fact that I'd promised myself I would fly under the radar when I returned to Michigan. I had barely been back seventy-two hours and almost every magical trick in my arsenal was on display. "I don't like to talk about it."

"Why?"

"Because ... people think I'm weird. I don't like being weird. Do you know how weird you have to be to be termed 'the strange one' in New Orleans? I don't like standing out."

"I don't think you have much choice in the matter." Braden surveyed the room as we entered, his eyes landing on Oliver and Renee. They toiled in the far corner, their attention on a computer, and they were out of hearing distance. "It's not so bad to be unique."

"It's not always a good thing either," I countered. "You're a reaper. Do you go around announcing to the women you pick up at the bar what you do for a living?"

He narrowed his lavender eyes. "First, we sign confidentiality agreements. We're not allowed to tell random people what we do."

"That's convenient," I groused under my breath.

"Second, I would never tell a random hookup what I do for a living because the assumption is that I won't see her again," he continued. "I'm curious as to why you think I pick up a lot of women at bars."

"It was a topic of conversation during dinner last night. At least three of your siblings teased you about what I believe was described as a 'lazy' selection process. Aisling even said you wait for women to approach you because it's too much work to go to them."

Braden had the grace to be abashed. "Right. I forgot that came up. I didn't even think about it."

"It doesn't matter," I said hurriedly. "I'm not trying to insert myself into your personal life. I simply mentioned it because we both know that it's necessary to keep secrets in this line of work."

"I think it's necessary to keep secrets no matter your line of work," he countered, leaning his hip against the long rectangular table to his left. "I think that's healthy. You can't know everything about one person. It's impossible. Even Griffin and Aisling, who are codependent as hell, don't know everything about one another."

"You could've fooled me."

"Yes, well, there are still some dark corners for them to plumb if they get in the mood." Braden chuckled, the sound warm as it washed over me. "I didn't mean that you should volunteer what you can do to virtual strangers. But the people here know about the world we live in.

"Heck, there's a merrow here and I always thought they were a myth," he continued. "I at least thought they lived by the ocean. I've known Madame Maxine since I was a kid. I'm well aware of what she can do. Your abilities aren't exactly shocking to me."

That was an interesting point. "You don't like my aunt."

"I used to like her."

"Something happened that caused you to change your mind. What was that?"

"Maybe you should ask her."

"I did." There was no reason to lie. "She said it was your secret to tell."

Braden worked his jaw, his mind clearly busy. "She didn't tell you?"

"No."

"She had a hand in what happened."

Worry at the way he said it bubbled up. "If you don't want to tell me ... ."

"It's not that." Braden shook his head as he turned his back to me. It was a defensive reaction — one I recognized because I often did it myself — and when he turned back his eyes were on fire. "My mother died when I was barely out of my teens. I was already working full time as a reaper by then, but I was still basically a kid.

"I spent my days working, thinking I was a big shot, and my nights carousing with my brothers," he continued. "Aisling and Aidan weren't yet reapers. They'd just graduated from high school and my father gave them the summer off to decide what they wanted to do with their futures."

I wasn't sure where he was going with the conversation, so I simply let him talk.

"My mother was called out on an emergency job to a warehouse," he explained. "She got trapped inside, the roof fell and she died."

I felt sick to my stomach for making him relive this. "I'm so sorry. You don't have to tell me about it."

"It's too late now." Grim-faced, he pushed forward. "About two years ago, some weird things started happening. Aisling was getting pushed in a very specific direction, and through a little investigation she found our mother was still alive."

I was dumbfounded. "Oh. I ... um ... don't understand."

"I'm not sure I do either," he admitted, pensive. "It's a long story and I'm not going into all the details. Another reaper family took her, kept her, but she was weakened from the fire. They called for a renowned witch to save her. Genevieve Toth. She resurrected my mother, but it wasn't exactly a good life.

"Eventually my mother took off with Genevieve and they did a lot of bad things," he continued. "I mean ... a lot of bad things. It turns out my mother's soul didn't survive what Genevieve did and she passed on. But her body remained behind. Her memories were intact. That woman had a plan, and it was to essentially kill Aisling and take over her body."

The story was fantastical, freaky even. I believed every word. The anguish etched on Braden's face could allow nothing less.

"Nine months ago, a little less actually, there was a big fight," Braden volunteered. "My mother's soul returned from the other side to help. Madame Maxine arranged for that to happen. The woman pretending to be my mother, she died. Aisling sacrificed her to save me."

"And you feel guilty for that?" I was floored. "Why would you possibly feel guilty for that?"

"Did I say I felt guilty?"

He didn't have to say it. The emotion practically oozed from his pores. "You didn't do anything wrong."

"No, but she's still dead. My mother's soul is gone again. Aisling seems to have no trouble dealing with the fact that she killed our mother's body. Everyone else has moved on. I'm the only one still thinking about it."

"I doubt very much that's true."

"Well, it feels true." He heaved out a sigh, briefly flicking his eyes to the vaulted ceilings before shifting to face the door. "I'm supposed to meet my father down by the water. He should be here any minute. I'm sure he'll stop in and talk to you before he goes."

I straightened. "Okay, well ... ."

Braden didn't give me a chance to finish, or collect my thoughts. "I'll see you later." He pushed through the doors and disappeared, leaving me with a mountain of thoughts I couldn't quite organize.

"I'll see you later," I murmured even though he was long gone. I wanted to add that I was sorry for forcing the issue, but I wasn't. The information helped me understand him a little better. Of course, I had no idea where to go now. That was a worry for a different time, though. For now, I had to focus on work, so that's what I did.

I turned to Oliver and Renee and found them watching me with unveiled interest.

"What have we got?" I forced myself to appear chipper. "Update me on everything we have going on. I expect I'm going to have to answer some serious questions this afternoon and I want to be ready."

SERIOUS QUESTIONS WAS an understatement. Cormack, a team of men dressed in expensive suits trailing in his wake, didn't wait long to put me on the hot seat.

"Izzy." There was no warmth behind Cormack's smile as he regarded me. "We need to know exactly what is going on here."

"I thought Braden would've told you," I hedged, uncertain.

"He did, but you're the authority here. We need the report from you."

"Right." I snapped my heels together, which seemed like a ridiculous thing to do, and nodded. "So, should I start from the beginning?"

Cormack folded his arms over his chest and nodded. For a split-second I thought I caught a hint of mirth wafting through his hardened eyes. The phenomenon was over as soon as it started, though, and I focused.

"So, here it is." I launched into the tale, internally congratulating myself when I didn't forget anything and managed to keep emotion out of it. Despite that, I was a nervous wreck when I finished and waited for the men to comment.

"So, what do we have?" The man who spoke looked to be in his sixties, distinguished, and in charge. If I had to guess, he was even higher than Cormack on the food chain.

"That's why we're here, Renley," Cormack replied. "We don't know what we have. We're trying to figure it out."

Renley? I recognized the name. Renley Hatfield was the head of the Michigan reaper arm. There was no position higher than his, except in the national office. The nerves I thought I had tamped down returned with a vengeance when I realized exactly who I was dealing with.

"You must have some idea," Renley pressed as he regarded me. "You're in charge of the gate. You must know what happened."

"I honestly don't." I hated — absolutely hated — the way my voice cracked as I tried to gather my courage. "I've never heard of anything like this happening."

"That doesn't bode well for us." Renley rubbed his chin. "What do you think, Cormack?"

"I'm not sure what I think." Cormack was a tall man, imposing, and he towered over Renley. There was also a warmth about him at which I couldn't help but marvel. When he offered me a wink I let loose the breath I'd been holding and forced myself to calm. I wasn't completely alone in this. He was with me, at least as much as he could be.

"The wraith isn't on Belle Isle any longer," I volunteered. "It clearly fled to the city. I don't know how to find it, but I think we should start looking there."

"We have ears to the ground," Cormack supplied. "We found evidence to suggest the man who died here was sleeping in one of the pavilion bathrooms, though we've yet to find an identity. We don't know if anyone is missing him. I'm sending my sons out to the nearest neighborhoods this afternoon. We're starting a grid to keep track of the buildings we search. We don't have nearly enough bodies to cover the area."

"So, what do you suggest?"

"Gargoyles."

Cormack's answer caused me to jerk my head in his direction. "Gargoyles? You mean ... like statues?"

Cormack smiled. "I'm referring to the live variety."

"I thought the gargoyles went underground after the fight at the theater," Renley countered. "We've had no reports of gargoyle activity since."

"We haven't," Cormack agreed. "I know where to find one, though. We'll need help if we expect to track down one mutant wraith in a sea of normal ones. The gargoyles hear more than we do."

"You're speaking of the creature that tried to help your daughter, the one you asked us to save."

"I am. Bub. He's ... a horrible little beast, but he's been known to help."

They couldn't be serious. Gargoyles? I had no idea they were real. Of course, I'd met a merrow only today. The fact that gargoyles were running around shouldn't have been that big of a surprise.

"Fine. Call in the gargoyles," Renley capitulated. "I don't like it, but the gargoyles are the least of our worries. If that wraith goes on a killing spree we all will be in a world of hurt."

"I agree." Cormack slid a sidelong look to me before continuing. "We might consider trying to reach out to other figures in the supernatural community as well."

"Who did you have in mind?"

"There's that coven over on Mack Avenue," Cormack suggested. "They're a bit nutty, but they're up on all the gossip."

"Oh, I don't like them." Renley turned petulant. "They try to bribe my men with sex whenever there's contact. It makes everyone uncomfortable."

"They do that on purpose," I interjected automatically. "They know it makes you uncomfortable, so they persist. They do it because they don't want you bothering them."

Cormack sent me an appraising smile. "I happen to agree with you. I'll send Aidan. They can't get him nearly as riled as the others. If the witches know anything, they'll tell him."

"Is there anyone else you want to bring in on this?" Renley asked.

The way Cormack shifted his shoulders told me he had a very specific idea, and it was something that neither Renley or I wasn't going to like.

"I do," Cormack confirmed. "I have an idea for help, although it might not go over well."

"Just spit it out," Renley instructed. "Time is wasting."

"Madame Maxine." Cormack spared me an apologetic look. "She's up on everything that's going on in this area."

"I thought you were on the outs with Maxine."

"It's a difficult situation." Cormack chose his words carefully. "I'm not exactly happy with her right now, but I don't dislike the woman. She's been a powerful ally throughout the years. I don't expect that to change."

"Will you talk to her yourself?"

"No." Cormack shook his head, his lips curving and causing my stomach to twist. "I have someone else in mind for that particular task."

"Fine. See what you can do." Renley made a tsking sound with his tongue as he surveyed the room. "What a mess. We've got to get this cleaned up as soon as possible."

"That's the plan," Cormack assured him. "We won't stop until we figure everything out. I promise. That's our highest priority."

Thirteen

If Cormack Grimlock wanted me to schmooze my aunt to get her help, he was going to be bitterly disappointed. I managed to maintain my cool until Renley and his cohorts disappeared into another part of the facility, and then I fixed the reaper family patriarch with a hard glare.

"You look angry." He folded his arms over his chest and regarded me with a look I couldn't quite identify. "If you want to yell, now would be a good time."

I wasn't quite sure what to say to that. "You want me to yell at you?"

"I'm used to people yelling at me. You've met my children."

"Your children love you."

"That doesn't mean they don't yell."

"Probably not." I shifted from one foot to the other, uncomfortable. "I love Aunt Maxine. She didn't raise me because my grandfather wouldn't allow it — he set strict rules for when I could see her — but she did her absolute best for me. She fought for me after my parents died. I'm not going to manipulate her."

Cormack cocked a dark eyebrow. "Is that what you think I want you to do?"

"I know you have issues with her. Braden told me what happened with your wife." I planned to barrel forward and lay down the law, but something about the way Cormack's features twisted gave me pause. "I'm sorry if you don't want me mentioning your wife. I didn't do it to upset you. I understand why you're so careful about talk of her, and I don't blame you. That doesn't mean I'm willing to manipulate Aunt Maxine."

Instead of immediately responding, he held up a hand to quiet me. I'm not big on being shushed, so it had the opposite effect.

"I will ask her to help us, but I'm not going to play games with her," I argued. "She's a grown woman and my family. If you expect me to play games ... well ... I won't. You might as well fire me now."

"Oh, good grief." Weariness evident, he slapped his hand to his forehead as he exhaled heavily. "You're kind of a mixture of my children. Do you know that?"

I was fairly certain that wasn't a compliment. "I'm my own unique person."

"You certainly are," he agreed. "You also have Cillian's need to soak up knowledge ... and Redmond's tendency to rush in headlong before the level of danger is ascertained ... and Aidan's capacity to give ... and Braden's tendency to turn sullen when things don't go his way ... and Aisling's mouth. Although, you're nowhere near Aisling. I shouldn't put that on you. You remind me of her a bit."

"I like her. I'll take that as a compliment."

Cormack let loose a loud chuckle that echoed throughout the room. "That's something she would say."

I folded my arms over my chest and waited.

"You helped her," he said after a beat. "Do you have any idea how much perkier she was last night? I guess I didn't realize how much discomfort she was in until you made things better. I owe you for that."

"Is that your roundabout way of saying you're not going to try to force me to manipulate my aunt?" My heart dropped when he shook his dark head. "No?"

"I don't want you to manipulate Maxine. That's not what I'm

pushing for. I do want you to talk to her, see if you can get her to help. My guess is she'll be receptive to your request."

"And she wouldn't be to yours?"

"Things are ... rough ... between Maxine and my children right now. I don't blame her for what happened, but Braden is furious and the others are leery. That's the best way I can think to put it.

"Redmond, Aidan and Cillian will come around, and probably soon," he continued. "Aisling always had issues with Maxine because your aunt insisted on giving her cryptic readings that drove her batty and my daughter has a bitter streak. Braden, he is dealing with a mountain of guilt."

"He mentioned some of that to me." My stomach twisted. "I'm not sure I understand what he was telling me. He breezed through it and then walked out, as if he couldn't breathe and needed some air. I didn't follow because I assumed he needed space."

"The fact that he talked about it with you at all is amazing," Cormack countered. "He won't talk to me about it. He needs to talk to Aisling because they were together when it happened. He won't talk to her, even though he seems to be playing caretaker for her more than usual. They have a new bond, which I don't know how to take because they've always been the first to fight. It's interesting ... and alarming."

He was babbling, maybe more to himself than to me. I was learning a lot. "Why did they fight?"

"Because they're the most alike. Aidan may be Aisling's twin, but Braden and her share more personality traits. Aidan is easier to get along with. Aisling and Braden are my moodiest children."

"Do they believe that?"

Cormack snorted. "They admit to their faults, if that's what you're asking. Since it happened, Braden has been something of an enigma. He participates in family gatherings, spends time at the bar with his brothers, and sits with Aisling when she's upset or not feeling well. He's been good ... and yet he's distant."

"Maybe you simply need to give him some space."

"Perhaps." He nodded once. "Or maybe he needs something else entirely."

His pointed stare made me uncomfortable, so I quickly changed the subject. "I'll talk to Aunt Max, tell her what's going on. I'll ask if she can help. But I won't manipulate her. I won't use her for what I think she can give me. That's not who I am."

"I don't want you to manipulate her. We need help, though. That means tapping Maxine as a resource. You're in the best position to do that."

"I'll do my best."

"I'm sure you will."

MAXINE MET ME AT a cute Italian restaurant on Royal Oak's main drag. I was forced to take an Uber — something that would get expensive if I didn't get a handle on my vehicle situation — but I had no other options, so I settled in and enjoyed the ride.

Maxine was already seated when I arrived. I greeted her with a hug and kiss on the cheek before sitting across from her.

"Thank you for meeting me."

My aunt was many things, and intuitive was one of them. "You clearly had something on your mind when you made the call. I'm here for you. I told you that when you mentioned moving back, despite what your grandfather said to the contrary ... in rather vicious words."

Yes, that was an ugly business. My grandfather, who I adored, wasn't happy when I informed him I was joining the reaper academy after I graduated high school. Given who my father was, I had a spot waiting. My grandfather wanted me to live a normal life — or as normal as I could being the granddaughter of a powerful sorcerer. He was a former reaper. He was born into it, like my father before me. He changed his mind about the righteousness of the job after my father and mother died. I guess I couldn't blame him.

When I told him I was considering becoming a reaper he had a meltdown. I joined the academy anyway, aced all my classes and then got a side job as a secretary at the New Orleans home office when I graduated. He wasn't thrilled with the development, but the fact that I was doing clerical work was a great relief to him. I knew it would be, so I bided my time.

Slowly, I moved to a variety of different positions, each one slightly more active than the previous. When it came time to apply for my position as gatekeeper in Detroit, he barely batted an eyelash ... until I delved into the nitty-gritty of the decision. I still remember the way he howled. He wasn't happy, and yet there was nothing he could do to change my mind. This had always been the plan. He simply didn't realize it.

We'd barely talked since, although he'd taken to emailing me weather updates from New Orleans every morning. He didn't want to talk about anything other than the weather, but it was a start. He would eventually forgive me. He always did.

"I do have something on my mind," I agreed, sipping my water before continuing. "We have a situation." I told her about the wraith and the discovery of the body. She knew part of the story, but the death was an added worry that none of us expected. "We have to track it down, but we have no idea where to start looking. I don't suppose you have any ideas?"

Instead of immediately answering, Maxine leaned back in her seat and stared at her wine glass. "Did Cormack ask you to approach me?" she asked finally.

I refused to lie to one of the few family members I had left. "He did. I thought initially he wanted me to manipulate you, which I was against, but he said that he preferred I was upfront. He seems to be ... troubled ... where you're concerned. I don't know how else to phrase it."

"He's troubled because of his children and how they perceive me," Maxine corrected, her lips curving down. "We've always been close, shared tea and coffee here and there. He's been unusually distant since it happened."

Even though Braden explained what "it" was, I still felt out of the loop. "Braden told me about it, although I'm not sure I understand everything."

"What did he tell you?"

I related his tale, almost word for word, and when I was done, my aunt heaved a sigh.

"That's mostly it, but not entirely." I'd never known Maxine to be fidgety, but she ran her fingers through her hair now, as if she needed something to do with her hands. "I did what I had to do. You must understand that."

I didn't understand any of it. "He said a lot of things that made sense to him, but not to me. I'd like to understand, but there are too many holes. I can't get there."

"And you're asking me to get you there."

"It would be nice," I confirmed. "If I'm going to be working with these people I'd prefer not sticking my foot in my mouth at every turn."

Maxine offered a dismissive wave. "Oh, don't worry about that. All the Grimlocks suffer from Foot-In-Mouth Disease."

"You know what I mean."

Because she did, Maxine simply nodded. "Fine. I'll explain it to you, but I don't want to hear any lip."

I mimed zipping my mouth, something she taught me when I was a kid and she shared "secrets" that I wasn't supposed to tell my parents. They weren't really secrets, of course. She slid me candy when my mother insisted I'd had enough sugar for the day, promised adventures in the wilderness that my father would have frowned upon, that sort of thing. It was still our special thing and I remembered the afternoons spent in her care.

"Lily Grimlock died years ago, at least for all intents and purposes," Maxine started. "Genevieve Toth was trying to master soul-walking. She failed."

"Braden mentioned that name. I don't recognize it, yet I feel as if I should."

"She was evil and she sacrificed others for centuries to sustain herself. She's gone now. Cormack killed her when she attacked Aisling. The damage she left behind sustains."

"Braden said that in the course of trying to save his mother, Genevieve severed her soul. I don't understand how that works."

"It's more that she shattered her soul," Maxine corrected. "One piece was big enough to hold together and pass over. That was the real Lily, a woman who loved her children and husband and wanted to protect them at all costs.

"The other portion, a much smaller sliver, remained with her body," she continued. "That other woman had all of Lily's memories but none of her emotions. Genevieve Toth concocted a plan to take over Aisling's body — she thought she needed a female reaper to turn back the soul-walking mistakes — but Aisling fought her off, and the rest of the family wiped out Genevieve's minions.

"At the time, no one realized Lily was still walking and talking," she said. "That became evident months later. Aisling discovered it, but had the most trouble accepting it. Braden immediately embraced his mother, trusted her, and tried to wedge her back into the family."

I tried to the picture the man I'd only recently met acting the way my aunt described and came up empty. "I'm guessing that didn't go over well."

"No. At least not with Aisling."

"Did they fight?"

"They always fight." Maxine's lips curved as she shook her head. "That's how they communicate. The Grimlocks love each other, but they get off messing with one another. Braden and Aisling most of all like to push."

"At some point it became clear that the woman masquerading as their mother was a fraud," I noted. "Braden said that himself. He said there was a big fight."

"There was," Maxine agreed. "Lily took over Genevieve's plan and decided to take Aisling so she could anchor herself to this plane with a human body that wasn't as tattered as the one she was trying to control. I wasn't completely sure what was happening, but I knew the Grimlocks needed help."

"And you somehow resurrected Lily Grimlock's soul," I mused. "That must have been an interesting bit of magic."

"I *borrowed* her soul," Maxine corrected. "It was a basic transporter spell with a bit of oomph. Lily's soul was really here, though only reapers could see it. Aisling was the first, but Lily revealed herself to all her children at the end. She helped save them."

That didn't sound so bad. "So ... why are they so angry?"

"Because she couldn't stay."

"Is that the only reason?" My aunt's answer didn't seem to jibe with the vibe I got from Braden. "I think there has to be more to it than that."

"Nothing in life is ever simple," Maxine agreed, a hint of a smile playing around the corners of her lips before she sobered. "Basically, the fight went down in an old theater. The half-Lily tried to escape, but Aisling stopped her. The floor gave way and Aisling had a choice of saving the creature pretending to be her mother or Braden."

My heart skipped a beat. "She obviously chose Braden."

"She did. Braden still feels guilt for his mother dying, even though he understands that woman wasn't really his mother. He grapples with it, which means the others struggle, too. They're a co-dependent lot."

"I had dinner with them last night. They're all loyal to a fault. Co-dependency is definitely a thing in that house. They all grouped around Aisling when I tried to ease her foot discomfort as if they were waiting for me to try to hurt her so they would have something to kill."

"That sounds exactly like them," Maxine said. "They're a force to be reckoned with when they want to be."

"And yet they blame you for what happened, and it wasn't your fault." My temper flashed bright and hot. "That doesn't seem fair."

"They don't really blame me," Maxine countered. "They need someone to blame, and I'm the most convenient target. They'll get over it."

"And you're okay with that? You helped them. You shouldn't be punished for your good deed."

"I gave them their real mother for a very brief period of time. She was ripped from their lives again. Do you think that's easy for them?"

I shook my head as tears pricked the back of my eyes. "I know what it's like to lose a mother."

"You do. Still, what happened to them was different," Maxine stressed. "No one should have to deal with what those children did. Can you imagine getting your mother back only to find out she wasn't your real mother? Can you imagine being responsible for her death? The Grimlocks are dealing with a lot."

"That doesn't make it your fault."

"They'll get over it in time. Until then, I will offer help wherever I can. But ... I need to see the gate. I haven't been in that room since your mother and father were in charge, but I need to see if I can get a reading. If we're going to find this wraith, I'll need something to go on."

"That's against the rules."

"I'm well aware."

I capitulated almost instantly. "You'll have to be quiet. If I get caught showing you the gate I could get fired."

"I'll be quiet as a mouse." She mimed zipping her lips, causing me to smile. "It will be just like old times. I snuck in there a time or two with you when you were a child, but I don't suppose you remember that."

My stomach gave a little flip. "I remember." In truth, I remembered almost all of it. The only thing I didn't remember was the most important thing. I hoped that would change.

Fourteen

Maxine didn't spend much time staring at the filmy gate opening when we reached the aquarium. I found that odd because it's all I wanted to stare at. Instead, she murmured a spell I didn't recognize and started pacing the outside boundary of the room, keeping close to the cinder block walls.

"What do you think is on the other side?" I asked, easing a hip onto the table and watching her. "Do you think we go on?"

"Of course we go on." Maxine seemed so sure of herself it gave me pause. "How can you be a reaper and not believe in the afterlife?"

"It's not that I don't believe in it," I said. "It's just ... do you think Mom and Dad are over there?"

"Why wouldn't they be?"

"Because I can't remember what happened the night they died and I've been doing a little research." It was hard for me to admit but now that I'd started I couldn't stop. "If something came through the gate, then maybe their souls were destroyed during the fight. I didn't know that was a thing until I started reading up on the possibilities."

Maxine stopped whatever she was doing and focused on me. "Are you really worried about that?"

I nodded without hesitation. "Just tonight you told me a story about a body coming back without a soul. If the soul and body get separated, there's always a chance something bad can happen to the soul."

"I guess that's true." Maxine didn't look convinced. "You know, you have ready access to reapers who could look that up for you. Cormack would've been the one in charge of Belle Isle at the time of their deaths. You could ask him to check his records."

That hadn't even occurred to me. "He was in charge even then?"

"He's been in charge a very long time. His parents retired early and moved to Florida. Cormack took over when he was barely in his twenties. He's an important figure in this organization."

I rubbed my cheek, uncertain. "Do you think he would be upset if I asked?"

"No. You've met his children. He's largely unflappable."

"I'll think about it."

Maxine returned to her spell, allowing me to watch. When she was finished, I asked the obvious question.

"What was that?"

"I was searching for a trail, but there doesn't seem to be anything," she replied. "I thought maybe if we could find the wraith's essence that we could follow it."

"Oh." That was better than any idea I'd come up with. "Why do you think we can't find a trail?"

"There are two possibilities. The first is that the wraith's lack of a complete soul makes a trail impossible because it doesn't read as a complete entity."

"And the second possibility?"

"That it's so strong it managed to mask its trail."

I didn't like the sound of that. "Which do you think it is?"

"I have no idea." Maxine planted her hands on her hips as she huffily looked around the room. "I don't know what to tell you. I need to think."

MAXINE TOOK HER THINKING plans home. She offered to walk back to the boathouse with me, but I waved her off. I had my golf cart, which meant I could zip to my new home in a few minutes. The island was empty, the wraith seemingly gone, so I wasn't overly worried about making the trek myself.

I had no reason to stay near the gate. Our logs were cleared for the afternoon thanks to Oliver and Renee, which meant we wouldn't have souls to monitor again until the morning. Still, I couldn't drag myself from the shimmering surface.

I sat cross-legged on the top step next to the opening and stared at the rippling doorway. The surface was reflective, and I saw a distorted image of myself, but I could see nothing on the other side.

Perhaps that was for the best.

"I know you're not there," I said softly, speaking to no one in particular. "I know you can't hear me, but this is as close as I can get."

If anyone were to catch me, to ask what I was doing, I would lie and say I was talking to myself. That was less embarrassing than the truth. I was alone, which meant I could be bold. I had things to say to my parents that I didn't want Renee and Oliver to hear. I was under no illusion that they could hear me. I still wanted to talk.

"I've never forgotten you," I offered. "I was young, but you ingrained yourselves in my memories. Grandpa kept photos of you all over the house so I wouldn't forget what you looked like. He would tell me funny stories. Sure, they were mostly about Dad, but he tried to include Mom as much as possible.

"Even though he wanted me to live with him, he didn't keep me from Aunt Maxine," I continued. "She came to visit every six months. He wouldn't let me stay with her for the summers, and I was bitter about that when I was younger, but I get it now. He was always afraid I would find my way back here.

"I can't remember what happened," I said, furrowing my brow. "I try. Hard. I remember us screwing around in this very room. Dad was making a joke — I think it was one of those lame Dad jokes that made me roll my eyes even back then — and we were planning to do something as a family over the weekend. I'm pretty sure it was the zoo.

"I remember the gate flickering, and it made a sound like a skipping record," I said, trailing my fingers close to the shimmering surface but being careful not to touch it. "I think something came through, but I can't remember what. Everything in my head is jumbled after that. I hear screaming and nothing else."

I lapsed into silence for several minutes before continuing.

"They questioned me – the reaper council and police officers, I mean. Aunt Maxine stepped in when they got a little overzealous," I offered. "They wanted answers. I get that. I didn't have answers to give. I was in shock. That's what the doctors said. It took days for me to snap out of it.

"By then, Grandpa had arrived in town," I continued. "He sat by my bed in the hospital and never left. He argued with Aunt Maxine, made her cry, but he refused to back down. She threatened to take it to court, but when she realized I was listening ... and crying ... she immediately backed off.

"After that, they shared me to the best of their abilities," I said. "They didn't always get along with each other, but they did the absolute best they could for me. You don't have to worry about me having a bad life. I had the best life."

I tilted my head, hoping for a familiar whisper to join the babel of strange ones floating through the room. It didn't happen. Even though I knew it wouldn't happen, I was disappointed all the same.

"Anyway, that's all I wanted to tell you." I dusted off the seat of my pants as I stood and moved away from the gate. "I'll be around. I'll keep talking even though you can't hear. You always said I was a chatterbox, Dad. That hasn't changed."

Still nothing, which allowed the weariness to overtake me.

"I'll see you later." I was halfway across the room before I registered the hair on the back of my neck standing on end. I jerked up my head, slowly swiveled to search every corner of the room, and then swallowed a gasp when I heard the doors behind me swing open.

I spun so fast I almost lost my balance, my eyes going wide when I realized three wraiths had entered the room. They stood tall, somehow stretched, and their black robes billowed thanks to the overhead fans.

"What are you doing here?" It was only after I asked the question that I realized it was stupid to waste my time with words. Wraiths didn't communicate. Occasionally they babbled, or said a single word.

The only thing I'd managed was to draw their attention to me ... and that wasn't good.

"Bruja." I recognized the word as the middle wraith focused on me. "It's the Bruja."

They knew who I was. It made no sense that they would recognize me, yet they did. "Get out!" I extended a finger toward the door, a move I remembered from my childhood when I invaded my mother's personal space. I realized I was channeling her, which was a comfort ... until the wraiths moved in my direction.

They almost looked as if they were floating, mostly because I couldn't see any feet, and their bony hands were pasty white as they extended them in my direction. I didn't have a weapon, so I backed up and considered my options.

"Bruja." The wraith's voice was a harsh rasp that sent chills down my spine. "Bruja."

Son of a troll! I was in a pickle now. This was the last thing I wanted. "I don't suppose you guys would simply call this a draw, would you? We could go our separate ways and no one would have to get hurt."

The wraiths continued to advance.

"That's what I figured. I was beside myself as I shook my head. "Okay. Well, I guess that means ... ." I didn't finish the sentence, instead bolting to my left and heading toward the supply closet. I had my security card in hand as I waved it in front of the scanner. Surprise was my only weapon, and I was banking on the wraiths being shaken enough to give me time to slide inside.

I knew better than to waste precious time glancing over my shoulder. I grabbed the storeroom door handle and opened it far enough that I could slip inside, twisting quickly to throw all my weight on the bar on the opposite side in an effort to yank the heavy door closed.

There was a small window at the top of the door. From my vantage point, crowded toward the floor, I didn't miss the hiss of disgust on the other side as a ghastly face filled the frame and stared into the dark depths of the room.

Carefully, I released the door handle, but not before testing it to make sure the locking mechanism held. I heard the wraiths pulling and prodding on the other side, but the door didn't budge. That was good, because this was going to be my new home if I didn't get some help. With that in mind, I pulled out my phone and searched through my contacts list. I didn't stop until I hit a familiar name.

He picked up on the second ring. "Who is this?"

"It's me. Izzy. Izzy Sage." I had no idea why I added the "Izzy Sage" part. He clearly knew it was me after the first three words. "I'm in big trouble. Wraiths broke into the gate room. I'm locked in a closet and ... I don't know what to do."

Instead of yelling and cursing, Braden was unnaturally calm. "Are you safe?"

"For now."

"I'm on my way. Stay where you are. Whatever you do, don't leave that room. Do you understand me?"

"Yes." I wasn't a fan of his bossy tone, but it wasn't as if I had a choice. "Please hurry."

"I'm on my way. I'll be there before you know it."

Somehow I doubted that.

THE WRAITHS SPENT SO much time trying to get at me in the supply room that they ignored the gate. That was for the best, because they were caught unaware when the Grimlocks — swords in hand — swooped in.

I watched with grim fascination as Redmond, Cillian and Braden dispatched the creatures within seconds of entering the room. They seemed practiced, as if this wasn't new to them, and Cormack was calm as he strode to the storage room door and attempted to open it.

"It's locked," I offered lamely as we stared at each other through the window. "You need a special keycard to get inside. I think I'm stuck here."

The look he shot me was pitying. "Or you could simply shove your keycard under the door and allow me to open it from this side."

Huh. He was cool in the face of a crisis. That was a good thing. "Great idea." My emotions were blunted as I slid the card under the door and watched as he swiped his way in. He smiled when the door slid open and caught sight of my face. I couldn't return the expression.

"Are you okay?" Braden brushed past his father and hurried to my side, ignoring the sidelong look Cormack shot him.

I nodded, clasping my shaking hands together. "I am. It happened fast. I'm sorry I had to call you. I didn't know what else to do."

"That's why we're here." Braden slipped his arm around my shoulders and led me toward the table. "Cillian, see if you can find a bottle of water in that fridge."

Cillian nodded without hesitation, offering me a friendly wink before turning on his heel. Redmond was busy prowling the room while Braden and Cormack invaded my personal space.

"You need to tell me what happened," Cormack instructed, his tone firm. "I need to know everything that occurred so I can fashion the appropriate report."

"They just appeared. I don't know how they got in."

"What were you doing here so late?" Braden asked gently. "I didn't think you guys worked overnight. That's why we're instructed to hang onto souls if they come in after a certain hour."

"I wasn't working," I hedged, decidedly uncomfortable. "I brought someone here to look around and was about to leave myself when it happened."

"Who did you bring here?" Braden's voice took on an edge. "Was it a ... date?"

"A date? Why would I bring a date here?"

"I don't know. Maybe that's your thing."

"It wasn't a date." My temper ratcheted up a notch. "I can't believe you'd even think that."

"What else am I supposed to think?" Braden challenged. "You're new to the area. You haven't made friends yet."

"No, but I have an aunt."

"Oh." He rocked back on his heels. The explanation was supposed to be placating, but it seemed to have the opposite effect on Braden.

"I asked her to talk to Maxine," Cormack supplied, taking the bottle of water from Cillian and passing it in my direction. "I thought she would be able to help. I'm guessing that's why she was here."

I nodded as I accepted the bottle and twisted the top. "She was hoping to be able to find a trail, but she came up empty. She says she needs time to think because she's never dealt with a situation like this before."

"I think we can all safely say that," Cormack said dryly. "How did the wraiths get in?"

That was a good question. "I don't know."

"Has the door been replaced?" Cormack turned his attention to Cillian, which made me realize he was looking to him for an answer. "That was high on our to-do list, but I didn't pay attention when we came in."

"It's the same door," Braden volunteered, his eyes remote as he shifted from one foot to the other. "It hasn't been switched out yet."

"Then the wraiths must have entered after Maxine left," Cillian surmised. "She didn't know to tug hard to latch it."

"That door must be replaced tomorrow," Cormack ordered. "The door is our biggest concern. After that, we have to track down the mutated wraith. " His eyes slowly tracked to me. "Did any of the newer wraiths cross the threshold?"

I shook my head. "That's what I was worried about, but they were distracted trying to get me out of the closet. I don't think they realized they were working on a limited timetable. They didn't even look in that direction once I was in here. I was all they seemed to care about."

"Well, we lucked out there," Redmond said as he joined us. "Still, I think we should keep a guard on this room and then have that door switched out pronto in the morning. We can't risk this happening a second time."

"Agreed." Cormack blew out a sigh as he regarded me. "We'll get Izzy back to her room, post a guard here and then pick this up in the morning."

That sounded like a workable plan to me. Of course, that could've been the exhaustion talking.

Fifteen

Despite the excitement, I slept hard. Braden and Cillian insisted on driving the cart back to the boathouse so they could walk back together. They didn't appear frightened at the prospect of wraiths attacking, but I was fearful on their behalf.

I watched from the upstairs window until they disappeared into the darkness, and then I climbed into bed. I was certain sleep would be elusive. I was wrong.

When I woke, I wasn't alone. My instincts told me that, and I was instantly alert, ready to fight in case my life was about to be threatened. I found Aisling sitting at my small vanity, playing with my makeup and studying her reflection.

"Do you think it's normal to look so bloated before giving birth?"

I wasn't expecting the question. "You don't look bloated."

"I look like a beached whale."

"You look like a woman who is about to expand her family," I corrected, dragging a hand through my mussed hair and regarding her with curiosity. "How did you get inside?"

"My brothers are masters at getting around locked doors." She swiveled in the chair and fixed me with an appraising gaze. "How did you sleep?"

"Better than I expected."

"Yeah. Adrenaline will do that for you."

"I guess." I kept up a continuous combing motion with my fingers. "What are you doing here?"

"Well, because everyone in my family planned to spend the day here to make sure the gate was secure, I insisted they include me. They didn't like it at first, but I'm betting you can guess who won."

It took everything I had not to smile. I figured that would encourage her, and I was under the distinct impression that was the last thing her family wanted. "I thought your husband wanted you out of the line of fire."

"That's why I'm here with you and not near the gate. My father insisted I serve as your chaperone, at least until lunch. That's when they figure the new door will be installed."

That was disheartening. "I don't need a chaperone."

"Don't worry. He played it up as if I would be the one looking out for you, but I'm well aware that he expects you to watch me. You've had a steady string of messages sliding across your screen." She pointed toward my cell phone, which was plugged in and resting on the nightstand. "I'll bet half of them are from my family, and my dad is explaining how you should go along with what he said without telling me differently."

"Really?" I cocked an eyebrow and leaned to retrieve the phone. I was curious as to whether she was right. She was. "Actually, I have instructions here from your brothers and father. I don't understand how they all got my number. I only gave it to Braden and Cormack."

"We share everything in the Grimlock family."

"That sounds invasive."

"You have no idea." Aisling's expression turned expectant. "Because they're being alphaholes, I thought we could take advantage of the situation. How does breakfast sound? After that, we can do some shopping. You need some warmer clothes."

"I'm on duty."

"Yes, but my father is the boss and he can shift your duties. Shopping will be a lot more fun than watching my brothers posture and test that door three million times."

She had a point, but still … . "I don't know." I chewed my bottom lip. "I'm pretty sure a good employee doesn't shirk her duties four days into a new gig."

"And I'm pretty sure that I want breakfast … and a trip to the mall. Once this kid comes, I won't see the mall for months. Everyone keeps telling me that. I want to shop until I drop now and get it out of my system."

"Okay." I saw no reason to argue. She was right about her family. Cormack's insistent message instructed me to keep Aisling busy and out of trouble. Shopping seemed a good way to do that. "Do you have a car? I don't."

"Really?" She pursed her lips.

"I haven't had time to purchase one."

"That's a form of shopping." Aisling grabbed her phone from the vanity. "I'll message Dad that we need a vehicle. He'll force one of my brothers to hand over his. I can't drive right now because I'm too big to fit behind the wheel. You'll have to do it."

"As long as you know where we're going."

"Oh, I know exactly where we're going."

"THIS IS A NICE AREA."

Aisling picked Somerset Collection mall or our shopping extravaganza. We ate a delicious breakfast at a cutesy diner in the parking lot and then hit the main building ten minutes later. The facility was filled with high-end shops, including a skywalk, and Aisling seemed at home, so I readily followed her.

"What are you looking for?"

"Clothes for you," Aisling replied without hesitation. "I like your style, and it's fine for summer, but you need something to get you through the next two months. Weather in Michigan is seasonal, which means you essentially need three different wardrobes."

I knit my eyebrows, confused. "Three? There are four seasons."

"Yes, but you get the same weather in much of spring and fall, so you need to plan ahead for three climates. Winter is a frozen tundra. We're mostly beyond that, so you can ignore it until the fall. Summer is hot and humid. You're probably used to that in New Orleans, and from what I can see you've got it covered. That leaves spring and fall. You need layers so you can bulk up and strip down."

"I can probably manage until summer hits," I hedged. I didn't have much money for shopping, especially because I needed to purchase a car. "I thought you were shopping for something specific."

"Oh, I'm shopping for everything." Aisling dug into her small purse until she came back with a black card. "It's on Dad. He said to get whatever we needed."

I balked. "I'm sure he meant that for you."

"And I want to get you things." Aisling wasn't the sort to back down, which made me uncomfortable. "Besides, this is what he gets for trying to trick me. If he thinks I'm going to be bamboozled by shopping, he has a rude awakening in his future."

I didn't like the look on her face one bit. "I think that we should focus on you and I'll handle my own clothes."

Aisling snorted. "Oh, we'll see about that."

IF I THOUGHT AISLING was a force to be reckoned with in the real world, watching her work in a mall setting was downright terrifying. She knew her way around the stores, to the point the concierge desk kept sending people out to collect her packages so they could be carried to Braden's BMW when we were done.

I was in awe. And, truth be told, I was a bit amused.

"Your father doesn't care that you're wearing out his black card?" I asked when we decided to take a break and catch lunch in the food court.

"My father is a wealthy man who likes to spoil me." Aisling dug into her bourbon chicken with zest. "Honestly, he won't care a bit. He'll blow smoke, complain a little and then he'll make sure I have the waffle bar of my dreams for breakfast tomorrow morning."

"It must be nice. Not the spoiling so much as knowing that he'll always be there."

Aisling studied me as she chewed, waiting until she swallowed to speak. "I know what happened to your family. I heard my father and Braden talking last night. I'm sorry. That must have been rough."

My skin prickled under her intense scrutiny. "I don't really remember it."

"I know that, too. It's better not to remember it. Trust me."

Maxine's words from the previous night filtered through my brain. "I know what happened with your mother. I'm sorry about that. I can't imagine what you must've gone through when she fell."

Instead of reacting with sadness, Aisling snorted. "Did Madame Maxine give you the details?"

"Kind of. She filled in the blanks after Braden told me."

The way Aisling's chin snapped up told me she wasn't expecting that. "Braden told you?"

I bobbed my head. "You seem surprised."

"He hasn't wanted to talk to anyone since it happened, including me, and we were there together at the end."

"You saved him, right?"

"We all worked together to save him."

She didn't strike me as the humble sort, but it was clear she didn't want to dwell on that moment. "Well, despite that, it had to be awful. I'm sorry."

"I'm pretty much over it."

I didn't believe that for a second. Still, it was probably best to change the subject. "Are you excited about the baby? Do you know if it's a boy or a girl?"

"I'm excited to get it out of me," Aisling replied. "We decided to be surprised on the gender. That was more Griffin than me. I already know it's a girl."

Her matter-of-fact delivery threw me for a loop. "Are you disappointed it's a girl?"

"No."

"You don't seem happy."

"Well, let's just say I'm a big believer in karma and I've got a whopping case of it heading in my direction. Believe it or not, I wasn't the best-behaved kid. That means I'm getting the devil to raise myself. It will definitely be a girl, someone to wrap Griffin around her finger while making me want to tear my hair out."

I had to bite back a chuckle. "I see you're a glass half full sort of person."

"Simply a realist. I ... ." Whatever she was about to say died on her lips when a woman moved in at our right and made a rather distinctive tsking sound. "Oh, you've got to be kidding me."

I was instantly on alert as I shifted my attention to the woman. She boasted pretty brown hair and a thin nose that was more ugly than flattering. The look she gave Aisling was straight out of a horror movie, and I had no idea what to make of it.

"Well, well, well. What have we here?"

If Aisling were a superhero, this is the point at which she would turn into Cyclops and burn holes into her villain. "Angelina."

"Aisling. You're looking ... fat."

"That's what your pimp said about you when he was filling out performance reviews," Aisling fired back, venom dripping from her tongue. "You got an A for laying on your back and an F for variety. Just FYI, if you expect to get the good tips, you've got to think outside the box. You won't be able to keep this up forever. Eventually you'll get shuttled off to the old whores' home."

I was stunned by the disparaging remark.

"Well, at least I'm not fat," Angelina shot back, her lips twisting into the approximation of an evil sneer. "What are you doing here during the middle of the day, by the way? Did Griffin dump you? Are you here drowning your sorrows in bourbon chicken?"

I had no idea what was going on, but I felt the need to stand up for Aisling. "She's pregnant, not fat."

Angelina shot me a withering look that made my blood pressure spike. "I know, you ninny. This conversation has nothing to do with you. Stay out of it."

My mouth dropped open as Aisling cursed a blue streak.

"Leave her alone, you slut," Aisling barked. "She hasn't done anything to you."

"I think being friendly with you is enough to prove she's an enemy," Angelina countered. "Unless ... what happened to Jerry the fairy? Did you finally replace him? That's probably best. He was dragging you down. If you sank any further those mutant ninja turtles were going to be forced to kick you out of the sewers."

"That did it!" Aisling struggled to get to her feet, but her stomach was so large it snagged on the table. "I'm going to totally yank your hair out of your head and shove it down your throat. Your pimp says you're used to things being shoved down your throat, so you'll probably like it."

My instincts kicked into overdrive as I touched my hand to Aisling's wrist and pulsed a burst of calming magic into her. The anger that was coursing through her dissipated, though only an iota.

"I hate her," Aisling hissed, her eyes firing. "She can't call Jerry a fairy. I don't like it."

I understood. I'd yet to meet Jerry — although the build-up was huge — but I felt protective of him, too. "She's just trying to get to you," I soothed, slowly sliding a hateful glare to Angelina. "She knows that's your trigger. She doesn't care that you probably shouldn't get worked up so close to giving birth. I care, so you need to calm down."

To my utter surprise, Angelina's aggressive stance relaxed marginally. "Why is she supposed to be taking it easy? Is she sick?"

If I didn't know better, I would think the woman was actually concerned. That only served to confuse me even more. "She's not sick. She's close to her due date. And she needs to remain calm."

"So why is she at the mall instead of being spoiled by her father? I'd think between her brothers, father and Griffin that they'd have her on lockdown."

Huh. That was interesting. "And how well do you know the family?"

"I almost married into them," Angelina replied, causing my heart to stutter. "We go way back."

"You didn't almost marry into our family," Aisling challenged. "Stop making things up. Well, unless you're role playing with your pimp and he wants you to make things up. Then it's okay."

"Knock that off." Angelina extended a warning finger. "I don't want to hear one more thing about my pimp. I don't have a pimp."

"Oh, did he cut you loose, too? I told you to take a class."

Angelina narrowed her eyes to dangerous slits. "I am good in bed.

In fact, I'm great in bed. You can ask anyone, because I've slept with everyone ... including your brother." She realized what she'd said too late, but that didn't stop her from trying to backtrack. "I mean ... that came out wrong."

"Everything you do ends up wrong," Aisling muttered, rubbing her hand over her stomach. She didn't look happy. "Listen, I can't fight with you the way I want to. No one is sadder about it than me. You're giving me indigestion, though, and I don't like it."

Angelina rolled her eyes and folded her arms across her chest. "And I should care because?"

"Because it's no fun for either of us if we're not on our game," Aisling replied, pragmatic. "That won't happen until I get this kid out of me. I think that means we need a truce until I give birth."

Angelina didn't look happy with the suggestion, but she acquiesced. "Fine. You have until one week after you give birth, and then it's on."

"That will give you plenty of time to think of new insults."

"Right back at you."

I gaped as Angelina turned on her heel and flounced to the other side of the food court, to where a young couple sat looking over what looked like brochures for a housing development. I had no idea what to make of the show. "What was that?"

"She's the devil." Aisling turned back to her chicken. "This is really good."

She acted as if she hadn't just participated in the snarkiest girl fight in the history of female bitchfests. "That's all you have to say?"

Aisling shrugged, unbothered. "We've hated each other since elementary school. We fight all the time. We've yet to kill each other, but it could happen one day."

"Uh-huh." I gave her a searching look. "Which one of your brothers did she date?" I was almost dreading the answer.

Aisling's smile was slow and sly. "Why do you want to know?"

I shifted on my seat, uncomfortable. "Just curious."

"Right. Well, you don't have to worry. It wasn't Braden."

"I don't care if it was Braden. Why do you think I would care if it was Braden?"

"Because you're not fooling anybody." She took another heaping bite of bourbon chicken, and this time she didn't bother swallowing before speaking. "Don't worry. I'll get all that information out of you, too. I'm just waiting for an opening."

I averted my gaze, cursing my burning cheeks. "There is no information to gather. We're colleagues."

"Yeah. We definitely have a few things to talk about."

Sixteen

Aisling ate all of her food and half of mine. She didn't seem bothered in the least when the people at a neighboring table took time to watch her chow down, amused looks flitting across their faces.

Once we were finished, Aisling insisted we return to shopping. I fought her efforts to buy new clothing ... and lost. Whenever she felt I wasn't embracing the program thoroughly, she faked crying. Her eyes were completely dry, but she put on a good act, which made the other people in the stores give me dirty looks. I didn't want to become known as the woman who mistreated a pregnant woman, so ultimately I acquiesced.

When we returned to Belle Isle, Aisling insisted on seeing the shoreline where the super-powered wraith entered the water. It was cold enough that I thought it was a bad idea. But Aisling refused to hear my concerns, and before I knew it we found ourselves staring at the steep hill that led down to the water.

"You're not walking down there." I was firm as I pinned her with a pointed look.

Aisling rolled her eyes. "Don't tell me what to do."

I grabbed her arm when she moved to crawl over the railing. "You can't walk down there. It's cold ... and dangerous ... and you're bigger than a Kardashian's lips when she starts pouting because a camera isn't around."

Aisling stilled, her eyes unreadable. Finally, when she spoke, her lips curved. "Did you just make a Kardashian joke?"

"I ... yes. If you like them, I'm sorry."

"I hate them with a fiery passion."

"You didn't let me finish." I was calm. "If you like them, I'm sorry you have such bad taste."

Aisling snickered as she rested her hands on the railing. "Yeah. If the Kardashians were the ring of power in *Lord of the Rings*, I would totally be marching them toward Mount Doom."

"Good to know."

"Yeah."

"You're still not climbing over that railing." I thought my Kardashian hate might earn me some points with Aisling. I was wrong.

"Oh, I'm climbing over the railing." Aisling clearly had no intention of backing down, because she slapped my hands away when I moved to grab her. "Knock it off."

Even though she had to be ridiculously uncomfortable, Aisling managed to slide her leg over the railing. Unfortunately, given her awkward position, she couldn't find the ground with her foot once she started, The panicked look she gave me two minutes later was almost funny enough to ignore her situation.

Almost.

"Do something!"

"What do you want me to do?" I grumbled as I moved closer to her. "I told you not to do this."

"Oh, you sound just like my father," she groused, grunting as she tried to find a spot to plant her foot. "He says things like that all the time." She shifted to a voice that sounded eerily like Cormack's. "Don't go outside in the rain because you'll get a cold. Don't pull that girl's hair because her mother is the type who will get you thrown out of school. Don't steal my car because I'll leave you in jail once you're caught."

I stilled, surprised. "You stole your father's car?"

Aisling made a protesting sound with her tongue. "He had it coming! He locked me in the house for doing the same thing my brothers did. Do you want to know why? Because I'm a girl. I refuse to be punished simply because I have a vagina. That one is on him."

"Uh-huh." I was understandably dubious. "Do you want to know what I think?"

"Not even a little."

"Well, I'm going to tell you anyway." I crouched so I was at eye level with her. "I think you're worried about being cut out of the action because you're having a baby. I'm not a psychologist — and that sounds like the absolute worst job ever — but it's clear that being one of 'the gang' is important to you." I used air quotes, which seemed to frustrate Aisling. "No one is going to kick you out of the gang."

"Ugh. I hate that you sound so reasonable." Aisling rested her cheek on the railing, clearly exhausted from her struggle. "We weren't going to have a baby so early in our relationship. We thought it would be better to wait."

"Well, accidents happen."

"Yeah." She looked lost in thought. "Our lives are going to be different."

"They might be better."

"I like being the center of the universe. That ends when the baby comes. I'll be forgotten."

"You won't."

"I'm at least going to be shoved aside."

I wanted to argue with the sentiment, but I knew there was a very real possibility that she was right. "I think you're overreacting because you're emotional. Your family loves you. Griffin clearly loves you. You won't be forgotten. You won't let that happen."

"I guess." Aisling briefly pressed her eyes shut and heaved a sigh. "I'm stuck."

"I know. I'm going to get you up ... somehow."

"We have another problem."

"We do?" I was instantly alert. If she was about to tell me she'd gone into labor I feared I would run screaming and leave her vulnerable to the elements. "What's the problem?"

"There's a body over there."

I straightened and craned my neck, staring at the location she pointed toward. "I ... are you sure?"

"Yeah. There's a dead guy over there. I've seen enough bodies to be certain."

Well, son of a troll! That was the last thing we needed.

BRADEN AND CORMACK were the first to arrive when I called to tell them what we'd found. I spent the next ten minutes trying to get Aisling off the railing — explaining her unfortunate position over the phone to her loved ones seemed a bad idea — but nothing worked because I couldn't find the proper leverage to lift her.

Cormack wasn't happy when he saw his daughter. "You have got to be kidding me!"

I pressed my lips together as I watched him stalk to the railing and grab her by the waist. When he realized he couldn't get his arms completely around her, he stilled.

"Oh."

"Did he think I didn't try that myself?" I complained to Braden, who looked both amused and concerned.

"He can't help himself," Braden explained. "All he sees is Aisling in trouble. He wants to help."

"It's not as if she's going to die there," I grumbled.

"No, but it's cold and that can't be comfortable."

He wasn't wrong.

"Braden, get over here," Cormack barked, hooking an arm around his daughter's torso to get a good grip on her. "You need to help me."

"Yeah, yeah." Braden made a face but acquiesced, climbing over the railing to position himself between Aisling and a potential fall. Once he found his footing, he carefully pushed Aisling so Cormack could tug her to his side. The loud grunting Aisling made caused her brother to bark out a raucous laugh as she burned holes in him with her glare.

"I hate you," Aisling hissed.

"You'll get over it." Braden left Cormack to deal with Aisling and shuffled toward the body.

Cormack immediately rested his hands on Aisling's huge abdomen. "Are you all right?"

"I'm fine." Aisling made a face that told me she was anything but as she turned her eyes to Braden. "Don't you think you should be focused on the dead body?"

"No. I think I should be focused on my idiot daughter," Cormack fired back. "What were you thinking coming down here?"

"She was thinking she wanted to be part of the group," I automatically answered. "She doesn't want to be cut out of the family antics."

"She's not going to be cut out."

"That's not how she feels. She's allowed to feel what she feels."

"Oh, well, thank you for that," Cormack muttered, rolling his eyes.

I ignored him and focused on Braden, who looked legitimately puzzled as he stared down at the body. "Is it someone we know?"

"Kind of," Braden hedged, shifting uncomfortably from one foot to the other.

"Who is it?"

"The same body we found yesterday."

His answer confused me. "Come again?"

"This is the same body we found yesterday," Braden supplied. "I have no idea how it ended up out here, but it's the same dude."

"So ... what do we do?"

"There's only one thing we can do." Braden was grim as he glanced at his sister while digging in his pocket for his phone. "You're going to be in big trouble when he gets here."

Aisling frowned. "This isn't my day."

"You'll survive." Cormack rested his hand on her shoulder. "Where is my credit card, by the way? Did you max it out?"

"No, but it's tired."

"I guess there are worse things."

GRIFFIN'S EXPRESSION WAS MURDEROUS when he parked thirty feet down the road thirty minutes later and immediately turned to his wife.

"What happened?"

Instead of putting his hands on Aisling's belly, Griffin pulled her in for a soothing hug. He was angry, but she was his first priority. I found his reaction interesting ... even though I knew it was wrong to analyze them.

"Hmm."

Braden slid me a sidelong look. "Hmm, what?"

"What? Oh, nothing." I shook my head to dislodge the serious thoughts. "I was simply thinking."

"About something specific," he prodded. "What were you thinking?"

"It's not important."

"I still want to hear it."

I met his pointed gaze for a long beat before giving in. "Your father immediately went to the baby bump when he helped your sister from the railing. Griffin worried about her first. I think that's what she needs because she's feeling displaced."

"How can she feel displaced by the baby she's carrying?"

I shrugged. "Hormones are a funny thing. I don't think she can help herself."

Instead of laughing at my take on things, Braden stroked his chin and studied his sister. "I'll talk to my father."

I was surprised and gratified by his reaction. "Thank you."

"What are you doing out here, baby?" Griffin smoothed Aisling's hair, pressing his hands to either side of her head to cover her ears. "You're freezing. You should be inside."

"I'm fine," Aisling countered, struggling to move away from him. "I spent the day at the mall. There's nothing safer than that."

"Other than the fact that you picked a fight with that Angelina woman," I offered. It wasn't that I was tattling as much as my mouth often had a mind of its own.

"Angelina?" Braden cocked a brow and made a face. "Oh, geez! You didn't touch her, did you? I heard you can get herpes from accidentally brushing up against her."

I didn't want to laugh — now was not the time — but I couldn't help myself. "You and your sister have a lot in common."

Braden was clearly offended by the comment. "You take that back. I'm nothing like her."

"More than you realize."

"We'll talk about Angelina later," Cormack growled, shaking his head. "Even pregnant, Aisling can handle Angelina. I want to know about the body down there."

"It's the same body we found yesterday," Braden volunteered.

"You mean ... the body looks the same as the one you found yesterday?" Griffin asked as he wrapped his arms around Aisling to keep her warm.

"No, it's the exact same body," Braden replied. "It's exactly the same, but he's wearing different clothes."

"I don't understand." Griffin brushed a kiss against Aisling's forehead before striding to the railing so he could climb over and shuffle down the embankment. When he reached the body and knelt, his expression reflected confusion. "Huh. He's wearing what looks to be a jumper from the morgue."

"I told you." Braden radiated smugness as he folded his arms over his chest. "It's the same guy."

"It's definitely the same guy," Griffin agreed, sliding on a pair of rubber gloves before leaning forward to touch the body. "I don't understand how he got here."

"Maybe the wraith collected him from the morgue," I suggested. "Maybe the wraith wasn't done with him."

"Like the wraith was keeping him by the swings so it could snack on him whenever the mood struck?" Braden slid me a sidelong glance. "That doesn't sound likely."

"Well, there has to be a reason this body showed up here after being transported to the morgue yesterday," I persisted. "It certainly didn't walk back by itself."

"I wouldn't be so sure about that," Aisling argued, frowning when Cormack stepped in to cut her off from the railing when she shifted closer. "What are you doing?"

"Stay here," Cormack ordered, refusing to show fear in the face of his daughter's glare. "You can make your opinion known from here without risking a fall. You don't want to hurt the baby."

"Right." Aisling rolled her eyes. "What was I saying?"

"Stay here," Cormack repeated.

"Listen to your father, Aisling," Griffin interjected, earning a growl from his wife. "This embankment is steep. I don't want you to fall. If you twist an ankle you'll be stuck in bed for days. Is that what you want?"

"No."

"Then ... stay with your father." Griffin was firm. "Later, I'm going to have a long discussion with your father because it was my understanding you were no longer in the field. I'm going to yell ... and he's going to yell. When we're done yelling, I'm willing to bet you're going to get something special as a reward because that's how your father operates."

"She's not in the field," Cormack argued. "I sent her to the mall with my credit card. That's as far from the field as possible."

"Then what is she doing here?" Griffin challenged.

"She came down here herself. She suckered poor Izzy into bringing her to the spot where the wraith made its escape."

Wait a second! "She didn't sucker me," I countered, annoyance bubbling up. "She simply said she wanted to see the spot where the wraith disappeared into the water. I didn't see the harm in bringing her."

"Was that before or after she got stuck on the railing?" Braden asked.

"Before."

"I think you answered your own question."

"Whatever." His smug nature was starting to grate. "This isn't my fault. I told her not to climb over that railing."

"Ugh, and here we go." Aisling smacked her hand to her forehead. "I can't tell you how happy I am to hear you guys talk about me as if I'm not here. It's a true highlight of my day."

"Baby, I'm going to yell at you later for being stupid enough to come down here," Griffin offered. "You'll definitely be there for that conversation. Until then, we need to figure out how this body got here. I'm not sure I should even call the morgue for this one because if the body showed up out here via supernatural means I'll be filling out paperwork and answering questions until the kid has its first birthday."

"Someone had to drag it here," I pointed out. "Bodies don't simply get up and start walking."

"They do if they're zombies," Aisling argued.

My mouth inadvertently dropped open. "What?"

"You heard me."

"And here we go," Braden muttered, shifting his eyes to Griffin. "We're back on the zombie train. Are you happy?"

"Hey! She wasn't wrong about the zombies." Griffin extended a warning finger, his eyes flashing as he glared at his brother-in-law. "Give her a break. She's tired ... cranky ... and about to produce a baby. She doesn't need you giving her grief on top of everything else."

"Well, excuse me for living." Braden held up his hands in mock surrender. "Let's all bow to Aisling's whims and go on another zombie hunt. That won't be a waste of time."

"She was right about the zombies!" Griffin exploded, causing my head to fill with a collage of memories as his anger bubbled close to the surface.

I sucked in a breath as I rested my hands on my knees and tried to absorb the images, which were coming fast and furious. "I don't understand," I murmured.

"Join the club," Braden groused. "Apparently zombies are real, in case you're wondering. I have no idea if that's what we're dealing with here."

"How do we find out?"

Cormack scrubbed the back of his neck as he watched Griffin return his full attention to the body. "I have no idea. I can't believe this is happening again."

That made two of us. Er, well, I honestly couldn't believe it happened a first time, if we're being sticklers for detail.

Seventeen

Aisling's refusal to budge from her zombie hunch caused me to worry for her mental health. When Cillian stopped by the scene long enough to see the body for himself — and listen to his sister rant — he collected both of us for a special task.

"Wait ... where are we going?"

I sat in the back seat of Cillian's truck as he navigated the busy streets of downtown Detroit. I had no idea where we were ... or where we were going, for that matter, which meant I was beyond curious.

In the front seat, her fingers splayed in front of the heating vents, Aisling's reaction was blasé. "We're going to the home office so Cillian can keep an eye on me," she grumbled.

Amused, Cillian snickered. "I wish I would've seen you stuck on the railing. That must have been funny."

"It wasn't funny. It was uncomfortable."

"Poor Aisling." Cillian had his role as big brother down pat; he was sympathetic when he reached over and patted her shoulder. "Did someone take a photo?"

"I'm done talking to you." Her penchant for being a pouty little sister on full display, Aisling folded her arms over her chest and stared out the passenger window. "I'm done talking to anyone who shares the last name Grimlock for the rest of the day."

"Oh, that's such a punishment." Cillian's eyes twinkled as he met my gaze in the rearview mirror. "What about you, Izzy? What's on your mind?"

"I'm curious as to why we're going to the home office," I admitted, my nerves kicking into overdrive. "You don't think they're going to take me in a back room and beat me with a stick for falling down on the job during my first week, do you?"

"No," Cillian answered immediately.

"They don't have any sticks free because they're all shoved up ... ." Aisling trailed off when Cillian fixed her with a warning look.

"You'll be fine," Cillian said after a beat. "We're going straight to the library. They probably won't even notice that we're there."

That was a relief. "And what do you think we'll find in the library?"

"Men who have never been laid," Aisling muttered. "The only reason Cillian manages to get some is because he's a handsome geek. Trust me, when you see the other people in that library you'll wonder how reapers manage to procreate."

"Ha, ha." Cillian flicked his sister's ear. "We need to conduct some research. I can't figure out how that body got from the morgue back to Belle Isle. Griffin is checking with the medical examiner, but he's afraid to ask too many questions because it might cause someone to focus on the family. That wouldn't be good."

That was an understatement. "So ... he's not calling it in?"

"No."

"What happens to the body?"

"My father called out a crew," Aisling explained. "They'll collect the body and study it. Allowing Griffin to call it in puts all of us at risk."

I rubbed my cheek as I considered the conundrum. "Does he cover for you guys often?"

When Aisling didn't answer, Cillian smoothly stepped in. "Not really," he said. "He has covered for us on occasion. I don't think he minds because Aisling is his top priority, but I don't think he enjoys it either. It's difficult ... but necessary."

"I wasn't casting aspersions on his character. I was simply curious.

I've never heard of a reaper hooking up with a cop before. Did you get grief about it?"

"From my family or the other reapers?" Aisling asked.

"Either."

"The other reapers probably whispered about it, but my father is too important for anyone to risk saying anything to his face," she explained. "Besides that, if anyone did muster the courage to question him on it, he would've handled it without telling me."

"My father wasn't thrilled when Aisling first brought Griffin home," Cillian supplied. "It wasn't because he was a cop, although that probably gave him pause. It was because she's his baby and he always dreaded the day she would stop flirting with losers and find someone who might actually be suited for her. The rest of us never thought that day would come because she's not exactly easy to deal with. We were proved wrong."

The fondness evident on Cillian's face stirred me. It was clear he adored his sister. It was also clear he liked messing with her.

"So we're going to the home office library?" I decided to change the subject. "Do you think we'll be able to find answers there?"

"I'm not sure." Cillian turned serious. "Aisling is right about us facing zombies before. That was a very unique situation. I'm not sure we're dealing with the same thing."

"I certainly hope not."

"Yeah. I don't know what to think."

CILLIAN WAS OBVIOUSLY COMFORTABLE with the home office staff, so he signed us in and led us through the building. Aisling, who didn't seem happy with her assignment, glared at the woman behind the desk when she reached out to touch her huge stomach without invitation, quelling her with a bone-chilling look.

"You must get tired of that," I noted as I fell into step with her. "You know people don't do it to irritate you. They simply can't stop themselves because giving birth is something of a miracle."

"It doesn't feel miraculous."

"It will be over soon."

Curiosity flitted across Aisling's face as she pinned me with a look. "You see things. I know you do. When is the kid coming? Like ... is it today? Tomorrow? I would really like some warning so I can get an ice cream bar out of my father the night before."

A snicker bubbled up. "I don't know when you're going to give birth. I'm not a mystical gazing globe."

"No, but you see things," Aisling persisted. "Are you psychic? I know you said you don't like that word, but it's the only one I have."

"Aisling, stop being a pain," Cillian ordered as he led us down an empty hallway.

"I'm not being a pain." Aisling refused to back down. "I'm curious. Izzy and I have bonded. She knows I'm not trying to stick my nose into her business for the sake of being a busybody. I have a scientific reason for my questions. Chill out."

"You've bonded?" Cillian cocked an eyebrow and shifted his eyes to me. "Have you bonded with my sister?"

That was a thorny question. "Um ... ."

"I only ask because, other than our mother, I've never known Aisling to bond with a woman," Cillian continued, not waiting for me to respond. "Her best friend is a man. She spends all of her time with us. Redmond says she thinks like a dude, and that's true. If you two have really bonded that will be cause for celebration because we'll be looking to you to soften her edges."

I didn't like the sound of that. "Oh ... I'm not sure."

"We've bonded," Aisling repeated, seemingly unbothered by my reticence. "You're putting my new friend on the spot. I don't like it. In fact ... ." She trailed off as Cillian pushed open a door and led us into the biggest library I'd ever seen. It had to be four stories high, and the staircases that led to the various levels wound through the oddly-placed walkways that skirted the walls. I was completely enchanted. "Wow!"

"Yeah, I love it here, too." Cillian grinned at me. "There's a lot of good information buried in these books. Make sure you have hours to burn if you decide to visit. I've lost entire days here."

"Yes, it's lovely," Aisling said after a beat, dragging herself toward an overstuffed chair in the corner of the room. It was located in front of a roaring fireplace. "I'm not climbing the stairs. I'll sit over here and you guys can bring books to me."

Cillian pursed his lips. "Didn't you just go on a diatribe before we left Belle Isle about wanting us to treat you normally? We wouldn't wait on you under normal circumstances."

If Aisling was bothered by the teasing, she didn't show it. "I can't climb those stairs and you know it. I'm too tired." She flopped in the chair and rested her feet on the footrest. "You pick the books you want me to read and I'll wait here."

Cillian grinned. "Fair enough. I'll order some tea. You're not supposed to have caffeine, right?"

Aisling was affronted. "I can have caffeine if I want caffeine."

"I seem to remember Griffin saying otherwise."

"Griffin doesn't always know what he's talking about," Aisling grumbled. "He's a good man, but I know what I'm talking about ... and I want caffeine."

"Fine. I'll get you caffeine. Don't rat on me to Griffin if he asks, though." Cillian craned his neck to stare into the back of the room. "I wonder who's monitoring the library today. Usually, whoever it is sits behind the front desk."

I followed his gaze toward the empty space. "Maybe we're on our own."

"Maybe. Or ... ." He didn't get a chance to finish because a creature — there was no other way to describe what swooped down from the fourth floor on rubbery wings — dropped between the staircases and landed on the marble floor without a sound.

"You rang?" The creature asked dryly.

I wasn't sure what to make of the animal. Heck, I wasn't sure it was an animal. It looked more like a science experiment gone wrong. It had the face of a dog, the wings of an owl, and a tail (at least I hoped it was a tail) that was so long and pointy I thought there was a genuine chance it could put somebody's eye out.

"Bub?" Aisling jerked her head in the creature's direction, her expression twisting into something I didn't quite recognize.

"Hello, little Grimlock." The creature eyed her with an unreadable expression. "Are you still growing? It seems as if you've doubled in size since last I saw you."

Aisling scowled. "Oh, that's nice to say to the woman who made sure you had a hospital room to convalesce in. The reaper hierarchy wanted to try you for helping my mother, but I stepped in and saved you."

"You stepped in and told the truth," Bub corrected, making a tsking sound as he shook his head. "I helped you. In turn, you helped me. I'd say that means we're even."

Aisling didn't look as if she agreed. "I would say that means we need to sit down and have a talk once this baby is out of me," she corrected. "For now ... you look like you've recovered. How did you end up here?"

"That's what I want to know," Cillian said, his eyes never leaving the creature's face. He didn't look nearly as excited to see the squat little being as his sister was. "I didn't know gargoyles worked in the main office."

The single word set off bells in my head, as if alerting on a memory I couldn't quite drag into the present. "Gargoyles?"

Cillian nodded. "It's a long story, but suffice to say Bub has ties to our family. He ... helped, I guess would be the right word ... my sister a couple of times when we were fighting a rather intense enemy. He was cryptic and difficult while helping, but we're here because of him so ... he's not a bad guy."

"But he's a gargoyle," I pressed, racking my brain for something I'd read in one of my grandfather's books when I was a child. "I didn't think gargoyles were real, at least not anymore. I thought they all died when the old magic died."

"What's the old magic?" Aisling asked. "Oh, and come over here before telling the story. I'm too tired to stand and I'll make a scene if I can't hear what you're saying."

Well, at least she was honest. "The gargoyles I read about died when the old witches died. I had no idea any were still around."

"What's the difference between old witches and new witches?" Aisling asked, stretching out in the chair. Getting comfortable was clearly her main focus. "I mean ... what was Genevieve Toth?"

"That's the third or fourth time I've heard someone in your family talk about her," I noted as I sat on the couch across from Aisling. "I asked my aunt, but her explanation was rather limited and I didn't have time to press her. Who is she?"

"An old witch," Bub immediately answered, his tail slashing through the air. "Genevieve was absolutely an old witch. She lived for centuries."

"That sounds like a dark witch to me," I countered.

"She was both."

"And this is the woman who somehow kept your mother alive, right?"

"Her body," Cillian replied quickly. "Her soul passed over. We didn't find that out until right before the big fight, but it was only her body that remained."

"Something I didn't know," Bub volunteered. "I didn't realize she was soulless. Had I known … ." He trailed off.

"You wouldn't have done anything differently," Aisling finished for him. "You couldn't have done anything else. You were trapped in an untenable position. My mother thought she was controlling you. You had to be cautious. I get that."

"I know you came to see me in the hospital before you left for your honeymoon," Bub supplied. "I know you sent gargoyle treats, too. But because gargoyle treats aren't real, my understanding is that you paid someone to open cans of Fancy Feast and switch out the tins for bowls before delivering them to me."

Aisling smiled. "You're welcome."

"I don't eat cat food."

"You're still welcome."

Cillian chuckled, whatever strain he'd been carrying only moments before evaporating. "I can't believe you sent him cat food, Ais." He moved closer to his sister, grabbing a blanket from the back of the couch and draping it over her. "That's kind of mean."

"I called every single day," Aisling argued. "I wanted to make sure he wasn't dead. I thought he might like the cat food. How was I supposed to know what he liked?"

"I like steak," Bub barked. "I like steak and hamburgers."

"I'll know for next time." Aisling shifted in her chair to get more comfortable. "By the way, this is Izzy Sage. She's the new gatekeeper on Belle Isle."

His eyes keen, Bub focused on me with new interest. "You're the gatekeeper?"

I nodded, suddenly uncomfortable. "I am. You know about the gate?"

"I know a great deal about many things." Bub turned thoughtful. "Sage. There was a gatekeeper with that moniker before. It was twenty years ago, right?"

I swallowed hard. "My father. My mother helped, too, but technically my father was the gatekeeper."

"I see." It was a simple statement, but his words somehow hung heavy. "And now you're back."

"I am."

"And why are you here?" Bub flicked his eyes to Cillian. "What trouble have you found this time?" His eyes moved to Aisling. "Am I right in assuming this is your fault?"

"No." Aisling rolled her eyes as she burrowed under the blanket. If I didn't know better, I'd assume she was about to take a nap. It was something she wouldn't own up to — I barely knew her and recognized that — but I doubted very much she was going to help with the research when a snooze was on the horizon.

"It's nobody's fault," Cillian said hurriedly. "We have a situation at the gate. A wraith broke in and crossed the threshold."

"Really?" Intrigued, Bub leaned forward. "Why would it do that? I didn't think you could cross from this plane to the next without dying."

"I didn't either," Cillian said. "But it did. Not only that, it passed back over with no ill effects. It seemed stronger when it returned, as if it was somehow enhanced. We're trying to figure out what's going on."

"There was a body, too." Aisling looked sleepy as she clutched the blanket under her chin. "We assumed the wraith killed it during its escape, but the body was hauled off to the morgue yesterday and somehow returned today. We can't figure it out."

157

"Can you think of a reason for a body to disappear from the morgue and end up at the water's edge?" Cillian asked.

"Other than my theory that the zombies are back," Aisling added.

"That thing with the zombies was a fluke," Bub said distractedly. "That was a spell gone wrong, not zombies. As for what you're describing, I've never heard of it."

"I didn't know that things could cross from the other side of the gate," Cillian admitted. "That means I'm pretty far behind on this one. We need books to dig through, history texts. There has to be some explanation for what's going on here."

"Yes." Bub's expression was hard to read as he snagged my gaze. "It sounds like you have a full plate. Just a quick question, though: Did the wraith make his wild run before or after Ms. Sage took her new position?"

I balked at the question. "What does that matter?"

"I'm merely curious."

"After," Cillian answered. "My understanding is that the wraiths have been gathering in that area for weeks. I don't think this was a new plan."

"Then that means they have a specific endgame in mind," Bub said. "We need to figure out what it is. Whatever they're doing, I can guarantee it's not good."

"We figured that out ourselves." Aisling turned on her side to face the fireplace. "Wake me if you find anything good."

Bub turned exasperated. "You're not going to help?"

"I'm growing a human life here. I can only do so much."

"Oh, geez." Bub's exasperation was palpable. "I'm glad I missed most of your pregnancy."

"You have no idea what you're talking about. My mothering instincts are kicking in full throttle now, so you've missed out. I would've showered you with Fancy Feast."

"I'm not a cat!"

"You say potato."

Eighteen

We spent hours researching the gate. I learned a few things, though most of the tidbits were odd curiosities I made a mental note to come back later and research further. We had a specific purpose today, and nothing I found answered the myriad questions looming over us.

Aisling slept for hours, so deeply that her snoring filled the room. Bub suggested messing with her — he had a few ideas that I found both worrisome and intriguing — but Cillian vetoed it. He ordered Bub to leave her alone, and checked on her multiple times to make sure she was comfortable.

By the time Braden and Griffin made their way to the library toward the end of the afternoon, she'd been out so long I'd started to worry.

"Oh, it's the owl dog," Griffin noted as his gaze fell on Bub. "I wondered where you ended up."

"I've been listening to your wife snore for hours," Bub said dryly. "Clearly I'm in hell."

Griffin slid a gaze to the slumbering form in the chair and smiled. "How long has she been like that?"

"A long time," Cillian replied. "She tried to pretend she was interested in the research, but that lasted all of five minutes. You should take her home."

"That's the plan." Griffin dragged a hand through his long hair. It was clear he needed a cut, but other things took precedence. "I'm trying to decide if I should wake her for the ride back to Grimlock Manor."

"I think it's funny that you guys named your house," I volunteered, earning a snicker from Bub. "I don't think I've ever met anyone who named his or her house. Er, well, I met a woman in New Orleans. Bertie Button — yes, that was her real name — and she named her cottage the Clam Shack. She had a lot of excess hormones from menopause, though, and I'm pretty sure she was simply horny when she decided to do it. She painted it pink, too, with pearly white accents."

Braden's mouth dropped open. "Wow! And I thought we knew colorful people."

"Now I totally want clam chowder for dinner," Cillian said.

"That sounds good," Griffin agreed, kneeling next to Aisling's chair and gently brushing her hair from her forehead. "She hasn't been complaining about contractions, has she?"

"No." Cillian sobered, obviously horrified by the thought. "Is she supposed to be having contractions?"

"The doctor says soon. I just want to make sure."

"She shouldn't be here if she's having contractions," Cillian complained. "She should be back at the house ... or in the hospital."

"Which is why I didn't want her at the scene today," Griffin muttered.

"Hey, you can't blame that on us." Braden turned defensive. "You know how she is. She doesn't want to be left out. It's not our fault. Dad was trying to include her in a safe way. He told her she was babysitting Izzy, even though Izzy was babysitting her. We did our best."

"I know." Griffin pressed his lips to Aisling's forehead and waited to see if she stirred. She didn't. "We need to come up with a way to keep her under wraps. She can't help herself from finding trouble. It's important she rests."

"Is there something you're not telling us?" Braden looked concerned. "She's not sick, is she?"

"No. She's pregnant."

"Oh, is that what she's carrying around under her shirt? I'm so relieved to know it's not one of those monsters from the *Alien* movies."

Griffin scowled. "You're just like her."

"You take that back."

"No." Griffin was firm. "You're just like her, which is why I want to thump you so often. I can only take one of you."

"Well, I want to thump you, too."

"That's fine." Griffin clearly understood the Grimlock vibe. "No matter how much hot air you blow, I know you're worried about your sister. We're only a few days from her due date. She's probably not going to give birth on that exact date, but we're zeroing in on the big event. She needs to be protected, whether you guys want to admit it or not."

Braden scowled. "Do you think we would let something happen to her? Really?"

"No, but I don't think we always have control over these things. There's a powerful wraith running around. Until that situation is handled, we're staying at Grimlock Manor, even after she has the baby, if necessary. I want her protected."

Braden softened his stance. "We'll figure it out. We'll protect her. I promise we won't let anything happen to her."

"That would be a nice change of pace."

BRADEN VOLUNTEERED TO TAKE me back to Belle Isle, but he took a detour by Mexicantown first. He said he was starving, and the sound of my stomach growling was hard to ignore.

"You should acquaint yourself with this part of town," Braden suggested as he sat across from me in a cozy booth, a basket of chips and four different types of salsa resting at the center of the table. "The food here is amazing."

"It's weird," I admitted, dipping a chip in the green salsa. "I was a kid when I lived here before. I don't think I ever properly understood the geography."

"What do you mean?"

I shrugged. "I was seven. Everything I knew revolved around Belle Isle. I thought it was big when I was a kid. It seems a lot smaller now."

"I guess. I never really thought about it." He leaned back in the booth, the mood lighting emphasizing the hard angles of his face. "What do you remember about living here before?"

"I don't know. I have trouble remembering some things from back then."

"Like what happened to your parents?"

The question made me uncomfortable. "Why would you ask that?"

He didn't back down. "Did you think I wouldn't look up your parents after I found out about your background?"

"No. It's just ... what did you find?"

Instead of immediately responding, he furrowed his brow.

"I'm serious," I persisted, my temper ratcheting up a notch. "I don't remember what happened and I don't have the security clearance to read about it."

"Did you try?"

That was the first thing I'd tried when I got gatekeeper security clearance. I wasn't even back in the area before I started digging. "I tried. It's level four, which is good but not great. Only the bigwigs can access the files on my parents.

"Well, that's not entirely true," I conceded, sighing. "I can read the basics with my clearance, but there's nothing in those files I don't know. My grandfather was very big on making sure that I never forgot my parents, that I always remembered they were good people."

"I don't think that's something you can forget," Braden nodded. "In fact, I think it's the opposite. I always remembered what a good person my mother was. That came back to bite me when she returned. I didn't want to see that the person who came back wasn't the same person I'd lost."

He seemed nervous about opening up to me, so I treaded lightly when digging deeper. "When did you realize what was really going on?"

"Not until the end. I didn't want to see it. There were warning signs, but I refused to see them."

"And your siblings?"

"Aisling never trusted her. Right from the start, Aisling was certain something bad was happening. I hated her for it. I was so ... angry ... with her because she wouldn't simply open her arms and accept Mom back into our lives. That wasn't fair to her."

"I get the feeling she's over it, if that helps." I offered him a smile. "She doesn't seem to be carrying a grudge."

"Why should she? She was right."

"That doesn't mean you were wrong."

"My mother tried to kill my sister so she could use her body as a conduit and prolong her own life. I would say I was wrong."

He had a point. "Well, you weren't evil about being wrong or anything."

He chuckled, the sound low and throaty. "You're good at putting people at ease. I don't know how you do it, but you're good at it. Is that something you learned from your grandfather?"

"I guess. He's a strong man and he was big on not forcing me to follow gender roles. He said I could be anything I wanted to be, and he was right. I wanted to be a gatekeeper — something he didn't want me to be because of what happened to my parents — and he's still upset about it."

"Did you want to be a gatekeeper because you liked the work or because you thought you would be able to learn something about your parents in the process?"

Braden's gaze was probing, his lavender eyes seemingly running roughshod over my nerves. "I like the work."

"I think you would be able to maintain eye contact if that were true."

I sighed. "I don't dislike the work," I hedged.

"You came here because of your parents, though, didn't you?"

"I ... ."

"You don't have to come up with an excuse." He gentled his voice as he leaned forward. "I get it. I would've done the same thing. You don't have to worry about me tattling on you or anything."

Oddly enough, that was a relief. "Thanks."

"You're welcome."

"Would you really have done the same thing?"

Braden nodded without hesitation, his black hair gleaming thanks to the low lights. "Yes. But I don't know that you should take that as a good sign as most everyone in my family thinks I'm the one who makes the worst decisions."

"Even worse than Aisling?"

"She gets a pass because even when she makes bad decisions she always manages to figure things out and garner a good outcome."

"I think you're probably the same way."

"And I think you're back to making me feel better." He stretched out his legs under the table, his feet brushing against mine. To my surprise, he didn't move them. It was a strangely intimate moment, and I didn't know what to make of it. "I tried to look up information on your parents, too. I didn't find much. We can ask my father to do it if you're really desperate to know."

I jerked my head up, surprised. I'd like to say I forgot about his feet touching mine in the process, but I was keenly aware of his body language. No matter how I tried, I couldn't forget. "Do you think he would do that?"

"I think he would complain about doing it," Braden hedged, uncertain. "I think he would try to help, though. He seems to like you. Plus, well, you might be our only chance to ever see Aisling with a female friend. I don't know if you've realized it or not, but she doesn't play well with other girls."

"I noticed during lunch today. There was a lot of 'your pimp says this' flying when she saw that Angelina woman."

"Yes, well, everything Aisling throws at her, Angelina has coming. Angelina is pretty far from innocent, but my sister isn't squeaky clean as far as that relationship goes either."

"Yeah. I can see they hate each other."

"That's putting it mildly."

"Still, when your sister suggested tabling their problems until after giving birth Angelina readily agreed. If Angelina is as terrible as you say she is, why would she do that?"

"Because Angelina used to date Cillian."

I pictured the irritating brunette with the amiable Grimlock brother. "They don't seem to fit."

"They don't, and she cheated on him. Aisling hated her before that, but the cheating sent Aisling into a tailspin. I swear, she was arrested three weekends in a row for the things she did to Angelina."

"Do I even want to know?"

"Probably not."

I snickered. "How did your father react to that?"

"He bailed her out."

"She didn't get in trouble?"

"Aisling rarely gets in trouble. My father talks big, but when it comes down to it he's a marshmallow. He would die to protect any of us. More important, he would kill for us. He's good with the big things. When it comes to the little things, Aisling knows how to get exactly what she wants."

"Does that make you bitter?"

"No. I want her to get everything she's ever dreamed about."

His sincerity took my breath away. "If you feel that way, why do you give her so much grief?"

"Because that's how we roll. I give her crap. She gives it right back. There are five of us, so there are uneven numbers. We pair up and take each other on. We're extremely competitive when playing games. That doesn't mean I don't love her. It just means I love to mess with her, too."

He was so matter-of-fact all I could do was shake my head. "I guess I'm glad I don't have siblings. I don't think I'll ever understand your relationship with your brothers and sister. It's extremely odd."

"I've never known anything different. I can honestly say every good memory I have involves a sibling. We may fight, but we have a good time together, too."

"I guess." I realized Braden was moving his foot up and down my leg as he focused on my face. The gesture, which could've been considered innocent a few moments before, was decidedly more intense now. "Um ... what are you doing?"

Braden pursed his lips, causing his innocent expression to deepen. "Nothing."

"You know I can feel your foot on my leg, right?"

He didn't move it. "So?"

I was at a loss. "Listen, you seem like a nice guy ... ."

His eyes darted, irritation flashing in the purple depths. "Is this where you tell me I'm not your type?"

Actually, that was the problem. "No. You're exactly my type."

Braden's smile turned lazy as he relaxed. "I'll take that as a compliment."

I didn't have the best track record with men, so that probably wasn't a good thing. Now was not the time to bring that up, though. "I didn't come here for this."

Braden stilled, his foot remaining against my leg as his gaze sharpened. "For what?"

"A relationship."

"We don't necessarily have to engage in a relationship."

Whether he meant to be charming or teasing, I couldn't say. Either way, it turned me off. "I don't play the one-night stand game."

"Oh." He slowly retracted his foot and rested his hands on the table. "I guess I'm confused. Do you want a relationship?"

I hated being put on the spot. "Do you?"

"I can't remember the last time I had a relationship that lasted longer than two weeks. It's not really my style."

"And I don't embark on anything considered temporary," I clarified. "The thing is, even if I wanted to pretend I don't have rules, you were right about me coming here for a specific reason. I want to figure out what happened to my parents. I want to be good at my job. The rest of it ... well, it's simply not important to me right now."

"I see." He stroked his chin, his expression thoughtful. "Now might be the time to embrace something light and without strings. Have you considered that?"

"Not for an instant."

"Fair enough." Braden held up his hands in capitulation. "I won't pressure you. I was just messing around. I'll talk to my father about your parents' files. I don't want you to be uncomfortable, but I'm still willing to help."

I forced a smile. "We'll just pretend this didn't happen. It's not like it was a big deal anyway."

"Definitely not." He offered a wink, though it wasn't entirely playful. "So, tell me about the things you liked to do in the city before you moved out of state. I'll tell you what's changed and we'll have a very sterile dinner conversation. How does that sound?"

"Like a pretty good idea."

Nineteen

The bigwigs were back the next morning.

They didn't bother calling to set up an appointment, instead opting to arrive with no notice. The previous day had sapped my energy, so I slept for an extra thirty minutes – which turned out to be a mistake.

"What are they doing here?" I worked overtime to rein in my temper as five men — two of whom had clipboards — buzzed around the gate.

"They're taking readings," Oliver replied easily, leaning back in his chair and folding his hands across his stomach as he watched the action. "I'm not really sure what to make of it. It's almost like a nerd convention ... although they've yet to decide on a speaker."

I shot him a withering look. "I don't think you should say things like that."

"Why? Are you a closet nerd?"

"No. I simply don't want to get caught laughing at our employers at a time tempers are frayed. They might not find it funny to be considered the butt of the joke."

"Fair enough."

I pursed my lips as I watched the men work for a bit before shuffling across the room to get closer to Cormack. He was deep in conversation with Renley, a serious expression on his face, and he didn't so much as glance in my direction as I closed the distance.

"There has to be a reason this happened," Renley persisted. "We can't simply ignore what's happening here."

"I never suggested we ignore anything." Cormack was calm as he regarded his boss. "I'm simply suggesting that you authorize my family to hunt the wraith, take us out of the soul collection rotation for a few days, and let us do what we do."

"You're not hunters."

"No, but that doesn't mean we can't control a wraith."

"You're down a man."

"I'm down a woman," Cormack corrected, causing my temper to flare at his nonchalant delivery. "The male contingent of my team is intact. They're ready to go. We simply need to pick an area and start hunting."

"And how exactly do you expect to pick the right area when we have no idea why this wraith is choosing the locales it seems to be targeting?"

"I want you to let Cillian do the research. He'll figure out the pattern and narrow the scope."

"I don't know." Renley rubbed the back of his neck as he considered the option. "I need to think about it. Give me some time. I'll get back to you before we leave the island later this afternoon."

"Of course." Cormack's nod was perfunctory, but I didn't miss the shift in his aura, the way red zinged through and caused orange ripples thanks to the previously yellow base. "I'm looking forward to our next discussion." He waited until Renley crossed to the other side of the room to viciously curse under his breath. I couldn't make out all the words, but "idiot" and "hope he trips over his own shoelaces and smacks his head into a wall" were easily picked from the din.

"Are you okay?" I asked him, momentarily wary. "Do you want something to drink?"

Slowly, he slid his eyes in my direction and sighed. "I knew you were there."

"I'm sure you did."

"I'm not sorry for what I said."

"I'm sure you're not."

"If you want to tell him, be my guest."

"I'm good." I bit the inside of my cheek to keep from laughing at his hangdog expression. "I have no interest in telling him what you said, especially because I agree with you."

Cormack raised an eyebrow, his surprise on full display. "Really? You agree with me?"

"I don't know if your family is really the world-famous wraith hunters everyone makes you out to be, but I happen to believe that someone with specialized knowledge should lead the hunt for this particular wraith."

"Yes."

"I don't suppose you know where the wraith has been hanging out, do you?"

"We know it's been in the heart of the city," Cormack replied, choosing his words carefully. "We know it's been in the busier areas. The night after it escaped from here, a hooded figure was seen in Hart Plaza. Two people ended up dead. They're blaming it on gang activity, but no shots were fired and it wasn't a territorial dispute."

That was interesting. "And where is Hart Plaza from here?"

"I keep forgetting that you're from here but haven't visited since you were a child," Cormack said. "It's several miles to the west, not far from the Windsor tunnel and the Renaissance Center."

I furrowed my brow as I ran the information through my memory. "I think I remember the Renaissance Center. It's right by the river, right? Has good restaurants?"

He nodded. "Basically."

"Okay, so why would the wraith want to be in that area?"

"That is the question of the day." Weariness momentarily overtaking him, Cormack folded his arms over his chest and leaned against the table. "The wraith has also been seen near Cobo Center and Greektown Casino."

"Is it moving in a specific direction?"

He smiled, quick and easy. "I like the way your mind works. We were interested in that, too. We're dealing with a relatively small area. You can circle back and forth with minimal effort without getting caught.

"The wraith was seen at Hart Plaza first," he continued. "Then it circled west to Cobo Center. Greektown Casino is to the east, though. I'm not sure why it circled back to that area."

I turned away from him and focused on the map affixed to the wall. "Can you show me?"

He nodded as he moved closer, extending his finger. "This map is older. A few of the newer buildings aren't on here, but that's okay. Hart Plaza and Cobo are both on here. The casino is over here."

I followed his finger, vaguely interested in the circular pattern he was making. "Do you know what's interesting about the area you've indicated?"

"It's essentially the cleanest part of the city," he answered without hesitation. "It's a target-rich environment."

"I'll have to take your word for it, but that's not what I was thinking."

He waited.

"That area may be busy, but that's hardly the only place a wraith could hunt if hungry," I pointed out. "I mean, think about it. Wouldn't it make more sense to go into one of the areas where the people are considered at risk? Those people would be easier to hunt."

Realization dawned on Cormack and his eyes lit with interest. "I get what you're saying." He slanted his gaze at the map. "The people in the area where the wraith has been hunting are more likely to be missed. If the wraith wanted to fly under the radar, it would hunt in the rundown areas."

"It's not just that," I countered. "The wraith is also making sure not to travel too far from Belle Isle. There's only one way on or off the island. The wraith is sticking relatively close to the bridge."

"Why do you think that's important?"

"I don't know. I simply find it interesting. Maybe the wraith isn't done with the island."

"Then why leave in the first place?"

"Because your son was here when it came back," I replied without hesitation. "Braden was armed. The wraith seemed surprised. I think its fight-or-flight response kicked in and that's why it took off. There might have been a different plan at one point. We need to find the wraith to figure it out."

His expression turned thoughtful as he stared at the map. "I don't suppose you've ever done any map analysis, have you?"

"I can't say as I have."

"Well, you're going to start." He was grim as he dug into his pocket for his phone. "You have a keen and analytical mind. You see patterns. I'm going to pair you with someone I think you'll work well with."

For a brief moment I thought he meant Braden and excitement coursed through me. I tamped it down quickly, chiding myself for the way my heart leaped. I was not here to play footsies under the table with some guy who believed one-night stands were the standard. I had other things to focus on.

When Cormack started speaking into the phone I realized right away that he had no intention of pairing me with Braden.

"I need you to put on your thinking cap, son," he said. "I also need you out on Belle Isle. I have an idea, and I want you to work with someone this afternoon to see if you can bring it together. I'll see you soon."

CILLIAN DIDN'T LOOK THRILLED to be forced out to Belle Isle so early in the morning.

"I hate it when you have ideas, Dad." He scowled as he stared at the map. Cormack explained what he wanted, and then sat back. He seemed expectant, as if he wanted Cillian to applaud his grand scheme. "This map doesn't even have the right buildings on it."

Cormack's smile slipped. "I know that. Use your imagination to add the buildings. We need to figure out where the wraith is going to be ... and why."

Cillian stared at his father, unblinking. "I was in bed. Maya had a morning off for the first time in five days because she's trying to arrange an extended weekend at the end of the month so we can go on vacation. There's a nurse shortage, which means she's averaging sixty hours a week. Do you know how rare it is for her to have a morning off?"

Cormack met his son's accusatory gaze without flinching. "I'm sorry for dragging you away from Maya."

"You're not sorry." Cillian made a face. "You think I'm being a big baby."

"I do think you're being a baby," Cormack agreed, winking at me in an effort to convey his mirth. "That doesn't mean I'm not sorry for ruining your day. I like Maya. You know that."

Cillian heaved a sigh. "Whatever. You're fixated on this wraith. And I know I need to focus, too. So far its movements have been random. There's no way to track it."

"Don't be a defeatist." Cormack slapped a hand on his son's shoulder. "I have faith you can figure it out. We have to find the wraith and eradicate it before it gets a foothold.."

Cillian tilted his head to the side as he stared at the map. "Fine. I'll see if I can figure out a pattern."

"That's all I'm asking." Cormack nodded. "I'm leaving Izzy to work with you. She has a keen mind. Perhaps together you can figure out the missing piece of this puzzle."

"Yes, we'll turn into superheroes while we're at it." Cillian's tone was dry as he rolled his eyes. "We'll do our best. Don't expect miracles from us."

"I would never expect miracles."

"You're full of crap. You want a miracle. Don't bother denying it."

"Your sister went to bed at nine last night and didn't whine once. I've already witnessed my miracle for the week."

Cillian snorted. "We'll figure something out ... although I have no idea how."

WE APPROACHED IT scientifically.

We used pushpins.

"What do you have?" Cormack asked as he stared at the plastic markers on the map.

"I called the home office," Cillian explained. "I asked for any and all wraith-sighting reports, whether they were confirmed or not. We didn't have enough data points."

"If the sightings aren't confirmed, how does that help us?"

"We can't make a pattern with only four data points," Cillian explained. "We needed more, and even though some of them don't make sense, I think we've put something together."

"Like what?"

"Well, for starters, we color-coded it." Cillian pointed for emphasis. "Red is confirmed sightings. White is potential sightings that seem to make sense given the data we have. Blue is the outliers."

Cormack stared hard at the map. "And?"

"And the wraith seems to be sticking to a relatively small area," Cillian replied. "It's been seen by the People Mover, Joe Louis Arena, Saint Andrew's Hall and Ford Field."

"All areas where a lot of people visit."

"True," Cillian conceded. "Look at the blue tacks, though. They're the ones I find interesting. The train depot ... the children's hospital ... the Heidelberg Project."

"I don't get what you're trying to say," Cormack said. "If those are outlier locations, it seems to make sense that they're false sightings."

"What if they're not?" Cillian pressed. "What if they're sightings of different wraiths?"

Cormack's face was blank. "I don't think I'm following you."

"That's because my brain is a busy place." Cillian smiled. "Between the confirmed sightings and the likely sightings, we basically have a square. The muted wraith is sticking to one area, and it's not far away."

"Okay."

"The outlier pins form another line beyond that square on three sides," Cillian explained. "The fourth side is water, so it makes sense there's no line."

"I'm still not following you."

Impatience finally got the better of me, although I held on much longer than I usually did. "The mutated wraith isn't working alone," I volunteered. "The wraith sightings outside the immediate area seem to indicate that other wraiths are forming a buffer around our wraith. They're a form of security, if you will. Our wraith is still close, in a focused hunting zone, but it has backup."

"Ah." Realization dawned on Cormack's face. "That means, in theory, it shouldn't be terribly hard to find."

"In theory," Cillian agreed. "The problem is, no matter how small the area, there are tons of buildings down there for the wraith to hide in. We need more bodies to search ... and it wouldn't hurt to have some aerial help."

"I don't understand what you're saying."

"The gargoyles," Cillian replied. "They've been sidelined since Mom ... did her thing. I think now is the time to dust them off."

"There's a very good reason they've been sidelined," Cormack argued. "They can't be trusted. They're mercenaries, selling their services to the highest bidder."

"Which is why we should lock them in now," Cillian pointed out. "If the wraiths secure their services first it will be all over. We need them."

"Well, great." Cormack made a face as he rolled his neck until it cracked. "I can't tell you how excited I am to be the one to tell Renley we need to make nice with the gargoyles. He won't find that request ridiculous at all."

"Suck it up." Cillian mimicked his father's tone as I tilted my head and stared at the back side of the room. There was something off about the dimensions, and I couldn't stop from momentarily kicking myself for not noticing before. "You're the one who says the job comes before comfort. We need Renley on our side, so you'll have to be the one to snag him."

"Yes, yes." Cormack waved off his son's amusement as his eyes turned to me. "What are you looking at, Izzy?"

I extended a finger. "That's the storage room I hid in when the other wraiths showed up."

He followed my finger with his gaze. "I remember. But those wraiths are dead. We don't have to worry about them."

175

"I'm not worried about the wraiths. I'm wondering why they came back in the first place."

"They wanted to cross over," Cillian said. "They wanted to enhance their abilities, like the first wraith."

"Except they didn't cross the threshold," I pointed out. "They didn't even look at it."

"That's because they were focused on you."

"That's what we assumed," I corrected, moving away from Cormack and Cillian and focusing on the wall. "The thing is, what if we were wrong? What if they came back for something else entirely? We assumed that the wraith was hanging close to remain near Belle Isle. What if there's something here that it wants?"

I lightly rested my fingers on the wall and leaned my head closer to listen.

"I don't think I'm following you," Cormack said as he watched me move my fingertips over the wall. "What are you saying?"

"The dimensions in this room are wrong." I knocked on the wall and came up with a solid echo.

"Are you suddenly an architect?" Cillian teased.

I shook my head. I murmured as I continued along the wall, "The storage room should be located in the center of the wall. It's not. Why?"

"I don't know. Why?"

"There's something else here." I knocked again. This time the sound was hollow. "There's another door on the other side of this drywall, and it's right here."

Cormack moved to my side, intrigued. "Why do you think that matters?"

"I don't know, but what if the wraiths didn't come back for the gate? They came to this room for a reason. Maybe they came for what's on the other side of this door."

Cormack licked his lips and slid his eyes to Cillian. "What do you think?"

"Hey, I'm a Grimlock." Cillian's smile turned sheepish. "I need to see what's on the other side of this wall now that I know something was covered up years ago. There has to be a reason for it."

"I agree." Cormack fumbled with his phone. "We'll need a construction team."

"Get a big one," Cillian instructed. "We have no idea what we're dealing with and I don't want to wait forever for them to get through there."

"I'm on it. We shouldn't have to wait long."

Twenty

It was a library.

Well, it was what probably doubled as a library fifty years ago.

It was basically a room with a long rectangular table at the center, and four huge shelves filled with oversized tomes. There was also a thick layer of dust, which caused Cormack to continuously sneeze as he surveyed the find.

"Knock that off."

A man I didn't recognize strode into the room and openly glared at Cormack, causing me to press my lips together to keep from laughing given the annoyed look on the eldest Grimlock's face.

"Pardon me?" For a moment, I got to see the look I'm sure Cormack used to liquefy his children's innards when they were teenagers and had missed curfew. However, the man it was directed at didn't seem impressed.

"Don't sneeze on the books," he ordered. "You'll ruin them."

"They've been holed off in a secret room for decades. I think they'll survive."

"They've been holed off in a temperature-controlled room and not exposed to the elements," the man fired back. "They're delicate."

"Uh-huh." Cormack wrinkled his nose as he looked the man up and down. He was young — late thirties or early forties by my estimation — and he was dressed in one of those blazers with the patches on the elbows. His narrow face wasn't exactly handsome, but it was dignified, and offset by a pair of scholarly glasses. "And who are you?"

"Edgar Mason," Cillian answered for the man, his face awash with awe as he stepped into the room. He'd disappeared not long after the construction crew managed to open the door and I hadn't seen him since. "You're Edgar Mason, aren't you?"

"I am." Mason bobbed his head as he looked Cillian up and down. "Who are you?"

"Cillian Grimlock. I'm a big fan." Cillian thrust out his hand so Mason could shake it. "I just read about that tomb you found in Africa several months ago. That was a terrific find."

I loved history as much as the next person, but I was legitimately confused. "Are you an archeologist or something?"

Mason flicked his eyes to me. At first, I thought they would cruise right over my dirty features — getting into the room was a messy endeavor — but his blue eyes snagged with mine as interest shone bright. "I guess you could call me an archeologist." His smile was so wide it threatened to swallow the bottom half of his face. "I'm the lead environmental investigator for the reaper council."

I had no idea what that meant. "Okay. Um ... what does that mean?"

"It means I do this." He gestured toward the room. "I make discoveries."

"You didn't make this discovery," Cormack pointed out. "We made this discovery."

I cleared my throat. "Technically, I made this discovery," I corrected.

Cormack was unruffled. "You're part of my team."

I opened my mouth to argue, but Cillian's tight-lipped smile and almost imperceptible headshake told me that wasn't a good idea.

"Mr. Mason has been cited in numerous scholastic magazines," Cillian volunteered, clearly hoping to take control of the conversation before things shifted too far to steer them back on course. "He's an expert on all sorts of things."

Cormack didn't look impressed. "Like what?"

"Well, for starters, I discovered a species of bat long since thought extinct in the caverns of Kentucky," Mason volunteered. He was so prim and proper I could practically see the disdain dripping from his tongue. "What do you think about that?"

"I think that's great for the bat," Cormack drawled. "I'm much more interested in what you're doing here. Why are you visiting our neck of the woods?"

"I was called to check out this library."

"But ... why?" Confusion etched itself over Cormack's distinguished features. "We don't even know what we have yet. Until we know if this find is significant, I would think your talents would be better served someplace else."

"And yet I'm here." Mason bared his teeth. The way he looked at Cormack almost reminded me of a male dog about to mark its territory. The weird thing was that this particular piece of land was a dingy hole in the middle of a building.

"I'm sure we can all work together," I interjected hurriedly, flicking a glance to Cillian so he could help control his father. "There's no reason for things to get out of hand."

"I quite agree," Mason said. "There's plenty of work for everybody ... as long as those volunteering to help realize that I'm in charge."

A muscle worked in Cormack's jaw and I was certain he was about to lose the world-class calm I'd become so fond of in such a short amount of time.

"We all know who's in charge," Cillian said as he rested a quelling hand on his father's arm. "We all want answers."

"Yes, well ... let's get those answers." Mason paused long enough to wink at me and then moved farther into the room. "Nothing is to be removed from this space before I have a chance to okay it. Is that understood? Great. Let's get started."

I WORKED ALONGSIDE Cillian, sitting on the floor to focus on the books on the bottom row of one of the shelves while he shifted through tomes at the top. The room had an eerie atmosphere thanks to a large window that was located right above us. It didn't look outside, instead offering a glimpse of a dark hallway that appeared to lead nowhere.

Cormack removed himself from the situation and stood at the back of the room. His attention was fixated on Mason, and he seemingly had no interest in anything else. Given the find, I was confused by his reaction, but I wisely refrained from questioning him.

"Don't worry about him," Cillian said as he dropped onto the floor next to me and opened a book. "He won't fly off the handle and kill Mason or anything. You don't have to worry about that."

Embarrassed to be caught staring, my cheeks burned as I turned my attention back to the book resting on my lap. "I wasn't worried."

"You were worried a little." Cillian's expression was cheeky. "My father has a temper. He'll get over it. Mason is a revered figure in certain circles. His ego is obviously an acquired taste, but that doesn't mean he's not brilliant."

"You're clearly excited about meeting him," I noted. "Let me guess: He's your version of a celebrity, right?"

Cillian shifted, uncomfortable. "I happen to like science."

"I do, too. That doesn't mean I don't like a good dose of celebrity gossip either. You're much more interested in Bill Nye the Science Guy than the Kardashians, right?"

"If I was interested in the Kardashians, my sister would kill me. She wishes they would be beamed to television oblivion."

"I kind of wish that, too," I admitted, flipping a page. "Braden mentioned you were interested in research above all else. I bet this is like a dream come true for you. An old room full of books no one has seen in a long time. That's like discovering gold to some people."

"Uh-huh." Cillian's gaze didn't shift from my face. "When did Braden tell you that?"

"Um ... I'm not sure. I just remember him saying it."

"Was it last night?"

I recognized the edge in Cillian's voice and shook my head. "No. It wasn't last night. Why are you asking about last night?"

"Because I happen to know you two were together after our trip to the research library." Cillian tilted his head so his long hair dipped low over his shoulders. "You guys went to dinner afterward, right?"

The question caught me off guard. "We got food. I don't know that I would call it dinner."

"You had a meal after six in the evening. Most people call that dinner."

I sucked in a calming breath. "Fine. We had dinner. It's not as if it was a date or anything, so if that's what you're thinking, you can stop right now."

"I don't believe I said the D-word."

"You were thinking it."

"Are you a mind reader now?"

"No, but ... I can read facial expressions, and you were trying to decide if dinner last night was something you could use against your brother the next time you're in the mood to fight. It's not, for the record. We had Mexican food, and that's it."

"Mexican, huh? Armando's?"

"How did you know?"

"That's Braden's favorite place to eat," Cillian replied, leaning his back against the wall and giving me his full attention. "I've never known him to take a woman there before. He's generally against it."

"And why would he be against it?"

"Because he doesn't want his favorite place tainted," he explained. "Our brother Redmond has a tendency to date women for a week and then ghost them. He's always got a favorite restaurant of the moment, and he takes his flavor of the week to those restaurants. Do you know what happens after he ghosts them?"

"Hopefully they kick him in the nuts because ghosting is a horrible thing to do."

Cillian's chuckle was low and throaty. "Good point, but no. Redmond always gives up the restaurant, essentially ceding it to the woman he's crushed as something of a parting gift. It's not nice as much as cowardly because Redmond doesn't want to risk running into those women again. Braden has heard the stories for years. He decided that he didn't want to risk losing his favorite restaurant, so he never takes dates there."

"Well, I hate to blow your theory out of the water, but we weren't on a date," I pointed out, hating the shrill tinge to my voice. "We merely stopped for something to eat after a long day."

Cillian furrowed his brow, unconvinced. "Here's the thing ... I think my brother likes you."

The statement was so simple, so ridiculously junior high, I couldn't stop my laughter from bubbling up. "Are you seriously playing matchmaker? I mean ... we're adults. I think we can make decisions on our own."

"I don't deny that." Cillian didn't back down. "My brother hasn't shown much interest in anything since my mother died. You know about that. Aisling said she filled you in. Braden has been struggling since that happened."

I sobered. "And that's terrible. I wouldn't wish that hurt on anyone. That doesn't mean he's interested in me. We're simply working on the same problem with a joint end goal. That doesn't lead to dating."

"It could."

"Except I just started this job," I argued. "I don't have time to date anyone. I need to focus on this. We have a rogue wraith running around killing people. Your father told me this morning that the main office believes it can attribute ten deaths to this wraith, and they're deaths that aren't showing up on the reaper rolls. That can't be a good thing."

"Definitely not," Cillian agreed. "I would never argue otherwise. That's not how I roll. But scheduling your life around outside factors isn't a good idea. On top of that, it rarely works."

"You sound as if you're an expert."

"I don't think I'm nearly the expert that Aisling is, but I've had a little experience with it. I met my girlfriend about a year and a half ago. We fell in love and moved in together despite everything that was going on.

"I don't regret it and it didn't split my focus," he continued. "She makes me a better man. That's always a good thing."

"Well, I'm happy for you." His intense scrutiny made me uncomfortable. "That doesn't change the fact that I'm not looking for a relationship."

"Fair enough." Cillian held up his hands in capitulation. "I'm not trying to tell you how to live your life."

"But?"

"But ... I love my brother." Cillian turned earnest. "He hasn't shown interest in anyone for what feels like a very long time. The fact that he took you to his favorite restaurant feels significant to me. I'm sure it doesn't to you, but I can't help but hope. You might be good for him."

I asked the obvious question. "And how is he going to be for me?"

"I ... what do you mean?"

"How is he going to be for me?" I repeated. "By his own admission he prefers focusing on a woman for one night and moving on. That is not how I want to live my life."

"Oh, he talks big." Cillian made a face. "I can guarantee he doesn't mean that, though. He's found a reason to stick close to you for the past three days. That isn't a coincidence."

"And it's not something I'm in the mood to explore." I was firm. "I'm never going to be the type of woman he's interested in. That's not how I'm built."

"I think you're already that type of woman."

"And I think you're seeing what you want to see." I refused to back down. "I'm not getting involved in this. We have other things to deal with."

"Fine." Cillian turned morose as he focused on his book. "I'm going to let this go until after we catch the wraith. When that's done, be prepared, because we're totally going to revisit this."

"That sounds like a threat your sister would make."

"Well ... I learned from the best."

I pursed my lips to keep from laughing. That would only encourage him. "There has to be something good in these books for them to be locked away the way they were. Let's find out what that is, shall we?"

"That's the plan."

"I BELIEVE I'VE DECIPHERED this book," Mason intoned, drawing multiple sets of eyes in his direction as he moved toward the center of the room. The book in his hands was large, opened to the middle, and looked to have a wall of text spread from top to bottom. "I believe this is ancient Sumerian."

Cillian cocked an eyebrow as he leaned over and looked at the page in question. "That's Italian."

Mason turned haughty. "And how do you know that? I think I know a bit about dead languages."

"Because I'm fluent in five languages," Cillian replied without hesitation. "That word right there? *Fantasma*. It means ghost. *Spettro* means wraith. *Anima* means soul. That book is in Italian."

"So you say," Mason grumbled under his breath.

"It's also a dictionary of sorts," Cillian added, refusing to engage in an argument. "That book is merely a dictionary of magical beings. There's nothing out of the ordinary in there. In fact, none of these books are out of the ordinary from what I can tell."

Cormack, who had disappeared into the gate room to make several calls, looked intrigued as he returned. "What do you think that means?"

"I don't know."

"Theorize."

Cillian threw his hands in the air and shrugged. "I don't know what to tell you, Dad. They're basic research books. I mean ... I obviously haven't been through all of them, but I don't see anything that stands out here."

That made no sense to me. "Why would someone close off this room and hide these specific books? There has to be a reason."

"Maybe it was laziness," Cillian suggested. "Maybe it was easier to close off the room than heat it. These books all have copyright dates from before 1960 as far as I can tell, although I haven't checked each one. It's cold down here. This room is even twenty degrees colder than the gate room. There could be a practical reason for why the room was closed off."

"But just to abandon these books?" Mason challenged. "That makes no sense. These books are obviously important."

"I don't think they are," Cillian challenged. "I think they're just books ... and you have no idea how difficult that is for me to say."

"I'm not simply going to abandon these books," Mason argued. "I think there is important information here."

"Then you should definitely continue going through them," Cillian supplied. "I don't think they can help us." He focused on his father. "I think we should go back to the map. This room is a distraction. We need to consider this in a practical manner."

Cormack nodded. "Then that's what we'll do."

Twenty-One

The whispering was at an all-time fever pitch when I exited the newly discovered library hours later. I stayed long enough to keep looking through the books, determined there had to be something worth discovering, but I came up empty.

Cillian, seemingly at a loss because his hero wasn't who he'd expected, spent the better part of the afternoon talking to his father in the main gate room. They both looked up when I exited, offered smiles, but didn't make a move to join me.

I was fine with that. I had other things to focus on, including the intense whispering I heard on the other side of the gate. It was so loud it bled into the other room and I couldn't ignore it. I hoped Cormack and Cillian wouldn't find my reaction odd, but the voices were drawing me toward the shimmery opening ... and calling to me.

"Do you hear something from that thing?"

Braden took me by surprise when he moved in at my right. I wasn't even aware he'd arrived until he stole my breath and caused me to stumble.

"Hey!" He caught me around the waist and stopped me from falling headlong into the opening. "What are you doing?"

I inhaled through my mouth and exhaled through my nose to calm myself as I tried to keep from cursing a blue streak.

"What happened?" Cormack called out from the other side of the room, confusion evident.

"I tripped," I replied hurriedly, grateful to have found my voice. "I was walking up the stairs and caught my toe. Thankfully Braden saved me before I did a header through the gate."

"Yes, well, be careful." Cormack's gaze was weighted as he glanced between Braden and me before turning his full attention back to Cillian. That allowed me to deal with Braden on my own terms.

"So ... um ... thanks for that."

"Don't mention it." Braden's demeanor was awkward as he released me, making sure I wasn't wobbly before completely pulling his hands away. "Are you okay?"

"I'm fine."

His cocked eyebrow told me he was dubious. "Do you hear something from the gate?"

I should've expected the question. That was what he'd asked right before I tripped. I wasn't prepared to give him an answer. "Why would you ask that? Do you hear something from the gate?"

His expression was hard to read, those lavender eyes probing as he looked me over. "You know, my sister says that answering a question with a question is a surefire way to recognize that someone is lying ... or trying to cover up some big secret."

"I believe you told me at dinner last night that your sister believes you have snakes in the basement. You mentioned that toward dessert, if I remember correctly."

"That's Redmond's fault. He used to hide pot down there and she was a real tattletale so he lied about the snakes to scare her away from the basement."

"Did it work?"

"Kind of."

"Well ... I guess Redmond was smart then."

Braden shook his head. "You still haven't answered. Do you hear something from that gate?"

I wasn't keen on lying. To be fair, I wasn't morally against it or anything. I lied throughout my teenage years without feeling a lick of guilt. For some reason — one I couldn't explain — I didn't want to lie to him. That was a sobering thought ... and it also made me want to smack myself around because engaging with him on a truly personal level seemed a bad idea.

"You do." Braden came to his own conclusions before I could wrap my head around a sensible lie that I was willing to utter. "You hear something, don't you?"

I decided to stall for time. "Why do you think that?"

"Because you tilted your head, as if you were hearing something, and you were so engrossed you almost didn't notice that you were about to walk to the other side ... of life."

That seemed a bit dramatic. "I wasn't going to walk to the other side of life."

"You were so."

"I was not."

"You were."

"Wasn't."

"Oh, this is easily the dumbest argument I've ever been involved in," Braden groused, dragging a frustrated hand through his hair and causing it to stand on end. "Seriously, I grew up in a house with Aisling, and she once argued that she was queen of the world because Dad told her it was true."

"She was clearly queen of your world, so she wasn't wrong."

"Whatever." Braden wrinkled his nose in a dismissive way, something I'm certain he thought made him look disappointed. Sadly, it made him look cute. The last thing I wanted was to sit around and think about how cute he looked. "What do you hear on the other side of the gate?"

The question made me uneasy. "I didn't say I heard anything on the other side of the gate. You assumed that."

"And you've been very careful not to deny it." Braden leaned closer, his eyes lasering into mine. "What do you hear? Can you hear the people who died and passed over? Like ... can you hear your parents?"

A surprising lump formed in my throat. "No. It's not like that."

"What is it like?"

"I .... ." My heart rate picked up a notch. "I don't hear anything. I don't know why you think that."

Disappointment lowered over Braden's handsome features. "You can trust me. You don't have to lie."

"I'm not lying." I held his gaze for what felt like forever and then shifted my eyes to the left. "Your brother and father are over there. I think they're waiting for you."

Braden glanced in their direction but didn't immediately move to leave. "Izzy ... ."

"I have work to do." I kept my voice even, but just barely. "Your brother needs you. He met a hero today and it didn't go well. Apparently Edgar Mason is not the superhero your brother fancied."

"Cillian will get over it." Braden took a deliberate step back. "I guess I should leave you to your work."

"That's probably best. I'm behind because of everything that's going on. I'm guessing that my job performance review for the first week won't be worth framing."

"You might be surprised." He heaved out a sigh. "I won't tell anyone about what you can hear. If that's what you're worried about, don't."

"I don't know what you're talking about." It was difficult to get out the words. "I don't hear anything."

"Yeah, well, I don't believe you."

I didn't blame him.

MASON PACKED UP MOST of the books before leaving. He stopped by my computer station long enough to tell me that he would be in contact if he found anything of importance ... and he was certain he would find something of importance because he always did.

After he left, the workers who had uncovered the room packed up their tools and vacated the premises, too. The Grimlocks were the last to leave, Braden lingering by the door and watching me as I made a big show of going over reports with Oliver and Renee. Finally, he disappeared through the opening. I was almost sad to see him go. Relief warred with my disappointment and ultimately won out.

Once I was certain I had the facility to myself I decided to let my magic out to play. It was rare that I could take over the gate room and experiment without worrying about someone stumbling upon me. I wanted to take advantage of an opportunity I might not have for some time.

I strode to the spot in front of the gate — the place where Braden had managed to grab me before I tripped and fell into oblivion — and raised my hands to send wisps of magic through the opening. The first bolt glanced harmlessly away. When I focused, the second zipped through what looked to be a small fissure in the shimmering opening.

I reached out with my senses, opening my mind, but came up empty. I meant for the magical jolt to serve as a drone of sorts, a way for me to see what was on the other side without risking myself. My connection to the magic was severed as soon as it disappeared through the filmy barrier, though, and there was no way for me to call it back.

"Well, that was stupid." I rubbed the tender spot between my eyebrows. "I wonder … ." I extended my fingers toward the surface, intent. I knew it would probably hurt when I touched the gateway, but I was prepared to absorb it … right up until the moment I felt a presence move in behind me.

"Don't jump."

"Aunt Max!" I sucked in a calming breath as I slowly turned to face her. She looked amused more than concerned, which only served to increase my irritation. "That wasn't funny."

"It was mildly funny." She pulled her purse strap over her head and left the bag on the table before drawing closer to me. "What were you doing?"

"Trying to see if I could sense anything on the other side."

"Like what?"

I shrugged. "I'm not sure. I was experimenting."

"You always had a scientific mind."

"That's not what Grandpa says. He maintains I'm prone to fits of whimsy. He's said it for as long as I can remember. I actually had to look up the word 'whimsy' when I was in junior high to figure out what he was saying."

Maxine waited a beat. "And?"

"And I don't think he meant it in a complimentary way."

Maxine snorted as she looked around the room, her eyes drifting to the newly-created door that was hidden only five hours before. "That's new. What happened there?"

I related my day, leaving nothing out except my fluttery reaction to Braden's presence. When I was done, she seemed intrigued.

"Well, isn't that something?" She strode across the room and poked her head inside the forgotten library. "What happened to all the books that were on the shelves?"

"Someone named Edgar Mason took them."

Maxine furrowed her brow. "Edgar Mason? Are you serious?"

"Why would I be anything other than serious?"

"I don't know." Maxine was clearly at a loss as she leaned her hip against the door jamb. "I don't understand why he would be here. This isn't normally his idea of a prime location."

"Do you know him?"

"I've met him."

I expected her to tell me more. When she didn't, I fixed her with a serious look. "Would you like to tell me what you thought about him?"

"I don't know that I really thought anything about him," Maxine replied after a beat. "He's a ... dandy. I guess that's the word that most closely fits his personality."

"Are you going to make me Google that word?"

Maxine snorted. "It's not necessarily a bad thing. It's more that he's kind of a prima donna."

"How is that not a bad thing?"

"I think it comes down to perception."

"You're still the same word maestro you were when I was a kid, Aunt Max," I offered. "No matter how you butter that bread, though, I don't think prima donna is a compliment."

"Fair enough, but I didn't necessarily mean it as an insult."

"What did you mean?"

"I meant that he has a certain reputation," she replied, her eyes shifting back to the empty shelves. "Even in reaping circles, where people are supposed to keep their profession on the down low, he thinks an awful lot about himself. He's one of those people who constantly wants to seem bigger than life, even if he's done nothing of note."

"You're saying he's a braggart."

"That's a fair assessment," she confirmed. "He likes to be the big man on campus when he's really the freshman who can't find his way to the university center."

"And you still have a way with words." I winked at her as I crossed to join her in the doorway. "Cormack and Cillian Grimlock were here for the discovery. Cillian was thrilled when Mason first showed up, but he grew disillusioned quickly."

"Cillian has a giving heart and a thirst for knowledge. If he'd never met Edgar before, he probably thought the man had something to offer. In truth, on his worst day Cillian is smarter than Edgar on his best."

"I think he figured out fairly quickly that Mason was full of himself," I noted. "He grew agitated when Mason said some of the books were in Sumerian."

"Sumerian?" Maxine made a face. "Edgar thought books squirreled away in the Belle Isle Aquarium dated back two thousand years before Christ?"

I shrugged. "Apparently so."

"I'm guessing Cillian didn't take that well."

"He pointed out that the language was Italian."

Maxine pressed her lips together as mirth flitted through her eyes. "Oh, well, that is just priceless."

"Pretty much," I agreed. "Cillian said the book that Mason was holding was some sort of paranormal creature dictionary or something. That it wasn't anything important. Mason didn't happen to agree, so they spent the rest of the afternoon ignoring one another."

"Well, I don't like to cast aspersions on people ... ."

"Yes, you do."

"I do," Maxine agreed, grinning. "In this particular case, I would align myself with Cillian. He's a good boy and he knows a great deal about a variety of different things."

"I got that feeling myself. He's back to focusing on the map." I gestured toward the wall, to where the pins remained. "He thinks we might be able to outthink the wraith and figure out where it will show up next."

"That map isn't correct," Maxine noted after squinting a bit. "The casinos aren't even on it."

"Yes, well, he's working around that."

"And what did he find?" Maxine abandoned her post by the door and moved to the map. "What's with the pins? Does he think the blue pins are outlier wraiths serving as a buffer to protect the new alpha?"

It took me a moment to translate what she was saying. "Pretty much."

"I guess that makes sense. If the enhanced wraith is the smartest game in town, of course the displaced wraiths will start sniffing around. Now that Lily Grimlock is gone and her band of rogue reapers in hiding, the wraiths want leadership. This new wraith is filling a vacuum of sorts ... and things could get seriously worse if we don't find that creature."

"I'm open to suggestions," I said. "My understanding is that the Grimlocks were going to hunt in the area where they believe the wraith might show up tonight. They have no way of knowing it will be there, but they're going to try. If you have a better idea, I'm all ears."

"Well, I might have a better idea." Maxine tapped her chin as she adopted a far-off expression I remembered from my childhood.

"Oh, I don't think I like that look," I complained, my stomach lining turning acidic. "You're about to suggest something weird, aren't you?"

"Define weird."

"I can't even come up with a good definition."

"That means you're overreacting." She adopted a pragmatic tone that told me I was right to be afraid. "I simply think I have an idea about how to find the information we're looking for."

"And how is that?"

"By conducting a seance, of course."

Whatever I was expecting, that wasn't it. My mouth dropped open as I ran the words through my busy brain. "You can't be serious."

"Oh, I'm completely serious."

"Aunt Max ... ."

"Don't worry about it." She patted my head as if I were three years old and had just asked why the sky was blue. "This is going to work. I think we're going to get answers and ... hey .... we might even come up with a way to help the Grimlocks."

Now she was just talking to hear herself talk. "Why do I think this is going to blow up in our faces?"

"Because you're a worrywart."

"Why else?"

"I have no idea."

"Are you sure about this?"

"I've never been more certain of anything in my entire life."

Oddly enough, that didn't make me feel better.

Twenty-Two

This wasn't the first time I'd participated in a seance with Maxine. She was always the fun one when I was growing up. That's not to say that my parents weren't fun. They were. But in simple terms, they also were rule followers. Maxine didn't have that problem.

"Do you remember when we held the seance in your living room during that storm?" I asked as I sat cross-legged on the floor in front of the gate. "There was a storm raging and you claimed that I'd called a ghost to your place."

Under the dim light of the candles she lighted, Maxine's face was hard to read. "I remember. You *did* call a ghost to the house. It took weeks for me to get rid of it."

"Yeah, right."

"You did call a ghost over." Maxine's voice was soft but firm. "You didn't realize what you were doing during the seance and you opened a gate. Heck, I didn't even know there were other types of gates until you managed to call something from the other side. That ghost — his name was Roger and he kept singing — was a real pain in the butt."

I stared at her for a long beat, dumbfounded. "You're joking."

"No. You opened a door for Roger instead of talking to him through a window, and it was a mess to clean up."

I had no idea what to say. "I always thought you were making that up."

"No." She took pity on me and leaned closer to pat my hand. "You were strong even then, Izzy. Your parents were worried about how strong you would become. The mix of your genes was ... interesting. I think we always knew you would turn into something special."

"I'm not special."

"You are." Maxine kept her eyes on me as she tightened her grip. "Your grandfather says you spent some time reading tarot cards and palms in New Orleans when you were working your way through school."

I battled back surprise. "I guess you two were in touch more than I realized." A twinge of sorrow hit me. "I didn't charge a lot. I remembered what you said about being responsible. I was careful when I read their futures."

"I'm sure you were." Her answer was a little too perfunctory for my taste. "Once you open certain doors, though, you can't close them. I wish you would've talked to me before you opened your own shop. You could've found yourself in a dangerous situation if you weren't careful."

"I was careful." My temper bubbled up before I could control it. "I was always careful."

"I know you were." She made a tsking sound before holding up her hand to cut off whatever I was about to say. Even I didn't know what it was, but there was no doubt it would be hot and mean. "We're here to see if we can find answers, not dwell on the past. I simply wanted to make you aware that even as a child you were powerful. This gift you try so hard to hide, it was always there."

I gazed into her eyes for what felt like forever and thought about Braden. "Can you hear the gate?"

Maxine shook her head. "No. Can you?"

I nodded. "There are voices on the other side. They talk to me, call for me."

"Is this new?"

"No. It happened when I was a kid, too."

Maxine was all business. "What do you remember?"

"Just that I heard voices."

"Did they tell you to do things?"

"No. They ... showed me things."

Maxine wrinkled her nose. "Not, like, gross things, right?"

I was amused despite myself. "No. Just pictures. I can't quite remember them. I remember Dad seeing what I was drawing and freaking out. He picked me up and ... that was it. I can't remember anything other than that."

"That's probably for the best."

"That's easy for you to say," I countered. "It happened to me. I need to remember."

"I think that if your subconscious was ready to remember you already would've done it. When you're ready, you'll know."

"I'm ready. Trust me ... I'm ready. That's why I came back here."

"I know, but I don't think things will happen on the timetable you seem to imagine. I believe the universe has a way of getting what it wants. It wanted you back in this place, and it won. That doesn't mean you'll get the answers you want right away."

That was the last thing I wanted to hear. "Well ... awesome." I dragged a hand through my hair and focused on the candle flickering on the floor between us. "What do you expect to achieve here? What do you think is going to happen?"

"I don't know that anything will happen," she replied, resting her hands on her knees as she got comfortable on the floor. "I'm hopeful that we'll be able to find a spirit, one that's anchored to this place, and ask it some questions."

"And how does that work?"

Maxine wrinkled her forehead. "Haven't you talked to spirits since you were a kid? I mean ... you grew up in New Orleans. That place is crawling with spirits. You grew up amongst the Bruja, not my Bruja, but others of the same ilk ... and your grandfather was a sorcerer. How can you not know about spirits?"

I averted my eyes. "I guess it never came up." That wasn't exactly true. I'd called a ghost one other time, not long after Katrina had ravaged the city. I was younger then, but I remembered. My grandfather swooped in and saved me ... and then we had a very long talk about what was and wasn't allowed. Ghosts were essentially off the table. "Just tell me what you want me to do. I'm ready."

"I want you to follow my lead." Maxine extended her hands and waited for me to press mine to hers, palm to palm.

I did as she wanted, smiling when the candle flickered the second skin touched skin. "Did you do that?"

Maxine ignored the question. "I want you to focus on your feelings, Izzy. It's not about what you know. It's about what you feel."

"Okay." I pressed my eyes shut and opened my mind, allowing the whispering to increase tenfold. "What am I supposed to feel?"

"There's no right answer to that question. Although ... I thought I just heard something. What was that?"

"They're talking to me." I didn't bother opening my eyes even though I felt Maxine's gaze on me. "They're excited. I think they can sense something is about to happen."

"In a good way or bad way?"

"I don't know. Let's find out."

When Maxine didn't immediately respond I wrenched open one eye and found her staring at me. "What?"

"You seem awfully excited, Izzy."

"Since when is that a bad thing?"

"I didn't say it was a bad thing."

"Last time I checked, you were the one who insisted we do this," I pointed out. "If you want to stop, just say so. I don't have time to screw around. In fact ... how did you even get in here?" I didn't ask the obvious question when she showed up, but I had no choice but to utter it now. "They replaced the door."

"I ran into Oliver when he was leaving. He let me in."

"You mentioned before that you knew him. It's fine that you're here. I would've let you in myself. I'm not sure it was a good idea for him to let you in, though."

"Probably not," she agreed. "But Oliver and I go way back. We need to focus on the seance. You're desperate for answers and I'm curious about what will happen because we're so close to the gate."

"Do you think the seance could pull souls through the gate?" The idea was horrifying. "That would be dangerous, right?"

"I don't think even you can pull souls through the gate."

That wasn't exactly comforting. "Aunt Max ... ."

"We're just going to test it." She flexed her fingers against mine. "If I feel as if something is about to go off the rails I'll pull the plug."

"Fine." I wasn't thrilled at the possibility of unleashing ghosts on the unsuspecting island populace, but I was eager to find answers. The sooner we took care of the enhanced wraith, the better. "Let's do this."

Maxine nodded. "Close your eyes," she prodded. "Go back to the place where you were. Try to ignore the whispers and focus on individual voices."

"Okay." I pressed my lips shut and inhaled through my nose. "Okay."

Briefly, while going through my rebellious teenage years, I'd decided to focus on yoga. My grandfather was big on magic and wanted me to flex my mental powers in a different way, so I knew the yoga would drive him crazy. It did, and I enjoyed watching the way his eyes rolled when he thought I wasn't looking. In truth, the yoga helped center me. It taught me a few techniques for calming myself. I used those techniques now.

"Do you hear anyone?" Maxine asked. Her voice sounded as if it was traveling over a great distance. "Is anyone out there?"

"Someone is here," I replied, opening my mind wider when I felt a presence brush against my subconscious. I felt, rather than saw, my own internal image flicker. It was something I'd witnessed firsthand with the New Orleans Bruja, and I knew my countenance reflected a skull – a Catrina, almost – even though I couldn't see it. "I feel ... someone."

"Is it a man or a woman?"

"Woman."

"What is she saying?"

Maxine was intent. I recognized that, even though my mind was still floating. It didn't feel as if it was attached to my body, more that my subconscious had somehow managed to climb to a spot ten feet above my head.

"She's not saying anything. She's ... trying to show me something."

"What?"

"I don't know. It's something with her mind. In fact ... ." I let go of Maxine's hand and raised my fingers into the space above my head. I expected to make contact with the spirit's ghostly form, but instead I touched nothing but air. "She's trying to warn me."

Maxine's demeanor shifted and I felt her lean closer. "Warn you about what?"

"Something is coming. Some ... creature. It looks like a snake."

"What creature?"

My eyes never opened yet suddenly I saw all around me. "Oh, my ... ." I blew out a terrified breath and forced my eyes open, scrambling back when a kaleidoscope of ethereal faces filled my vision. "What the ... ? Aunt Max!"

"I see them." Maxine sounded grim as she slowly rose to her feet. The spirits — who looked angry and ready for retribution — shifted quickly to fill the space between us. "Where did they come from, Izzy?"

Was she seriously asking me? "How should I know? You're the one who thought it was such a great idea to have a seance. You should know where they came from."

"Your magic drew them here."

"No." I vehemently shook my head. "I didn't expel any magic."

Maxine tilted her head to the side, her expression chilling. "You did."

"I did not."

"You did so."

"I did not." I shook my head when I realized this was essentially the argument I'd had with Braden earlier in the evening. "I did not," I repeated, my voice lower. "They're not here because of me."

"Oh, Izzy, don't be an idiot. Of course they're here because of you. I certainly didn't call them."

"But ... ." I wanted to challenge her assessment but I knew she was right. "What am I supposed to do? I don't like this. I don't like the way they're looking at me."

As if on cue, I moved to the side to avoid the nearest female ghost.

She seemed intent as she stared. When she extended a finger to touch me, I knew that was beyond the scope of what I could tolerate and jerked away from her. "How do we get rid of them?"

"I guess that you get rid of them the same way you called them," Maxine replied, swatting at a younger ghost, one who looked to be in her teens. "You called them, so you need to send them back." She lashed out again with her hand. "And, the sooner you evict them, the better."

"I didn't call them!"

"Yes, you did!"

"I did not!"

"Oh, don't start this again." Maxine was beside herself as she smacked down a short male ghost who looked to have wandering hands. "You need to call them off, Izzy. I can't stop them. I don't even know what you did to get them here. You have to be the one."

I didn't enjoy being the one required to do anything. "I didn't call them here! Stop saying I did."

"Oh, this is unbelievable." Maxine hopped off the step and twisted to evade one of the ghosts. "Izzy, do something!"

"I don't know what to do."

I felt helpless, frustration washing over me. I didn't think things could get worse. I was wrong.

At that exact moment, the door to the gate room opened and Braden strolled through it. He looked lost in thought, as if he wasn't expecting an audience, and he pulled up short when he caught a hint of movement out of the corner of his eye. "What the ... ?"

"That was going to be my line," I gritted out, hopping to my right to put space between the insistent female ghost and myself. "What are you doing here?"

"I forgot my sunglasses."

"Oh, well, that's convenient." I tilted to my side. "This isn't what it looks like."

Braden took a long moment to glance between Maxine and me. "It looks as if you're being overrun by ghosts, which I don't get since you're half reaper. Why are you surrounded by ghosts?"

"Aunt Max thought it would be a good idea to conduct a seance so we could perhaps get answers about what the wraith did on the other side ... or why those other wraiths showed up."

The ghosts were growing more aggressive, and the woman who refused to be separated from me actually managed to put her ghostly hands on my shoulders, sending a shiver down my spine.

"Oh, geez!"

"Are you okay?" Concern washed over Braden's features as he took a step in my direction. When the ghosts flooded toward him, acting as an intimidating barrier, he stopped. "How do we get rid of them?"

"Izzy has to do it," Maxine offered, gasping as she tried to escape from two ghosts at the same time. "She accidentally called to them. This wasn't what I had in mind when I suggested a seance, by the way."

"Well, you should've been more specific." My temper ratcheted up a notch. "Knock it off!" I yelled at the ghost closest to me, widening my eyes when she stopped moving and merely stared. "Huh."

"Did you just order that ghost around?" Braden asked.

"Yeah."

"And it listened?"

"Yeah."

"So, order them back to where they came from," Braden snapped. "If you can control them, now is the time to make them go away."

That was easier said than done. "What if they don't do as I ask?"

"There's only one way to find out." Braden took two long strides in my direction, frowning when three ghosts changed course to cut him off. "They don't want me close to you." He almost sounded as if he was talking to himself as he glanced around the room. "They don't want Madame Maxine close to you either. They're trying to isolate you."

His words had a chilling effect. "What is that supposed to mean?"

"They're attracted to you." Braden managed to keep his voice calm. I thought that was mildly impressive given the panic running through his eyes. He was a master at maintaining control, I had to give him that. "Izzy, you have to order them away." He almost sounded as if he was pleading.

"I'm not sure I can," I admitted, my stomach twisting. "I don't even know how I called them here in the first place."

"Then we have to experiment until you get it right," Braden prodded. "For now, order them away."

I licked my lips and nodded. "Okay." I focused on the frozen ghost, at the way her nearly transparent lips twisted into a sneer. "Go back to where you came," I whispered.

The ghost merely stared at me, unimpressed.

"You'll have to be louder than that, Izzy," Braden chided. "You need to be more forceful. Let them know who the boss is."

"I guess, in that scenario, I would be the boss."

"You are the boss," Maxine stressed. "You have to act like the boss. Order them to go back where they came from. Be specific."

"Right." I gathered my courage. "Go back where you came." My voice was stronger this time, but not loud. "Go back where you came," I repeated, this time louder. A brief shimmer moving through the ghost told me something was happening. "Go back," I ordered, my courage growing when I saw another shimmer. "Go back. Go back. Go back!"

I repeated the phrase multiple times, allowing my words to run together until there was no end or beginning of the chant. I felt my image flashing, the internal Bruja emerging as power washed over me. I focused on the ghost directly in front of me, channeling all my energy into her. I continued chanting as she disappeared.

"That's enough, Izzy." Braden was at my side before I realized it was over. He grabbed me around the waist when I listed to the side, my head suddenly heavy. "You did it." He gentled his voice. "They're gone. Good job."

"Good job." I ran the words over my tongue. "Is it bedtime yet? I think I need a nap."

"Definitely." He caught me before I fell to the floor. "I'll make sure you get to bed."

"That's good." My head rolled to his shoulder, my mind heavy. "You smell like ... limes."

"That's because Aisling likes limes in her iced tea instead of lemons."

"Hmm. That sounds good."

"I'll get you some when you wake up tomorrow." Braden directed me toward the door. "Come on. I'll get you back to your room. You're in the boathouse, right?"

"Yeah. My old house is gone. It was destroyed."

"I know. I'll take you to the boathouse."

"Okay. Nighty-night."

And just like that, I was dead to the world.

Twenty-Three

I woke in my bed, which was still too new to feel comfortable. I was dressed in the same clothes I'd worn the previous day. When I rolled to a sitting position, the first thing I saw was my shoes neatly arranged on the floor near the door.

The second thing I saw was Braden sleeping in the chair in the corner of the room. He looked uncomfortable, his lanky frame contorted in such a way that he couldn't possibly have gotten any sleep. And still, his eyes were closed and his breathing easy.

"Holy bats in the belfry." I clutched my blanket closer to my chest, as if covering myself, and glared at Braden as he stretched and opened one eye. "What are you doing in my bedroom?"

"And good morning to you, too," he drawled sleepily.

"You want me to say 'good morning' to you?" I was incensed. "You're in my bedroom. I didn't invite you into my bedroom."

"Well, given the fact that you essentially passed out while I was dragging you through the aquarium last night, that's hardly surprising."

"Passed out?" I wrinkled my forehead as my mind drifted to the previous night. "Something happened last night? Something ... oh!" The female ghost, the unhappy one with the dark glare, infiltrated my thoughts. "We had a seance."

"Yes, and that was about the dumbest thing I've ever heard of." Braden groaned as he sat upright and raised his arms over his head. "I think I'm too old to sleep in a chair."

"Why did you sleep in the chair?"

"I was worried about you."

His answer was so simple it made me feel guilty. "You didn't have to worry. I just ... was tired. I'm fine now that I've slept for a few hours."

"You slept for eleven hours," Braden corrected, causing my eyes to widen. "I got you back here at about seven last night. It's almost six. You were more than a little tired."

He wasn't wrong. The aftermath of the botched seance was misty in my mind. I remembered seeing him, talking to him, and then everything became a blur. "Well, I'm sorry you felt the need to babysit me." I swallowed hard. "That shouldn't have been your responsibility."

He rolled his eyes, managing to irk me even though I knew I should be grateful. "It wasn't all that bad. Your golf cart was outside, so I used that to transport you. Luckily for you, I happen to love driving golf carts."

"Should I take that to mean you were hot dogging all over the island?"

"I never hot dog ... unless at a ball game and they're on the menu." He winked, his full arsenal of charm on full display. "I drove you straight here. Madame Maxine offered to do it, but she wasn't certain she could get you up the stairs. I sent her home and handled it myself.

"I planned to watch you for an hour and then leave you with nothing but a note and a lot of guilt, but some freezing rain rolled through last night," he continued. "Oliver warned it wasn't safe to drive across the bridge. I was stuck here anyway, so I decided to keep watch over you. I figured it couldn't hurt after the ghost ordeal."

"Freezing rain?" The term meant very little to me. Of course, I understood that it was a weather condition that made for hazardous travel, but I couldn't remember ever seeing it. "I guess I'm sorry I missed it."

"You're a Michigander now." Braden's tone was teasing. "You'll put aside that notion fairly quickly."

"I guess." I rolled my neck and lifted my hands to study them. "All the ghosts are gone, right?"

"Don't you remember?"

"Kind of. It's all hazy."

"I think that's because you expended so much power there at the end that your mind shut down. That's probably normal, or maybe I'm just hoping that because I don't want to see you suffer."

My stomach threatened to revolt. "Power? What do you mean by power?"

"I mean that you have magical abilities." He was matter-of-fact as he got to his feet. "I don't know why you insist on lying about it — frankly, I would be screaming it to the skies if I had magic to wield — but I recognize what happened last night."

That was interesting because I had no idea what had transpired. "I don't think ... ."

"Shh." Braden's eyes lit with amusement as he pressed his finger to his lips and admonished me to shut my mouth. "I know it. You can't change the fact that I saw you in action. I know you can do more. I know you can hear something when you're around the gate."

I opened my mouth to argue, but no sound came out.

"You can trust me." He turned plaintive. "I know you don't believe that. Your grandfather probably told you to keep your abilities a secret. That was smart on his part. But you can trust me."

I found my voice. "It's not that I don't trust you."

"Then what is it?"

"It's that ... I don't know what to tell you." That was mostly the truth. "I don't fit into one group. I'm more than one thing."

"There's nothing wrong with that."

"There is in the reaper world," I argued, my voice becoming stronger. "You're supposed to be a reaper and nothing else. That's why I was so interested in your sister's relationship with her husband. Marrying outsiders is frowned upon. I don't remember much, but I remember that.

"My mother wasn't a reaper and she got a lot of grief for it," I continued, warming to my topic. "She always felt like an outsider. She worried I would feel like an outsider. My grandfather warned me when

I decided I wanted to work for the reaper council that they wouldn't accept me if they knew everything. That's why he left the fold. He was more than one thing, too."

Braden looked as if he was struggling to understand everything. "Okay, I get that," he said after a beat. "Reapers aren't always the most welcoming bunch. That's a given. I don't think it's for the same reason you think it is."

"Oh? Why do you think reapers are such jerks?"

"I think that reapers are militant about keeping their secret," he replied, refusing to allow himself to be drawn into a needless argument. "Can you imagine the panic that would go through the populace if they found out there was a group of people who sneak into their homes and places of business to absorb souls after they died? That we get lists of who is going to die before it happens?"

Oddly, that hadn't occurred to me.

"I mean ... think about it," he continued. "There's very little we can do about some of the medical emergencies, but in a lot of cases people could be saved through intervention. But that's not our job. And think about the murders. If people knew we were aware when a murder was going to happen, how do you think they would react?"

"That's a fair point," I admitted as I combed my fingers through my hair, grimacing when they snagged. I figured, given the way I'd passed out the previous evening, I'd slept deep. That meant my bedhead was probably out of control. "That doesn't change the fact that they see me as an outsider."

"I don't think anyone sees you as an outsider but you."

"If people knew ... ."

"What?" Braden held his hands out. "What would they say? I know. I'm not bothered by it."

"You haven't had a chance to really think about it."

"Perhaps, but I don't think anything will change."

I had a feeling he was deluding himself. "If people find out, the odds of me losing this job are much greater. I can't lose this job."

"Because you want to find out what happened to your parents?"

"Partly."

"Well, I asked my father about that," Braden volunteered. "I figured he would know something. He doesn't. He doesn't know what happened to your parents because no one knows."

"That's impossible," I protested, my anger returning with a vengeance. "Somebody had to find me. I was in the hospital. I remember being in the hospital. I doubt very much I managed to get there myself."

"They found you in the rubble of the house," he corrected. "Search crews went to the house because it was clear something very bad had happened. They found your parents right away. They were dead. They couldn't find you, and there was debate about whether you'd been kidnapped. Then someone — I'm not sure who, the report was vague — but someone found you. You were unconscious and transported to the hospital. Once there, Madame Maxine was called and the reaper council lost interest ... mostly because when they asked the obvious questions you couldn't answer. You couldn't remember anything."

I shook my head. "How can they not know what killed my parents?"

"They weren't there. They know your parents died — and they were ugly deaths — but they don't know who or what did it. They only know you somehow survived."

That wasn't what I wanted to hear. I was certain the reaper council knew what had happened and simply refused to share the information with outsiders. Now it seemed I had been wrong ... and apparently about a great many things. "I came back to find out what happened to my parents. I'm not going to turn my back on that mission even though I'm going to have to dig harder than I initially envisioned for answers. I'm not simply going to let it go."

"I don't blame you. I wouldn't give up either."

"Well ... that's good."

Braden's lips quirked. "As for the magic, I don't care that you're more than one thing. I'm fine with it. You mentioned my sister and her husband, and you're right. My father wasn't especially thrilled when she brought him home. It wasn't because he was a normal man. It was because my father could tell there was something different about him.

"I know you think the reaper council is full of a bunch of stodgy old men who want things a certain way," he continued. "They do like history, and there are rules for a reason. They're also willing to change if necessary. I've seen it happen. We had so much going on with my mother and other stuff that was happening that the council had no choice but to get with the program or be left behind."

"And you think they would accept me no matter what?" I was beyond dubious. "I don't feel that's true, and I'm not willing to risk my future on your hunch."

"I don't want you to risk anything either," Braden supplied. "It's okay if you want to hide who you really are and what you can do. I don't blame you. But keep in mind that everybody has secrets. You're not the only one hiding something. Half the people in this business are hiding something and the other half are too stupid to realize they need to hide something."

"Yes, well, I need to worry about my own secrets."

Braden's fingers were gentle as he reached over and slipped a strand of hair behind my ear. He hesitated a moment before pulling away. "You don't have to worry about me sharing your secret. I have no interest in doing so. I understand about loyalty. Whatever else you believe about me, I don't break confidences."

"I believe you."

"Good." He pressed the heel of his hand against his forehead as he regrouped and directed the conversation to something else. "You should probably get cleaned up. I need you to give me a ride back to the aquarium so I can collect my vehicle and then head home to shower."

"Oh, right." I rolled out of bed, taking a moment to make sure I was solid before shaking my head. "Thank you for staying with me last night. It wasn't necessary, but it was sweet all the same."

"That's my middle name."

"Sweet?"

"Yes."

"Is that something you tell your friends at the bar?"

He shrugged. "Maybe."

"Well, it won't work on me."

"I think it's already working on you."

"And I think you're dreaming."

"We shall see."

BRADEN WAS IN A good mood when we reached the aquarium. The roads were clear thanks to a warm-up, but his BMW still had a layer of ice on it that required some massive heating power from the vents.

While he was waiting for that to happen, he stepped into the aquarium lobby with me.

"If you need something today, you know how to reach me. I have to get home so I can change out of yesterday's clothes — I wasn't planning on spending the night — but I'll be available this afternoon if something comes up."

Tara, already behind the counter, widened her eyes. That let me know she heard Braden's statement, and she was clearly intrigued.

"Thank you." I felt like an idiot as I stared at the floor. "I'll be fine. I know how to take care of myself."

"I didn't say otherwise, but you don't have to do everything by yourself. It's okay to ask for help."

"I honestly can't see any reason why I'd need help today."

"I can think of one reason," Braden said grimly as Edgar Mason pushed his way through the doorway.

"Oh, good morning." Mason seemed chipper as he tugged each finger of his gloves to remove them. "I didn't realize I warranted a personal greeting in the lobby. That's rather sweet."

While I found Mason's reaction amusing, Braden clearly saw it differently. "Yes, we're sitting here to greet you," he drawled. "We thought that was the best way to spend our time when there's a rogue wraith on the loose."

That reminded me of something. "I take it your family didn't find the wraith last night."

"No." Braden shook his head as he glared at an oblivious Mason. "Cillian selected three likely places for it to show. It didn't."

"Cillian? That's the man who couldn't read the Sumerian texts yesterday, right?" Mason queried.

"I believe he said they were in Italian," I corrected, doing everything I could to keep from laughing at Braden's huffy demeanor. He clearly didn't like Mason ... an emotion I understood. "You'll have to take that up with him."

"Oh, I look forward to doing so." Mason offered me what I'm sure he thought was the most charming smile in his repertoire. "So ... you're the gatekeeper at this particular facility."

I nodded, unsure where he was going. "I am."

"Good. You'll be having lunch with me this afternoon. I have a number of things I want to discuss with you."

"Oh, well ... ." I was at a loss.

"What if she doesn't want to have lunch with you?" Braden challenged, his cheeks flushing as his temper made an appearance. "You can't just order her to eat when she doesn't want to eat."

Mason's expression was blank. "Why wouldn't she want to eat? Is there something I don't know about lunch in this area? Granted, I don't expect a panoply of choices. As far as I can tell, it's coney or bust. Still, I'm sure she can find something to her liking."

"First, coneys are awesome," Braden snapped. "Second, you're not in charge here. You can't just order her to go to lunch with you."

"I don't believe I ordered. I need to talk to her about a few things. In her job as gatekeeper she is the most likely individual to answer those questions."

"I haven't been on the job long," I hedged, uncomfortable when I felt Braden's eyes land on me. "I might not have the answers you're looking for."

"It can't hurt to try." Mason was back to being oblivious as he skirted around Braden and headed toward the hallway at the back of the room. "I'll meet you in the gate room so we can firm up plans. I have a full agenda today and no time for dillydallying."

I purposely avoided Braden's gaze. "I'll see you in a few minutes."

"Lovely."

Twenty-Four

Braden suddenly didn't want to leave the aquarium. He stalled, hemmed and hawed, and feigned a leg cramp to get rid of Mason so we could talk without an audience. Sure, Tara was still around, but Braden barely registered her presence.

"You can't go out to lunch with him," he hissed the moment we were alone.

I remained immovable for a long moment. "Why?" I asked finally. In truth, I knew why he didn't want me to go out with Mason. I couldn't help but wonder if he would admit it.

"Because he's a tool."

"I need more information than that," I said dryly. "When you say 'tool,' my mind immediately goes to a home improvement situation."

"That's because you're trying to drive me crazy," he fired back. "That dude's ego is so big he could float away. I don't want him to take you with him. You could die thanks to the fall back to Earth."

I pressed my lips together to keep from laughing at his serious expression. "I think I can take care of myself."

"I didn't say you couldn't."

"You're acting as if I'm an easy mark."

"I'm simply trying to protect you. That guy is a tool. You can't go out with him."

"I don't think he wants me to go out with him in the way you're suggesting," I argued, deciding to put my foot down in an attempt to end this ridiculous argument. "I think he wants to talk to me about the room and its proximity to the gate. He probably found something important."

"That guy couldn't find something important if I glued it to his face."

"Now, don't get bitter," I chided, amused despite myself. "You too can puff out your ego to the size of California if you simply stop trying to think rationally." I was trying to placate him, although I had no idea if it worked. "There's no reason to get upset. It's lunch. I'll answer his questions and that will be it."

Instead of immediately responding, Braden wrinkled his nose and shifted to look out the aquarium's front window. "Maybe I should see if I can get Cillian to take my charges today. That way I could go to lunch with you."

That seemed an overreaction. "I'm an adult who can make her own decisions." I debated continuing but ultimately decided he needed to hear it again despite the fact that he'd stepped in and saved me the previous evening. "Besides, I thought we agreed that getting too close was a bad idea."

"Yeah. Bad idea."

"So ... why are you freaking out about this?"

"What?" Braden jerked his head in my direction, alerting me that he hadn't been listening at all. "What did you say?"

My temper flared. "I said that we agreed getting close was a mistake," I repeated. "You agreed."

"No, I didn't." He shook his head, firm. "You said that, and I backed off because I needed time to think. Well, I've thought about it, and I've decided I don't want to do what you suggested."

My mouth dropped open. "Excuse me?"

"You heard me." He made a face. "I think we should try dating."

His about-face was so jarring I had no idea how to respond. "But ... you said that it was a good idea to stay friends and nothing more. You

215

don't like dating someone for more than one night anyway. I'm not a one-night stand girl. Our lives don't mesh."

Braden was unnaturally calm as he leveled his gaze on me. "I changed my mind. We can date for more than one night. In fact, we can date for a lot of nights. If that's what you need to hear, I understand. I've said it ... and I mean it."

I was flabbergasted. "But ... no. I didn't come back for this. I came back to find out what happened with my parents, to see if I belong here. Dating is not part of the plan."

"I'm going to help you figure out what happened to your parents." He was sober as he rested his hand on my shoulder. The weight, warm and heavy, was soothing. I hated the realization, so I immediately pulled away from him.

"I can figure it out myself!"

"Hey, I'm not in the mood to get into a screaming match with you." He raised his hands. "I'm going to help you. I know the area and I might know a few people who can help us answer the big questions regarding your parents ... like what came through that gate, because I'm pretty sure that something came through that gate and killed them no matter what you say."

I was taken aback. "What makes you say that?"

Caught off guard by my shifting demeanor, Braden pressed the heel of his hand to his forehead. "I really should've left this conversation until I got back. We could've talked about it over lunch ... when you're not eating with that tool Mason."

"We're not having lunch." I was huffy, my cheeks burning as I glared. "I want to know why you think something crossed over and killed my parents. I never told you that. I'm not even sure it's true because I can't remember what happened."

"You didn't tell me," Braden agreed.

"So how do you know?"

"Because you showed me."

"Showed you what?"

He rubbed the side of his face, clearly lost. "You showed me in your dreams last night. You showed me what you remembered."

"I most certainly did not." I straightened, the absurdity of the statement igniting my anger. "I didn't even know you were in the room all night. You saw me when I woke up this morning. I had no idea."

"You still showed me." His voice softened. "I don't know everything you are, but I know what you're not ... and that's a coward. I saw what you remember last night, and even though it was jumbled I could follow the narrative.

"You talked to something on the other side of that gate, and whatever it was decided to cross over," he continued. "Your father realized right before it happened that something was about to go very wrong. He carried you out, raced to the house you shared with the intention of packing a few bags and running, but it was already too late."

My heart pounded as he talked about the images I'd clearly put on display for him while my barriers were down. He was describing everything exactly as I remembered it. In other words, he was telling the truth.

"You saw all of that?"

"I did."

"Why didn't you say something sooner?"

"Because I wanted to give you time to settle. Because I wanted to give me time to settle, too." He smiled. "I get what you're up against. I know you can't remember. I want to help you find the answers you need."

"That doesn't mean dating has to be involved."

"Hey, if I'm going to spend a lot of time around you I'm going to get something out of it."

I scowled. "You're a pig!"

"Not that." His lips twisted into a sneer. "I'm going to get the pleasure of your company ... and, no, I wasn't talking about naked company. Although, now that you mention it, if you want to include naked time in the mix, I'm all for it."

I wanted to smack him ... and maybe kiss him. The realization that my heart was racing for a reason other than fury was frustrating. "I don't think it's a good idea."

"Yes, well, I'm going to convince you otherwise."

"By browbeating me?"

"No. I have a sister. I know that doesn't work. I'm going to do something else."

"What?"

He held his hands palms out and shrugged. "I'm going to woo you."

I choked on a laugh. "Woo? Did you suddenly turn into your father?"

"No, but he would definitely use that word. In fact, he might have used it during a conversation we shared last night. It's a lame word, but I'm still using it. I'm totally going to woo you."

"Stop saying that. It creeps me out."

"At least we're on the same page there."

I sucked in a breath as I took a moment to consider what he'd said. "I need to think about this," I supplied, shaking my head. "I'm not going to let you dictate what is and isn't going to happen."

"That's fair. We can talk about it some more over lunch."

"I'm having lunch with Mason." On this I refused to back down. "He has questions about my job, and I've fallen down so far this week that I might never be able to crawl out of the hole when it comes to this job. I can't just do what I want to do here. He's in charge of that room, and that means we're going to lunch together."

Braden clearly didn't like that suggestion one bit. "No."

"You have no choice in the matter."

"Well ... ."

I cut him off with a shake of the head. "You should know that I will never date a Neanderthal. If that's how you see yourself, you should leave right now."

"Oh, you're hitting below the belt," he grumbled, rubbing his chin as he flicked his eyes to the window. His BMW was running outside and the ice was completely melted. "Fine," he said finally. "We'll do things your way. I'll go to work ... and you'll go to work. We'll do our duty and not be irresponsible."

"Great." I moved to head to the back hallway. "I'll talk to you later?"

Braden nodded, his expression hard to read. "Definitely."

"Great." I felt awkward about sharing a goodbye with him in front of Tara, who I was certain heard most of our conversation, so I waved. "I'll talk to you later."

I could feel Braden's eyes on me as I strode away. "I'll call you after your lunch to see how things went."

"I'll be fine."

"I'm still calling."

"I might not answer."

Braden's voice turned smug. "Oh, you'll answer."

"I can see what your sister meant when she said you were a pain in the behind," I called out. "I'm just betting she has decades of good gossip for me."

"If you think you can frighten me with talk of my sister ... well, good job."

"I thought so."

"I'll call you later."

"I'm looking forward to it."

"THIS IS THE WEEKLY report."

Oliver was waiting for me by the gate when I walked into the back room. He had a clipboard in his hand and an agitated look on his face.

"Okay." I took the clipboard from him, curiosity getting the better of me when I realized most of Oliver's attention was on the opening that led to the newly-discovered room. "Is something wrong?"

"Something is definitely wrong," he shot back, his eyes firing. For a moment, I swore they looked as if they glowed, as if he had fire in his orbs. I figured that was a trick of the light, so I managed to remain calm.

"What's wrong?" I asked the obvious question, although I had a feeling I already knew the answer.

"I cannot stand that ... person!" He jabbed a finger toward the room. It happened to be his middle finger, something I was doubtful was a coincidence.

"Edgar Mason?"

"I don't like calling people names."

"Of course not. You're too professional for that."

Oliver barreled forward. "He is a turd. That's the best word to describe him. A turd. He's not even a polished turd."

"I've never understood the need to polish turds," I teased, grinning until I realized he looked as if he wanted to rip my head off. "You're not in the mood to have a good time, are you?"

"Not really."

"Good to know." I made a rolling motion with my hand. "Continue." I fixed my attention on the clipboard and let Oliver wind himself up. I still hadn't spent enough time with my co-workers to bond with them, but I figured this was as good a place as any to start the process. "I'm totally interested in hearing how he's a turd."

"Thank you." Oliver launched into a diatribe that would've made my grandfather proud — he once spent three hours explaining why anyone who didn't respect a handicapped parking space should be drawn and quartered — and I kept one ear on him as I checked each section of the report.

"So that's basically it," Oliver finished, his eyes never moving from the back room in case Mason dared make an appearance. "He's a complete and total tool."

"You're not the first person I've crossed paths with this morning to use that word to describe him," I mused. "Just a quick question: These numbers here, basically they're saying that this is the number of souls we expected this week, and this is the number of souls we collected this week, right?"

Oliver followed the tip of the pen I gripped and nodded. "Yes."

"Okay, good. I'm glad I'm not a complete idiot and can read a report. I have another question."

He folded his arms over his chest and waited. "Why is our intake number so much higher than our expected intake number?"

"What do you mean?"

"Here." I pointed toward the first number. "It says we were expected to take in four-hundred and eighty souls for the week."

"Correct."

"We took in almost seven hundred souls. Is that normal?"

"Oh, well ... ." For the first time since I'd entered the room, Oliver forgot about his Mason rant and focused on the clipboard. "The intake number is always greater than the projected number because of emergencies and last-second deaths that don't show on the lists. That's an inevitability in this line of work."

"I get that. That seems like a big difference, though."

"It is a big difference." Oliver looked baffled as he handed back the clipboard and strode to the filing cabinet. "Hold on." He opened a drawer on the far end and rummaged inside until he found what he was looking for. When he straightened, he had a report in his hand — and it looked a lot like the one I was holding. "This is the report from two weeks ago."

"What does it say?"

"Um ... ." He scanned the report. "Expected intake five-hundred and twenty. That makes sense because we get more deaths during big snowstorms and that was our last huge snowstorm. Actual intake ... five-hundred and fifty."

"That seems like a more realistic differential," I noted.

"I think that's the norm." Oliver dug into the cabinet a second time. "This is a report from November. Projected intake is four-hundred and sixty. Actual intake is four-hundred and seventy-seven."

"So the numbers from this week's report are way off," I mused.

"Way off," Oliver agreed, tilting his head as he considered the ramifications. "Before you ask, I have no idea why the numbers are so far off. I can't say as I've ever paid that close attention to them. I guess it's possible that we've had other weeks like this one where the numbers skew wide."

"Or maybe something happened this week to mess with the numbers," I suggested. "Like an enhanced wraith being unleashed on the populace."

Oliver balked. "You can't possibly believe that the wraith is responsible for more than one-hundred bodies."

"I don't know what I believe." That was the truth. "I think we need to report this number to someone. The question is, who?"

"We could send it up the food chain via email, but that's a bureaucratic reaction. I think it would be smarter to put the report in front of someone who will understand why this is such a concern."

"Who are you thinking?"

"There's only one choice."

I heaved a sigh. I knew exactly who he meant. "Cormack Grimlock?" I poked my fingers in my eyes and rubbed, weariness threatening to force me back into bed for the day. "That's who you're talking about, right?"

"Do you have a better idea?"

Sadly, I didn't. "Okay, but I'm not sure he'll see what we see in the report."

"At least we'll know we tried to warn someone."

Twenty-Five

When it came time for lunch, Mason thankfully suggested eating in the only restaurant on site. I wasn't worried about leaving the island with him. He didn't give off a creepy vibe, but I wasn't excited at the prospect, so staying close to the gate seemed the better option.

"This is a cute place," he commented as we sat at a corner table. The smile he graced me with was charming enough that I couldn't help but return it. "What's good here?"

"I've only eaten here once. The burgers are great."

"I'm a vegetarian."

"Oh, well ... ."

"We have vegetable pockets, too," a woman announced as she approached the table. She wore a cute uniform — the same one Tara wore to run the front desk — and she had an impatient look on her face. "What'll it be?"

"We haven't even looked at menus yet," Mason replied. "I'm no expert, but I believe that's generally how customers decide what to order at most establishments."

"Oh, geez." The woman rolled her eyes and stomped to the counter to grab two menus from the stack resting there. When she returned, she made a big show of doling them out. "Can I start you off with a beverage?" She asked with exaggerated congeniality.

I pressed my lips together to keep from laughing. "Are you Claire?"

She flicked a set of deep blue eyes to me. "I am. You're Izzy Sage, right? My husband mentioned you."

That was surprising because I got the distinct impression that Collin and Claire didn't often chat. Renee said they spent all their time screaming at one another. I couldn't imagine an instance in which my name came up in pleasant conversation. "That's me." I forced a smile. I didn't want to get on her bad side. "I've heard a lot about you."

Instead of being offended, Claire snorted. "I bet you have."

Intrigued, Mason glanced between us. "Am I missing something?"

"Nothing of importance," Claire fired back. "Do you know what you want?"

I didn't bother looking at the menu. "I'll have a cheeseburger with fries."

Claire nodded and focused on Mason. "And you?"

"What do you have that's gluten-free?"

"My foot."

"I don't believe I'm in the mood for roasted feet today," Mason shot back, grinning like a madman as he winked at me. "I'll have the vegetable pocket. Hold the fries. They're full of oil and carbohydrates. Do you have any apple slices for a side?"

"I can chop up an apple if that's what you want," Claire drawled. "How does that sound?"

"Lovely. Thank you."

"Happy to be of service." Claire grabbed the menus and lowered her mind barriers for a brief moment, allowing me to see a glimpse of her plans for the apple. There was licking involved, which grossed me out, so I struggled to keep a pleasant expression in place until she disappeared into the kitchen.

"She seems ... interesting," Mason said after a beat. "What do you know about her?"

That was a tricky question. Mason was seemingly high in the reaper hierarchy, but that didn't mean he knew every secret of the paranormal world. If he wasn't aware that merrow were not only real but also working in the aquarium restaurant he might blow things out of proportion. That was the last thing I wanted.

"Not much. I've only been here a few days. One of my co-workers says that Claire and her husband are known for their fights — I believe she called them epic — but I've yet to witness one."

"Oh, well, that sounds entertaining." Mason's eyes flickered with amusement. "You say you've been here only a few days. I was given the impression that you're the gatekeeper."

"I am. I just transferred from Missouri. I was working a clerical position there.

"In fact, I've worked a lot of clerical positions at a number of offices the past five years," I continued. "This is my first stint as a gatekeeper ... anywhere."

"Ah, well, you have to start somewhere."

"Pretty much."

"Did you choose Detroit, or was it chosen for you?"

"I requested the assignment."

"Why?"

I expected the question. Perhaps not in such a blunt manner, but I expected it. "Why not? Michigan is a lovely state. The water allows for freshwater boating and there's a lot of history associated with the area. I love history."

"And the city is notorious as the murder capital of the world."

I waited a beat. "I believe St. Louis is the murder capital of America."

"I think it's Detroit."

I narrowed my eyes. In all honesty, I knew the truth because that was my grandfather's biggest argument when he tried to exert control and keep me from moving to the area. "That's just one of those myths," I countered, keeping my voice calm and even. "St. Louis — the one in Illinois — is number one. That's according to a list I looked at a few months ago. Detroit is ninth on the list. It's behind Flint, which means it's not even the murder capital of Michigan."

Mason stared at me for a long beat. "Well, I didn't realize that. You learn something new every day."

"I guess so."

"That doesn't mean the city is safe," Mason continued, refusing to back down. "The city is run down; the people are fleeing. I don't think it's safe for a single woman to live in the city. You should consider a move to a different location."

"I asked for this location."

"Why?"

"I like the state." My temper threatened to bubble up. "Why do you care?"

"You have a lot of potential. I hate to see you squander it."

"And you're basing that opinion on what? You've spent exactly twenty minutes with me since you arrived."

"I like to think of myself as intuitive. I read people fairly well."

"You're clearly humble, too," I drawled.

"I am," he agreed. "I believe humility is necessary for a balanced life."

He was also clearly oblivious to sarcasm, but pointing that out seemed the wrong way to go. "I'm happy here. I have no idea if I'll stay, but I'm happy here for the time being."

"Because your parents lived here when you were a child? Did you come back because of them?"

The question threw me for a loop. "How do you know about my parents?"

"I'm privy to all personnel files."

"Yes, but ... why would you bother to even look me up?" And why did he pretend to know nothing about my past, including the time spent here, when that obviously wasn't true?

"Because I always like to know the people I'm dealing with," Mason replied without hesitation. "You're technically in charge here. The library discovery could be of significance. We're still going through all the books we collected. That could take months."

"My understanding is that the books, while potentially valuable, didn't offer anything new," I countered. "You seem to think they're a big find."

"I think there's definitely potential for a big find," he clarified. "I can't say anything with any degree of certainty until I have proof, but I feel in my bones that something big will come from the discovery."

He sounded sure of himself. "May I ask why you volunteered to come here?" I was honestly curious. "From what I've heard, you prefer spreading your talents to other finds ... ones that include talismans and one-of-a-kind items."

"You don't know we haven't found any one-of-a-kind items."

"I have a fairly good idea you haven't," I argued. "I saw the books. While some of them are beautiful, and will probably fit into the reaper library quite well, they don't seem to offer anything out of the ordinary."

"Do you read Sumerian?"

"No."

"Then how do you know that?"

His tone was so icy it made me want to jab him with a hot poker to loosen him up. "Let's just call it a hunch."

"Or you listened to that would-be researcher you were working with and he told you what to believe." Mason's lips curved downward. "You shouldn't listen to him. You should listen to me. I'm an expert."

He was also big on tooting his own horn. "I don't really care either way," I said finally, opting to take the conversation in a new direction. "I was interested when I thought the library might be able to help us figure out what the wraiths were doing, but that doesn't seem to be the case, so I don't really care where the books end up ... or what we learn from them."

"Knowledge is always important, no matter where it comes from."

"Sure. I'm a big fan of knowledge. I'm also a big fan of catching the enhanced wraith. I don't think anybody is safe as long as it's running free and feeding on souls at such a fantastic pace."

I realized my mistake too late to take it back. I shouldn't have let the increased soul collection tidbit slip in front of someone outside of the core group.

Intrigued, Mason leaned forward and pinned me with a penetrating look. "What souls are you referring to?"

Crap on a crap log. Why can't I ever keep my mouth shut? "It's a hunch," I offered hurriedly, hoping Mason was so self-absorbed he would believe the lie because boredom with a conversation that wasn't about him would force him to look elsewhere for entertainment. "I'm working on a theory that we can trace the increase in souls to the source and find the wraith. I plan to tell my boss about my theory tomorrow."

That was a complete and total lie. I'd already called Cormack with an explanation regarding what we'd found in the numbers — and he was definitely interested — but I had no plans to take it further than that. In truth, I didn't know what the numbers meant. Wraiths sucked souls so there was nothing to collect. An increase in souls would signify rampant death, but if the wraith was responsible, why wasn't it eating them?

"So ... you think that the wraith that escaped — and I've only heard a minimum about that because wraiths aren't my forte, so I apologize — but you think that wraith is killing people and a team of hunters will be able to track it that way."

I shrugged. That was as good an explanation as any. "Basically."

"What if you're wrong?"

I shrugged. "If I'm wrong, no harm done. If I'm right we'll be able to trap and kill it. That's what everyone wants, so ... that's the thing to hope for, right?"

"Of course." Mason bobbed his head, his expression thoughtful. "I guess I didn't give it much thought. You assumed the wraiths were after the books in the library. What would they want with the books?"

"I don't know. At first I thought they were going to try to cross over through the gate like the first wraith. They got distracted by me when I locked myself in the closet. When I discovered the library, I couldn't help but wonder if the wraiths were looking for answers there instead of the gate. Now I'm back to the starting point. I don't know what the wraiths wanted, but it's clear something weird is going on."

"We live in a paranormal world. Something weird is always going on."

"This is weirder than normal."

"Apparently so." Mason's smile turned indulgent. "I'm always up for a good tale. Tell me more about this wraith. As I said, I haven't heard much. I would like to know more."

"Okay, but it might take a while."

"We have an hour for lunch. Thrill me with your story."

I FELT DRAINED AFTER lunch with Mason. It wasn't that he was annoying — okay, he was, but it wasn't *only* that. He was also tedious, a constant questioner and so full of himself I couldn't fathom how he didn't explode under the pressure of his own hot air.

"You look beat," Oliver teased when I returned to the gate room. "How was lunch?"

"Terrible."

"Where's your friend?"

"He's chatting up Claire O'Reilly in the restaurant. He doesn't seem to pick up on social cues. I'm convinced she's going to hit him over the head with a frying pan and I don't want to be present because that will mean answering questions from the police when his body disappears."

"Good idea." Oliver beamed as he turned back to his computer. "By the way, you have a visitor."

I glanced around the room. It was just Oliver and me as far as I could tell. "Is my visitor invisible?"

He pointed toward the open door that led to the library. "In there."

I fixed him with a pointed look. "Who is it?"

"Black hair. Purple eyes. Loud mouth."

Braden. I wasn't expecting him to return until later this afternoon. Apparently he couldn't wait. That gave me a little thrill ... and I hated myself for it. I never fancied myself a girly-girl and here I was getting giddy at the prospect of spending five minutes with a man I hadn't even kissed. What was wrong with me?

"I'll take care of him."

I left Oliver to finish his work and strode to the library. I had to force myself to maintain a normal speed, which was another embarrassment, but I pushed it out of my head as I swung into the room. Instead of finding Braden — who I'd planned to congratulate for not interrupting my lunch — I found one of his doppelgängers perusing the empty shelves.

"Aisling?" I made a face, confused.

She turned slowly, her smile in place as she rested her arms on her stomach. If possible, it was even larger than the last time I'd seen her ... which wasn't very long ago. She seriously looked ready to pop.

"Hey, Izzy."

"What are you doing here?"

"I was bored." She shifted from one foot to the other, probably to alleviate the discomfort, and glanced back at the shelves. "My father said you found a library here with a lot of books. I don't see any books."

"Edgar Mason took them. He thinks they're a rare find."

"What do you think?"

"I think he thinks a lot of himself and it's best to let him believe whatever he wants to believe. Anything is better than listening to the man talk. He has only one topic he feels is worth conversation."

"Himself?"

"Yup. Do you know him?"

"No, but I know the type." Aisling sighed as she sank into the open chair to her left. The table and chairs remained dusty, but she apparently didn't mind. "My feet hurt again."

I couldn't hold back my smile. "Is that why you came? It's okay if it is. I understand you're dealing with a lot of pain and I want to help if I can."

"I came because I'm bored and sick of the men in my life telling me what to do," she fired back. "I'm pregnant, not an invalid."

Her huge stomach made me want to question that assertion, but even nine months pregnant I was certain she could physically take me if she put enough effort into the attack. "They're not trying to smother you with testosterone. They're simply trying to do what's best for you. They believe protecting you is the single most important thing they can do."

"I don't need protection. I'm not in danger."

"I think we're all in danger while that wraith is on the loose."

"That wraith isn't hunting in any neighborhoods I'm visiting, so I'm safe. For the first time in two years I'm not at the center of trouble. They should be happy about that."

"Because you're not happy about it?"

She shrugged. "It's not that I'm unhappy," she clarified. "I don't want anything to happen to the baby. I'm a little nervous about how my life is going to change. They should realize that locking me up does nothing but cause my irritation thrusters to fire on full. I need room to breathe."

The way she phrased it made me nervous. "Do they know where you are?"

"They think I'm taking a nap in my old bedroom at my father's house."

"How did you get here?"

"I stole my father's car. Don't worry. I didn't take one of the ones that looks like a penis, one of his midlife-crisis mobiles. I took one of the ones in the back. He won't notice."

"He'll notice you're missing."

"It's a huge house and I told him I was taking a nap. He's busy researching whatever you told him when you called earlier. He won't notice I'm gone."

I had my doubts, but I decided now wasn't the time to push her. "What do you want me to do?"

"Entertain me, of course."

Her grin told me that was going to be a painful prospect. "You're going to be obnoxious, aren't you?"

"You have no idea."

Twenty-Six

Aisling was a complaint machine. I had no idea if she was this way when she wasn't close to giving birth, but her personality grated in a way that set my teeth on edge.

"And then I told him that I won't wear that stupid watch because I know he wants to use it to track my every move," she continued with what I was certain was the longest story known to man. "It's an Apple Watch. That means it has GPS. He thinks he's smarter than me, but he's not."

"Hmm." I studied the graph Oliver was watching with interest. "The numbers seem normal so far."

"They do to me, too," Oliver agreed. "But that doesn't necessarily mean anything. The Grimlocks are the most active group, and they don't usually send until later in the afternoon."

A balled-up food wrapper hit the side of my face, causing me to swivel quickly and find Aisling's eyes lit with annoyance. "Do you need something?"

"Yes, I need attention," she drawled. "I came here to have an adult conversation, something that doesn't revolve around how many cases of diapers I think we should have ready for the big day and whether or not I want one of those bassinets with the handles so I can carry the baby around like a purse."

"Well ... how many cases of diapers do you think you need?"

"I don't want to talk about diapers."

"She was talking about her watch," Oliver volunteered. "She thinks her husband is trying to spy on her with it."

I looked at Aisling's bare wrist. "Obviously it's not working."

"That's because I put it on one of my father's giant lion statues. I don't want to be spied on."

"Have you considered he wants you to wear the watch so he can talk to you in case of an emergency?" I challenged. "You can place and accept calls on those things. Maybe he's worried that you'll forget your phone when you go into labor."

"Trust me. I never forget my phone."

"Fair enough. I still think he's simply trying to be an attentive husband. You should give him a break."

She narrowed her eyes to dangerous lavender slits. "Did he force you to say that? Bribe you, maybe?"

I didn't want to laugh. It would probably make things worse. I couldn't stop myself. "No. I've met him. He's devoted to you. I think most women would kill for a husband that devoted."

"I don't question his devotion."

"What do you question?"

"His methods. I'm not his child. *This* is his child." She pointed toward her stomach. "Sometimes I want to strangle him for doing this to me. And, yes, I blame him. She kicks and pokes constantly. I could never forget her."

I stilled, amusement and worry warring for supremacy. I decided to change the subject back to something familiar, something we'd already discussed, but I couldn't quite remember the specifics. "I thought you didn't find out if it was a boy or a girl."

"We didn't, but I know. It's a girl. She's going to be my penance for a childhood spent driving my father insane. He blames me for all his gray hair. I want to be upset about it, argue and stuff, but I know he's right. I'm about to get a whopping serving of karma and I'm not looking forward to it."

I risked a glance at Oliver and found him smiling. He was clearly amused by Aisling's show of petulance.

"A little girl might be fun," I offered, searching for the right way to soothe her ... or at least shut her up. "You were a girl. You turned out okay. Well, except for the whining. I think that should go away as soon as you give birth, though, right? That's not a normal thing, is it?"

Aisling's glare was back. "I don't whine."

Oliver and I snorted in unison.

"You've done nothing but whine since you got here," Oliver countered, shaking his head. "It's okay. I've dealt with a lot of whiners over the centuries. You're an amusing whiner, if that makes you feel any better."

I wrinkled my nose. "Centuries?"

"Years," Oliver quickly corrected. "I meant years. What? She keeps talking and it feels like centuries since we've had any quiet in here. Sue me. I said what I thought without thinking. I should fit right in with this group."

He wasn't wrong. Still, part of me felt bad for Aisling. "She's coming up on the big day. She can't help it if she's nervous. I think the edginess simply takes the form of whining. In a week or so, we won't even remember she acted like this."

"Oh, you'll remember," Aisling countered, her expression going dark. "I'll never let you forget. In fact, I'm going to make you babysit. You too, Mr. Talk Before You Think. I don't know you, but I'm guessing you're a fine babysitter. I'm going to line up babysitters so I can nap once this kid comes. She's never going to let me sleep. If you believe my father, he swears up and down he didn't sleep for a full four months after Aidan and I were born. I believe in karma, so that means I won't sleep for eight months."

"You and Aidan are twins," I pointed out, hoping to find something to calm her nerves. "Your parents didn't sleep after that because they had infant twins and three other children under the age of five. You won't have the same issues."

"I hope not."

"You won't."

"Are you saying that because you've seen something with your woohoo magic?" she asked hopefully.

"No, I'm saying it because it's obvious. You're not alone."

"My mother and father weren't alone either."

"That's not what I meant. You and Griffin aren't alone because you have a father and a bunch of brothers who are going to help you. Braden told me that your baby will be the most spoiled kid ever.

"He's actually looking forward to being an uncle," I continued. "He's going to help. I'm betting your other brothers are equally excited. They're going to do everything they can to make things easier for you. Your father wants to be the world's best grandpa, so he's going to help.

"So, despite all that, how do you figure you're alone?"

She blinked several times in rapid succession. "I guess I didn't look at it that way," she grumbled after a beat. "Still, I'm allowed to worry about these things. I can't do anything else. I can't work. I can't go shopping. My father says I can order things off the internet and he'll pay, but that's not nearly as much fun.

"He also says I can order whatever food I want, or put in a special request for candy, and he'll make sure I get it," she continued. "He's bending over backward to make sure I have everything I need."

"He sounds like an ogre," Oliver intoned, his fingers flying over the keyboard when a new batch of data started scrolling across the screen. "The Grimlocks are starting to dump their souls. It looks as if they had a busy day."

Aisling craned her neck to see the computer screen without getting up from the chair she insisted was now permanently melded to her butt. "What are you guys so interested in? You've had your heads bent together since I got here. What's up?"

"I don't know that anything is up. It's just ... we noticed a discrepancy with the soul numbers yesterday, between what we're expecting to get and what we actually get."

Aisling leaned forward, instantly alert. "Fewer souls?"

"That's what you would think given what's going on, but it's the opposite," I replied. "We're seeing more souls. Like ... a lot more."

"I don't understand." Aisling ran her fingers over her stomach as she leaned back in her chair, making a face that caused my heart to skip a beat.

"What was that?" I rolled my chair closer to her. "What was that?"

Bewildered, she glanced to her left and right. "What was what?"

"That. You made a face as if you were in pain. You're not in labor, are you?"

"You're the one who needs to calm down now," she chided, shaking her head. "I'm always in pain these days. If it's not one thing, it's another. These chairs aren't exactly comfortable. My back hurts. It's not the end of the world."

"Oh." I was embarrassed. "Sorry. I didn't mean to yell at you that way."

Aisling cocked a dubious eyebrow. "You haven't heard yelling until you steal my father's car and the police pick you up in it."

Oliver snickered. "Did that really happen?"

"Several times."

"No wonder your father blames you for his gray hair." Oliver pushed several buttons and slowly got to his feet. "The Grimlocks are sending another batch in about twenty minutes. Apparently they're waiting for two people to return. They're close."

I wasn't sure what he was getting at. "Okay."

"I'm going to run to the bathroom and then get something to drink," he volunteered. "I'll be back in time to watch you do the intake. You haven't handled it by yourself yet, and I think you need to get comfortable with the process."

Guilt coiled in my belly. "Yeah, I'm sorry about that. This whole week hasn't gone as I expected. I thought my biggest problem was going to be holding back my natural propensity to be a shrill busybody. That would've been a blessing at this point, huh?"

Oliver flicked my ear in a playful manner. "Things will work out. This week hasn't been easy, but we work in a field where death comes calling regularly. Nothing is ever truly normal."

He had a point. "Take your break. I'll stay here and entertain our guest. By the way, don't think I don't know what you're doing. You need a break from the mouth over here." I jerked a thumb in Aisling's direction and ignored her indignant grunt. "I don't blame you. I'll take watch this time. You can have the next watch."

"Oh, there's not going to be a next watch," he drawled as he moved toward the door. "I'm going to call her father and tell him where she is before that happens."

"Tattletale!" Aisling shouted.

"I like to think of myself as a survivalist."

Aisling watched Oliver escape the room with a dark glare, waiting until she was certain he was gone to speak again. "So ... what's going on with you and my brother?"

The question took me by surprise. "What?" I meant to sound innocent, as if I was truly surprised. Instead I sputtered, and almost tripped over the single word. "I have no idea what you're talking about."

"Yeah, you're a crappy liar," Aisling supplied. "We'll work on that going forward. If you plan to hang with my brother, you'll need to learn how to manipulate him. To do that, you'll have to be a much better liar."

I was flabbergasted ... and a bit uncomfortable. "What makes you think I'm doing anything with your brother?"

"I heard him talking to Redmond when he was getting ready for work this morning — I can't sleep for more than three hours in a row without having to go to the bathroom — and they thought they were speaking privately so he didn't hold anything back."

"So?"

"So, he said he spent the night with you."

A burning sensation crept up my cheeks. "It's not what you think."

Aisling studied my face. "He said that he slept in the chair by your bed."

"Okay, it's exactly what you think."

"He also said he was fine with it," she added.

"How was he supposed to feel?"

Aisling shrugged. "My brother isn't known for being the best date. In fact, there are times when I think he's something of a jerk when it comes to women. But he never just sleeps on the chair ... or the couch. He always gets some action."

"That must be those world-famous Grimlock looks," I muttered under my breath as I pretended to focus on the screen to avoid meeting Aisling's intense gaze. "He's handsome, so he thinks every woman wants to fall at his feet."

"All my brothers think that. It's not necessarily their fault because women have been throwing themselves at their feet since they were teenagers. We're talking grown women trying to get it on with sixteen-year-old boys. It was disgusting."

"I don't doubt it."

"The thing is, my brother is a horn dog and I've never thought otherwise," she pressed. "Last night, though, something happened that caused him to worry about you. He put you to bed, and instead of trying to put the moves on you he slept in the chair to make sure you were okay."

"It was a chivalrous effort," I agreed. It was also necessary due to the freezing rain, I silently added.

"It was a moment of growth," Aisling corrected. "He was more worried about you than he was about his own needs. That's huge for Braden."

"Well ... we haven't decided what we're going to do going forward." I was uncomfortable with the conversation. It felt like something I should be talking about with Braden, not his sister. "We need to get through this wraith crisis. Then we'll see what happens."

"What's going to happen is you're going to date my brother," Aisling said. "I'm going to give you tips on how to control him because I like you and I want this to work."

"You don't even know me."

"I know enough." Aisling smiled. "I think you're going to be good for him. I always assumed he'd bring home some bimbo to irritate me, so I'm happy with this development."

"I already told you that we don't know what's going to happen. I don't think you should bank on an outcome when it could go a different way."

"And you're deluding yourself because you're not ready to deal with what you're feeling," Aisling noted. "I find that just as cute as the way Braden asked Redmond if he would look like a schmuck if he bought you flowers."

My mouth dropped open. "You shouldn't be telling me this!"

"I have a big mouth. Everybody knows it. Braden should've made sure I wasn't eavesdropping in the hallway if he wanted to keep his secret. That's on him."

I wanted to shake her to keep words from tumbling out of her mouth. "I think we should change the subject. In fact ... ." As if on cue, my phone rang. I was relieved when I reached for it. Any distraction was welcome at this point. "Hello?"

"Izzy, it's Braden." He sounded frazzled, and I was instantly alert.

"Hi. Is something wrong?"

"We have a lot of somethings going wrong over here," he said, his voice devoid of all traces of warmth. "First, my sister is missing. She took off in my father's Bentley. He is spitting mad. We're searching every fast-food restaurant in a ten-mile radius."

Guilt threatened to overwhelm me and I swallowed hard. I really should've called to let him know where Aisling was. "She's with me. You don't have to worry about her. She's been sitting in the gate room watching us work all afternoon."

I could practically hear the string of profanity running through Braden's head on the other side of the call. "She's with you?"

"Yes. I fed her. Don't worry. She ate a burger and fries."

"I'm not worried about her eating. I'm worried about her dying."

"She's perfectly safe here."

"No, she's not," Braden barked. "That's why I called. We just had a confirmed wraith sighting. It was one of the gargoyles in Bub's group and we know where the wraith is heading."

Something about the way he phrased the statement caused my stomach to roll. "You're about to tell me something bad, aren't you?"

"I am," Braden confirmed. "The wraith is heading straight for you. It's probably already on the bridge, not far from the island. You need to find a place to hide ... and you're going to have to take my sister with you."

"What are you going to do?"

"We're on our way. We'll get there as soon as we can. It's storming, though. Traffic is a mess because the freeways are flooding under the overpasses. We're on our way, but it's going to be tight. You've got to figure out a way to hold off the wraith until we get there."

"Okay."

"I ... will be there as soon as I can." He sounded lost, but my mind was working at a fantastic rate and I couldn't worry about what he was feeling.

"Okay," I repeated. "I have to go now. I need to get your sister out of here."

"Good luck."

"I think I'm going to need it."

Twenty-Seven

"**W**e have to get out of here."

I intended to be calm, soothing and something of a protective figure when I informed Aisling it was time to flee. Instead, I panicked.

So much for being good in a crisis, something I'd always believed I was.

Aisling, who sat in the chair with her feet propped on the table and a package of licorice resting on her huge stomach, gave me a dark look. "I'm not leaving. Your friend Oliver bought me a huge stack of candy when he fetched my hamburger earlier. I'm eating it."

I pinned her with a serious look. "We have to go."

"Why? Do you turn into a pumpkin at eight or something?"

"No."

Aisling grew quiet as she gnawed her licorice and furrowed her brow. "Who was on the phone?"

"No one." It wasn't that I wanted to lie to her so much as I was desperate to keep her from panicking. Things were bad enough without adding Aisling's special blend of attitude to the mix.

"Who was on the phone?"

"A telemarketer."

"A telemarketer, huh?" Aisling chewed, thoughtful. "Was it Braden? You can tell me if it was. Do you guys have a date? I've already told you that I think it's great. You're much better than any of the other women he's dated, trust me."

"That's lovely." I made up my mind on the spot and strode around the table to grab Aisling's arm and force her to her feet. "You can tell me all about these women, but after I get you out of here. We can't stay."

For the first time since I'd ended the call with Braden, Aisling seemed to grasp that something had changed. Her expression turned serious. "What's going on?"

I wanted to lie, keep her from freaking out and making so much noise the wraith would have to be deaf not to find us. Instead, I realized that time was critical and I had no choice but to tell the truth. "The wraith is coming."

"Which wraith? The one who went through the gate?" Aisling did the opposite of panicking and instead bit into her licorice and calmly chewed while talking with her mouth full. "How do you know that?"

"Braden told me. It's been sighted on the bridge. It should be here any second."

She swallowed hard as she tilted her head, giving the appearance of great thought. "Are they coming? What am I saying? Of course they're coming. My brothers and father love a big rescue."

"They're coming," I confirmed, hoping that would make her feel better. "I don't know how long it'll take them to get here. There's a storm. Braden said the freeways are flooded in some places."

"Okay." Aisling forced a smile as she planted her feet on the ground and stood. The groan she emitted was enough to set my teeth on edge, but she was standing, and I considered that a win. "Where are we going?"

"I was thinking we should go to the casino." I put my hand to the small of her back to prod her toward the door. She waddled — there was no other way to describe how she moved — and her pace was slow enough that I wanted to scream for her to move faster. "There should be at least a few people there. I haven't visited the building yet, but it's got to be better than waiting here."

"Good point." Aisling was almost at the door when she pulled up short and froze in place.

I was so intent on getting her out of the room, I didn't notice she was no longer moving until I smacked into her back. "Don't stop!"

"Shh." Aisling pressed a finger to her lips and remained focused on the hallway outside the door. She was so serious, I knew right away something bad was about to happen.

"What is it?"

"Someone is out there."

"How can you tell?"

She shrugged. "This isn't my first wraith fight. Believe it or not, before I had a baby firmly planted on my kidneys, I fought them all the time."

"Great. I'll have a T-shirt made up in your honor," I drawled. "We need to get you out of this room right now except ... there's only one exit."

"I think it's too late for that anyway." Aisling remained rooted to her spot as a shadow danced in front of the opening. She didn't retreat, which would've been my first inclination in her position, and instead braced herself.

Thankfully for both of us, the figure that rushed through the doorway didn't belong to a wraith.

"Oliver?" I'd forgotten he was in the building, so I was understandably relieved. "I'm so glad you're here. We need to get out of this building. There's a wraith coming."

Oliver's eyes were blank as he glanced between us. Finally, he took me by surprise when he wrapped an arm around Aisling's waist and swung her heavy frame off the ground. He didn't look as if he was straining in the least as he curled her body against his chest. "It's not just one wraith. I counted five, and they're already at the front door. I saw them on the monitors when I was in the vending room."

My heart twisted. "Five? That can't be right."

"I don't know what the other four wraiths want — though I can hazard a guess — but the big one is with them. I recognize it from the day it came back through the gate. It seems even bigger than it did that day, if that's even possible."

I licked my lips as I glanced around the room. "What should we do? There's no way out of here."

"That's not entirely true." He strode toward the newly-discovered library. "There's one way out."

I scrambled to follow, casting a furtive look over my shoulder in case the wraiths attacked, and did my best to ignore Aisling's protests.

"Put me down, you Neanderthal," she groused, frustration evident. "I'm more than capable of walking."

"Not fast, you're not," Oliver shot back, his eyes narrowing as he searched the dim room. His gaze fell on a large window at the back of the space. I'd noticed it earlier — it seemed to look out into nothing — but Oliver seemed happy with the discovery. "There's a passage back there. It's old and probably dirty, but it leads to the outside. You should be able to escape that way, Aisling."

"You must be joking." Aisling glared into the darkness. "I'm not going in there. It's probably filled with snakes."

Oliver made a face. "Why would it be filled with snakes?"

"Because they prefer hiding in dark places ... and, yes, I heard how dirty that sounded the second it left my mouth. It's too late to take back, so we're going to pretend I didn't say it, okay?"

"I don't care if you turn into the filthiest talker in all the land," Oliver shot back. "You're going." He lowered her to the ground and pushed her closer to me before lifting a chair and aiming it at the glass. "Don't even think of arguing," he called over his shoulder. "I know you're thinking about doing some whiny thing that makes your father and brothers kowtow to your every whim, but I'm not one of them and it won't work on me."

I couldn't help being impressed as Oliver heaved the chair through the glass, the noise causing me to jolt as I focused on the door to see if anything — wraith or otherwise — would race in our direction. The doorframe remained empty.

"Hold on a second." Oliver poked his head through the opening he'd created and stared into the darkness. If I didn't know better —

truly, it was impossible for him to make anything out — I would think he actually saw something important. "You're clear." He grabbed Aisling again and started feeding her through the opening despite her protests. "You have a straight shot. The hallway is dark, but there's nothing on the ground to trip you. Take small steps. If you have your phone, use it as a flashlight. The corridor isn't long. Hopefully you won't have too much trouble opening the door at the other end."

Something occurred to me. "How do you even know there's a door at the other end?"

Oliver's eyes flashed with impatience. "Does that matter now?"

"It does to me."

"Well, we don't have time for a long story," he said. "Suffice it to say I've been here for a long time. I was here before this room was hidden from the world. I knew about this corridor before it was closed off ... and that was a good five years before the library was dry-walled over."

That couldn't be right. The room had been closed for at least fifty years. Oliver was thirty — maybe thirty-five if he moisturized a lot. There was absolutely no way he could've been around when the library was in use. "I don't understand."

"And I can't explain." Oliver's gaze was furtive as he balanced Aisling on her feet. "I'll stay behind and try to hold them off, try to keep them from jumping through the gate, which I think is their intention. You two need to run for safety."

I immediately balked. "No way. I'm staying with you."

"You're not." He was firm. "I have the best chance of surviving this. If the wraiths get their hands on you it will be over."

"Then I won't let them get their hands on me." I was grim as I focused on Aisling. She wasn't tearful or afraid. She was disgusted by her dusty surroundings, and anger seemed to be the emotion best reflected on her pretty face. I was amazed by that, and a bit reverent. "I have to stay. This is my job. The gate has to be protected. You need to get out of here. Your family will be here soon. Even if you just get in your vehicle and hide in the backseat with the doors locked, that should be enough. Be quiet and careful and you'll be okay."

The look Aisling shot me was withering. "Oh, this is such crap," she snapped. "I've fought wraiths before. I can help."

"You can barely walk," Oliver shot back. "Your reflexes are dulled. You'll hold us back."

I wanted to smack him for his thoughtless remark, but the way Aisling's eyes fired, I knew she had plans to do that herself.

"You have a baby to think about," I added, adopting a gentle tone. "You have to think of her. You're her mother, which means you put her safety above all else. You can't let her down the very first time you're challenged to protect her."

"Oh, well, that was just low," Aisling drawled, disgust positively dripping from her tongue. "I am going to wrap those words in toilet paper and set them on fire on your front porch the first chance I get."

"At least you'll get a chance," Oliver persisted. "You have to go. You've done nothing but fight for two years. We'll take it from here."

Aisling obviously wasn't thrilled with the order. "I'll be back to take my mantle. Don't get too comfortable in my shoes."

"We'll do our best."

I kept my eyes on Aisling until she disappeared into the darkness. I picked up a few stray thoughts as she used her phone to follow the wall and disappear around a corner. They were filled with murderous intent, and I had no doubt she would make us pay if the opportunity arose. I couldn't think about her now, though, despite the worry cascading through me. There were other things on our plate.

"So, how do we do this?" I focused on Oliver. "Oh, and what are you?"

Oliver refused to meet my gaze, instead turning his full attention to the door and striding back toward the gate room. "What do you mean?"

"You're at least sixty years old, from what I gather. Probably older. That means you're not human. Reapers age the same way as humans, so you're not a reaper either. What are you?"

"Does it matter?"

"I'd like to know since we're heading into battle together."

Oliver sighed and shook his head. "I'm a vampire."

The admission knocked me for a loop. "Excuse me?"

"Oh, don't give me that look. You're a worldly woman, Izzy. You're magical. I've seen you at work and I'm guessing you're going to be even more impressive tonight. You know other creatures exist."

"Yeah, but ... vampires aren't trendy. They're old. I thought you would be something trendy ... like another merrow or something."

"Merrow folk aren't trendy. They're old. Vampires never go out of style. Why do you think those *Twilight* books were so popular?"

"Because every teenager wants to believe she's special enough for a vampire to fall in love with and then serve as her personal bodyguard."

"Fair enough." Oliver rolled to a stop in the middle of the room and glanced around. "We need something to use as weapons."

"There are daggers in the closet." I pointed for emphasis. "I found a box when I was locked in there during that other wraith attack."

"Good. We're going to need them. Let's arm up. It's going to be a long night."

OLIVER WASN'T IN THE mood to talk, so we selected weapons in silence. Once finished, we positioned ourselves on the landing in front of the gate ... and waited.

"Do you think they'll try to cross the threshold?" I asked, my palms sweaty as I waited for a hint of movement on the other side of the door. "That's why they're coming here, right? I mean ... I can't think of a single other reason for them to cross."

"I can't either," Oliver admitted. "That makes the most sense. We can't let them achieve their goal. If one enhanced wraith is trouble, five could be the end of us all."

"The Grimlocks are coming." The idea made me feel better, even though my voice shook. "They'll be here as soon as they can manage it. The fact that they know Aisling is here should hurry them."

"It's storming out ... and hard. That's going to make crossing the bridge difficult."

"They'll come." I was sure of it. "That's what they do."

"We can't rely on them. We need to fight."

"Are you suggesting that I'm some weak female who needs a man to run to her rescue?"

"No, but you are doing a great deal of talking about five men running to our rescue."

"They'll even the odds." I refused to apologize for my pragmatism. "They'll even the odds and we'll be able to hold the wraiths off. That's the most important thing, no matter who does the killing and protecting."

"I don't disagree. It's just ... ." Oliver broke off, tilting his head as he lifted his nose. To me, it appeared he was scenting the air, which I found unbelievably distracting.

"What are you doing?"

"The wraiths aren't alone." He gripped his dagger tighter as he focused on the door. "There's at least one human with them."

The news took me by surprise. "A human? What human would be stupid enough to join forces with a cadre of wraiths?"

"I think he's talking about me," a voice drawled from the doorway, causing me to snap my head in that direction.

"Edgar Mason?" I was officially dumbfounded. "What are you doing here?"

"Creating a new world order."

I had no idea what that meant. "But ... why?"

"Because it's important. Allowing reapers to make all of the decisions when it comes to the start and end of the afterlife seems folly to me. I refuse to allow that to happen for one second longer."

I was having trouble wrapping my head around the notion that Mason, the world's biggest tool, was somehow the lead figure behind a wraith revolt. "I'm seriously lost. Do you understand what's going on here, Oliver?"

"Not even a little." Oliver wrinkled his nose as he regarded Mason. "I don't think he's the one in charge."

"Of course I'm in charge," Mason scoffed. "This was all my idea. I'm the leader."

"Someone might have led you to believe that, but you're hardly the leader." Oliver flicked his eyes to the door as another shadow appeared. "Here comes the leader right now, and I'm really sorry I didn't figure this out sooner, Izzy. I should have. In hindsight, I definitely should have."

If it was possible, I became even more lost. "What are you talking about?"

"He's talking about me," Renee said dryly as she strolled into the room, red leather pants gleaming under the limited light. "I'm in charge. I bet you weren't expecting that, were you?"

I was officially clueless.

Twenty-Eight

"I don't understand."

I looked to Oliver for help, but he was more angry than confused.

"Oliver understands, don't you, dear?" Renee sneered as she brushed past Mason and took a position in front of him, clearly showing her dominance. "You get it."

"Would you like to share with the class, Oliver?"

"She's a lamia," Oliver explained. "Basically a walking serpent. According to legend, lamia fed on children. They had serpentine traits — including tails — and could reanimate the dead to serve as soldier fodder during battles. They're rare now, almost extinct."

I'd never heard the term before. "They feed on children?"

"Only in olden times," Renee said, making a tsking sound that oddly sounded more like a hiss. Of course, now that Oliver mentioned serpents that could've been my imagination. "I'm not all that discerning when it comes to food now."

My mind was busy as I tried to wrap my head around the change of events. "So ... you eat people?"

"Not very often. I'm old. There are other ways to sustain myself."

"How?"

"Think about how the wraiths survive," Oliver prodded as he gripped his dagger tighter. "I often wondered if that's how she was sustaining herself. I watched when I figured out what she was, which wasn't until after I'd been around her for some time. But I didn't hear any reports of Detroit cannibalism, so I thought maybe she was snacking on other things."

"What? Like she was suddenly a vegetarian?" My temper lashed out. "You should have told me."

"You weren't ready to hear it," he snapped. "I'd planned to tell you when things settled — about her and me — but things have yet to settle. Now I see there was no chance of that happening as long as she was here."

"Oh, don't take that tone with me." Renee wagged a warning finger as she shifted closer to one of the wraiths. It seemed eager, agitated. I couldn't decide if it was excited about the prospect of crossing the threshold or feeding on us. Neither was appealing. "I never hurt you, Oliver. I never felt the inclination to do so. Had you stayed out of things tonight, it never would've happened. This is on you."

"I should've known when you called in sick." Oliver's fury was palpable. "You're a lamia. You don't get sick. I simply thought you were tired, maybe a bit overwhelmed from everything that's been going on. You played your part well, and for a long time. I have to hand it to you. You're right, that is on me. I should've realized what you had planned. All the signs were there."

"What signs?" I asked, frustration threatening to overtake me. "What signs?"

"The body," Oliver replied without hesitation. "The same body showed up on the island twice. He didn't die twice. His form was simply used a second time to throw us off."

"I admit that was my hope, but you didn't spend nearly as much time focusing on the body as I'd expected," Renee supplied. "I thought it would force you to look in another direction, perhaps toward a resurrectionist. I didn't realize the Grimlocks already dealt with a resurrectionist ... and recently. They weren't distracted by the body in the least."

"You spent a lot of time talking about the Grimlocks," I noted, racking my brain. "You pretended to be giddy about their looks, and harbored a few crushes. That was all an act."

"Not all," she clarified. "They're attractive men. They're also troublesome. I knew when they showed up that things would turn ugly.

"Initially, I thought that the wraith might be able to cross over without anyone noticing," she continued. "There was always the chance you would be too overwhelmed with first-day jitters to pay attention to the gate. That was stupid on my part. I didn't know about your ties to the gate until Oliver informed me ... and that was after the fact."

I felt sick to my stomach ... and furious. It wasn't as if I'd bonded with the woman. I didn't bond easily, and once I met the Grimlocks my attention was easily diverted. That didn't change the fact that I felt betrayed. It was sharp, like the dagger I gripped as I readied myself for a battle I was sure would come.

"The Grimlocks fouled things up for you. I'm glad for it."

"Of course you are." Renee's tone was dismissive as she sighed. "You fouled things up for me, too. I didn't realize you were the one who created the initial gate breach twenty years ago. If I had, things would've gone much differently. I would've tried to get you on my side before moving.

"I thought that because you were new to the job it would be easy to kill or baffle you," she continued. "I didn't know that you were the conduit that made traversing the gate possible. That was conveniently left out of the details regarding your parents' deaths.

"Oliver knew more than I realized, too," she said. "I was aware that he was here, with them, when you were a child. He could've warned me about what you were capable of, but he chose to keep it to himself. I thought he trusted me. That was also a mistake on my part."

I felt as if I was mired in quicksand. "What?" I flicked my eyes to Oliver, floored. "You knew my parents?"

"I did."

"Were you going to tell me?"

"Yes."

"When?"

"When you were ready."

His answer caused my temper to fire on all cylinders. "I've been ready for twenty years."

"No, you haven't." Oliver refused to back down. "You're not even ready now. We don't have time for this conversation. Renee is here to shove four more wraiths through the gate, if you haven't figured that out for yourself. She's building an army."

"But ... why?"

Renee shrugged, seemingly unbothered. "Why not? You heard Oliver. My kind is almost extinct. If the paranormal world has its way, we'll be completely extinct before another century ticks over. I won't allow that to happen.

"I might not have seen the beginning of time — even I'm not that old — but I refuse to have my time ended by some arbitrary decision that lamia are dangerous," she continued. "There was a time when we could've ruled the world. Now we're forgotten. I'm going to change that, for me and the few who remain."

"By creating an army of wraiths?" Even though the pieces were starting to fit together I couldn't grasp all of it. "Do you think you can control them?"

"I already control them. Wraiths are mindless beings, even when given super strength like this one." She poked the tallest wraith's shoulder and grinned. "They can't think for themselves. They need someone to do it for them. That's where I come in."

"And you think you can just order them around, make them do your bidding, and take over the world?" I'd heard better ideas on a Batman cartoon. "Are you the Joker now?"

"You don't have to be condescending," Renee shot back. "I understand that you don't agree with my methods. That's your right. We live in a free society, after all. That doesn't mean I'll put up with your mocking."

"You're going to kill us regardless. I might as well mock you."

"It doesn't have to be that way." Renee's tone turned innocent, smooth, as if she was about to offer me a pony. "You're powerful — perhaps more powerful than you realize — and you're an asset. We could work together. You could be my second in command."

"Hold up." Mason raised his hand and stepped in front of Renee, an obvious ploy to take control of the situation. "I'm in charge here. You're my second in command."

Renee shot him a withering look. "Who told you that?"

"Common sense," Mason puffed out his chest, which seemed to be his usual stance, and fixed Renee with what could only be described as a haughty look. "You approached me with your plan, if I recall. You needed my help because I was the one with access to old magic books that talked about crossing over. You couldn't have done this without me, which means I'm in charge."

"Oh, please!" Renee rolled her eyes. "You're unbelievable. While I did need the books, that doesn't mean I needed you. I could've found what I was looking for through other means. I chose you because manipulation of a human ego machine is easy. All I had to do was tell you how great you were and you fell for everything I said."

"That's because I am great."

"You're a tedious little lump with limited intelligence and a pomposity that makes everyone around you uncomfortable," she countered, her voice remaining calm, as if scolding a small child. "I kept you around because you make an excellent scapegoat. I mean ... who better to blame than the man who confiscated a roomful of hidden books and squirreled them away so others couldn't see them? That's so suspicious ... and people will easily believe that you're to blame for all of this."

"Not for the body," Oliver challenged. "Mason is a reaper. He can ferry the souls of the dead, but not raise their souls."

"As you so kindly pointed out, they're not focused on the body. They've paid almost no attention to it. I didn't kill him, by the way. That was my friend." She gestured toward the enhanced wraith, offering the creature a fond smile. "He didn't realize he wouldn't have to feed as much after his transformation. But he's learning. That's why he's been helping me move extra souls through to the other side. He understands things better than he ever did because his brain has been enhanced, too."

And that's when the final piece slipped into place. "You've been killing people, increasing the soul count on the sly, because you want extra souls in the waiting room ... or whatever it's called. The place right on the other side of the gate. They're close, ready to be accessed, and you brought your friends to take advantage of that today."

"Smart girl." Renee beamed. "Souls feed wraiths, but we're creating a species that is greater than wraiths. They need a charged essence. Souls don't get that essence until they pass to the other side."

"You see, this was all a theory we developed the past year," Mason volunteered, his lips curving into a smug approximation of a "we know more than you do" smile. "Renee and I ran into each other at a conference, got to talking, and we realized we both had the same desire: to live forever."

"You should simply watch *Fame* and live forever that way," I suggested.

"I prefer our way." Mason's smile disappeared. "If the wraiths can absorb the essence and return to what they once were, only stronger, then we'll be able to do the same. If Renee is stronger, she'll ensure the lamia line doesn't die out. If I'm stronger, well, the world will simply be able to enjoy my superior intelligence for a longer stretch of time. Who doesn't want that?"

"I can think of a few billion people," I said dryly as I glared at him. "What is wrong with you? I don't agree with Renee, but I can see why she's acting the way she is. She's selfish and going to fail, but her reasoning probably feels sound in her freaky corner of the world.

"You, though, are supposed to be smart, but you don't see what's happening around you," I continued. "You don't get that Renee was using you and you're not going to live to see your happy ending."

"Of course I am. Don't be ridiculous."

"She's not being ridiculous, Edgar," Renee countered, sliding a sidelong look in her comrade's direction. "She's right. You're not part of the endgame here."

He balked, fear flickering through his eyes for the first time since he'd walked into the room. "I am the endgame."

"No, but this is the end for you." Renee was calm. She took two steps, placed a hand on either side of his face and smiled. "Wasn't it fun while it lasted?"

Mason didn't get a chance to answer because the lamia viciously jerked his head to the side, snapping his neck and causing my knees to go weak as she released him and let his body drop to the floor, her expression never shifting. She didn't so much as give him a second look, instead focusing on me.

"Isn't that better?" Renee was ridiculously happy, which made me leery. "He never did understand about keeping his mouth shut."

"What's your plan?" Oliver asked as I swallowed hard. "Are you going to kill us, allow the wraiths to cross over and return, and then report that you stumbled over our bodies tomorrow morning?"

"You're good at this." Renee's smile never wavered. "That's exactly my plan. I was hopeful that you wouldn't be here, Oliver. I was even hopeful that Izzy wouldn't be here, because her past intrigues me and I was hoping for more time with her. I need to learn more about that breach."

"I don't remember a breach," I snapped, my temper building. "I don't remember what happened when I was a kid. I've already told you that."

"I don't believe that's true. The memories are there. You've simply blocked them out."

"Why do you even care?"

"I think we can be powerful allies."

"That's not going to happen." I readjusted my grip on the dagger. "We're not going to let you send those wraiths through the opening. You have to know that's not going to happen."

"I recognize you're not the type to back down," Renee corrected. "But you can't stop us. You don't have the strength. Oliver might be stronger than a normal human, but he's not a superhero. And you, my dear, have a lot of power, but you've never used it in battle.

"There are two of you and six of us," she said. "Who do you think is going to win?"

I hated the question, the sense of dread it caused to roll over me. That didn't mean I could back down. I opened my mouth to answer, tell her she would have to kill me to see her endgame come to fruition, but didn't get a chance.

"Well, I guess that depends," Braden announced as he stepped into the room behind Renee, his eyes molten lavender fire. "Now there are seven of us and six of you. How do you think that's going to end?"

Renee jerked her head to look over her shoulder, her eyes going wide when the other Grimlocks appeared in the doorway to flank Braden. They were all armed, and none of them looked happy.

"I guess we're about to find out," Renee said, resigned.

"I guess so," Braden agreed, raising his dagger as the nearest wraith moved closer. "Let's see who is left standing."

I openly gaped as the Grimlocks fanned out, watching in slack-jawed awe as they began dispatching wraiths with fantastic speed. Perhaps sensing that her small army was about to fall, Renee did the opposite of what I expected and moved toward the gate rather than the exit and freedom.

"What are you doing?" I asked, sliding to my left to cut her off. "You can't possibly think I'm going to let you cross the threshold."

"You have no choice." Renee's fingers ignited with flame as she shoved them in my direction, my heart stuttering as I jerked back my head to keep her from touching me. "I'm not going to let you stop me."

"Izzy!" Braden yelled out the warning, but I knew better than to look at him. All Renee needed was a moment of distraction to take me down. I had no intention of letting her.

Instead, I dropped my dagger and raised my hands, the tips of my fingers twitching as I called for the magic I always kept a firm lid on. *"Insandi."*

The fire that erupted from my fingertips was purple, much like Braden's eyes, and I caught Renee's wrists before she could touch my face. I had good reflexes, my grandfather made sure of it, and the lessons he taught me over the years stuck hard and fast.

"What are you doing?" Renee grimaced as the fire I conjured burned into her skin. "What is that?"

"The end," I replied without hesitation, catching a glimpse of my reflection in the mirror as my face shifted into the mask of my Bruja people. It was something I didn't even know I could do until I was a teenager, and it terrified me the first time. I wasn't terrified now. I felt powerful ... and ready. "Your end."

"What are you?" Renee's eyes filled with fury ... and fear. "You're more than a Bruja."

257

"We're all more than the sum of our parts," I replied, allowing the magic to whip free and take on a life of its own. "Even you are more than you were born to be. It's too bad you didn't try to be good rather than evil."

"Let me go!" Renee's panic was palpable as she fruitlessly struggled against my grip. "You can't do this! I'm not ready to go."

"You should have thought about that before you attacked." I gave her another jolt of magic before removing my hands, watching in grim fascination as the purple fire engulfed her body ... and swallowed her screams. She flailed, her mouth open and her hands searching for an escape, but it was too late. Within seconds, the only thing left of Renee was the distinct scent of burning flesh ... and the eerie veil of purple smoke.

"Holy moly!" Redmond appeared in the spot next to me, his eyes filled with wonder. "Did you just burn her with your mind?"

"No. I used my hands." As if to prove that, I shook my fingers to extinguish the flame. After a moment of staring, I dragged my eyes to the rest of the group and found our team unharmed. Everyone from the rival group — except for Mason, who was dead on the floor — was gone, turned to ash. "The enhanced wraith?"

"It took two of us," Braden replied, swiping at a smudge on his face with the back of his hand. "We managed to take it out."

"Good." I looked around the room. "Um ... what do we do now?"

"For starters, I'd like to know where my daughter is." Cormack's voice was demanding. "I thought she was with you."

"She was," Oliver volunteered. "We were worried about her being in a fight. I created an exit for her, told her to flee. She should be long gone."

"Aisling never does what she's supposed to do," Aidan complained. "We need to find her."

"That won't be necessary," Aisling announced, appearing in the doorway behind her family. She was drenched from head to toe and looked a little worse for wear as she leaned against the doorframe. She also appeared furious. "I'm right here."

"You were supposed to run." Oliver's tone was accusatory. "You weren't supposed to circle back. I get that you were trying to help, but that was stupid."

Aisling snorted. "Forget help. I knew you were fine. I didn't come back to help you."

"Why did you come back?" I demanded.

"Because my water broke and I'm in labor. I need you morons to help me."

"Oh."

My eyes widened as the Grimlock men erupted into chaos, the furious fight already forgotten as they closed ranks around their sister and daughter.

"Someone needs to carry her," Redmond bellowed.

"It's not going to be me," Braden shot back.

"I don't want to touch her because she's got, like, baby juice or something on her pants," Aidan complained.

"It's not baby juice," Cillian shot back, casting his father a worried look. "Right? There's no such thing as baby juice, is there?"

Cormack was grim as he stepped closer to his daughter. "You're in big trouble for stealing my car."

Aisling grimaced as she held her stomach. "Can we fight about it later? I think something is about to rip free from my loins."

"Oh, gross!" The Grimlock brothers groaned in unison.

"We will definitely talk about it later." Cormack gripped his daughter's elbow. "You'll be paying to get that car detailed. You've been warned."

"Yeah, yeah, yeah."

Twenty-Nine

The trip to the hospital was panicked hilarity. No one wanted to sit next to Aisling in the back seat because they were afraid to get any goo on them, but when she whined three brothers ended up cramming in with her as a wall of protection.

Once at the hospital, Cormack started flashing money to make sure she got a private birthing suite and was made as comfortable as possible. Griffin raced to the hospital as soon as Cillian called. He was so discombobulated when he arrived that he couldn't remember where he'd left his car.

Cormack promised to find it for him before sending the daddy-to-be into the suite, stopping long enough to comfort his daughter as she cursed all men for her predicament, and then slowly eased into the hallway.

"How long are we supposed to wait?" Aidan asked as he paced the lobby, a cup of untouched coffee in his hand.

"Until the baby decides to come," Cormack replied. He sat in a chair and stared at the hallway that led to the birthing suite. By all outward appearances, he was calm. I could read the anxiety washing over him, though. "First babies can take time. I remember when your mother went into labor with Redmond. I didn't think I was ready.

Thirty-seven hours later, I was definitely ready and he was still being stubborn."

Redmond snorted. "How long did it take for Aisling to come?"

"Quicker. By then we had some practice."

Cormack was an expert at shuttering his emotions, but his defenses failed him now. Instinctively, I reached over and gripped his hand. "She'll be fine."

He slowly slid his eyes to me, his lips curving. "Is that something you've seen?"

I opened my mouth, unsure how to answer. "It's something I know," I said finally. "She'll be fine ... although I'm sure the tale of this birth will haunt you all until your dying days."

Braden snickered as he lowered himself beside me on the couch. "You've got that right. She's going to milk this birthing thing until she bleeds Dad's bank account dry."

"I have no problem with that." Cormack's eyes moved back to the hallway. "I wish we knew how things were progressing, that she was okay."

"I'm sure she's threatening Griffin with great bodily harm," Cillian offered. "She'll be fine. She's strong. She's always been strong."

"She has," Cormack agreed. "This is something that's out of her control, though. She can't simply will herself through this."

"I wouldn't be so sure of that," I offered. "If anyone can, she can."

"Yes, well ... ." He tapped his fingers on the arm of his chair. "Let's talk about something else." He needed to change the subject. "Let's talk about what happened tonight. I've been in contact with the reaper council. The members will handle the removal of Edgar Mason's body. It's not being reported to the police, so make sure you don't mention it in front of Griffin."

"He has other things on his mind," Cillian pointed out. "He won't ask."

"Plus, he has the next six weeks off," Braden added. "He won't care about anything but Aisling and that baby for the foreseeable future. We caught a break there."

"We caught multiple breaks tonight." Cormack's eyes were thoughtful as they slid to me. "Just how powerful are you?"

Generally I preferred when people were upfront with their questions. This time, I couldn't help but squirm. "I don't know what you mean."

"You killed Renee with your bare hands," he pointed out. "Fire spouted from your fingertips. You were calm when you were doing it, too. I don't think this was your first time fighting an enemy like the one you faced tonight."

"I'd never heard the term lamia until tonight," I corrected. "As for what happened, I don't know how to explain it. I inherited the ability from my mother. As for the full extent of what I'm capable of, I don't know. I don't spend much time testing my abilities."

"You should. You might be very helpful in the future."

"Maybe."

"Definitely," Cormack pressed.

"Don't give her grief," Braden ordered, taking me by surprise. "She's had a long night. You can talk to her about the magic later. The thing that we care about most is that the wraith has been neutralized and no one is trying to cross through the gate. The rest of it can keep."

Cormack narrowed his eyes as he regarded his son. "I guess you're right. We will talk about this at a later date, though." His statement was aimed directly at me.

"I can't wait." In truth, they had no idea the scope of what went down during the course of the evening. They weren't there when Renee mentioned I was the one who fueled the previous breach, something I couldn't remember. They weren't there when I found out that Oliver was present when my family was killed. I wasn't keen to share that information. It was something that would have to be explored later ... like when the Grimlocks were busy doting on the new addition to their family. Then I could track down and extract the truth from Oliver, who'd conveniently stayed behind when everyone else hopped into Cormack's vehicle to transport Aisling to the hospital.

"You did good work tonight, Izzy," Cormack supplied, taking me by surprise. "You fought hard; you were honor and duty-bound despite overwhelming obstacles. If you thought you didn't deserve your position, I think you found out otherwise this evening."

Even though my nerves remained frazzled, my mind a beehive of thoughts, his words were like a warm blanket as they settled over me. "Thank you."

"You're welcome."

I FELL ASLEEP, exhaustion finally claiming me as my head rested on Braden's shoulder. He woke me with gentle prodding shortly before dawn.

"What's wrong?" I was instantly alert.

Braden smirked. "I guess that depends on how you look at things. Technically, nothing is wrong. But the baby is here."

"Oh." I rubbed my eyes to chase away the remnants of sleep. "I guess we're supposed to see her now."

"Aisling? Yeah."

"No, Lily."

Braden stilled, his jaw tightening. "What do you mean?"

"The baby. Lily. She wants to see us."

"The baby is a girl?"

I nodded as I slowly got to my feet. "Lily Grimlock-Taylor. She's going to run you all ragged."

"I have no doubt about that." Braden gripped my hand as he led me toward the maternity wing. His brothers and father were missing from the lobby, which told me they'd raced to Aisling's side the minute they heard the news. "You're sure it's a girl? The nurse didn't tell us that. Apparently Aisling wanted it to be a surprise."

"I'm sure. What's more important, Aisling was sure before she even gave birth. She knew."

"I'll take your word for it."

AISLING'S SUITE bustled with activity. Cormack, Aidan, Cillian and Redmond gathered around the bed as Griffin cradled his infant daughter — complete with pink hat and blanket — and rested next to his exhausted wife.

Aisling was alert, although she looked as if she'd been through a war. Her dark hair was soaked through with sweat and her eyes were red and puffy from crying. Still, in the center of it all, the queen seemed to be enjoying her reign.

"It's a girl," Redmond offered excitedly when he saw Braden.

"It's a little girl who will be sweet and cute," Cillian corrected. "Her mother never was. We can train this one from the start."

Aisling rolled her eyes. "She's not going to be sweet and cute. She's going to be a terror." She tipped her finger into the blanket to stare at the sleeping baby. "She does seem kind of sweet now, though, doesn't she?"

"Definitely." Aidan bobbed his head. "I called Jerry, by the way. He's supposed to be here any minute. He'll be so ticked he missed the birth — he was planning on being your surprise coach — but he'll probably forget that fairly quickly once he sees her. How could he remember his outrage now that she's here?"

"Oh, he'll remember," Griffin intoned, wonder etching across his face as he stared at the baby. "Look how pretty she is. She looks like you, baby."

Aisling snickered. "She's going to act like me, too. Don't kid yourself."

"I think you're building that up bigger than it needs to be," Griffin chided. "She's a baby. She'll want baby things. How hard can that be?"

"Famous last words," Cormack teased, clapping his son-in-law on the shoulder. "Now, hand her over. You've held her enough."

"I just got her," Griffin complained.

Cormack refused to back down. "I want to hold her. I'm the grandpa. That's my right."

"Fine." Griffin made a face before handing over his daughter, taking advantage of the fact that his arms were free to move his hands to Aisling's shoulders so he could shift her to rest against him. "She has black hair like you guys."

"What color are her eyes?" Braden asked. He'd been careful to stick to the other side of the room, not getting too close to the baby for reasons I couldn't quite ascertain.

"They're lavender," Aisling answered.

"I think those genes are pretty much unstoppable," Griffin added.

"It's probably good that I'm a fan of the black and purple combination."

Aisling nodded as she rested her head against his chest. "Yeah."

"What's her name?" Braden asked, focusing on the pink bundle in his father's arms.

"Lily," Aisling replied.

Braden briefly pressed his eyes shut. "That's a good name."

"I thought so." Aisling's eyes filled with tears. "I guess we didn't completely lose her after all, huh?"

"You never completely lost her," Cormack said, tilting his head to the side when the sound of a loud voice in the hallway assailed his ears. "Jerry is here."

Oh, wow, the famous Jerry! I could hardly wait. I turned to the door expectantly, widening my eyes when a flurry of movement barreled through the door.

His hair was dark, although not Grimlock dark, and his eyes bright. He wore a mint green suit that looked as if it should've been mothballed fifty years ago. His outfit was cheerful, but he didn't look happy.

"I can't believe you people cut me out of this! I'll never forgive you."

"The baby is here, Jerry," Aidan noted. "Her name is Lily."

"Of course her name is Lily." Jerry stomped closer to Cormack to see the baby's face, his expression gentling when he got his first look at his niece. "She's spectacular."

"She wasn't so spectacular when she was ripping me apart on her way out," Aisling argued.

"I want to hold her." Jerry reached for the baby, but Cormack turned his shoulder to keep him from grabbing his granddaughter.

"I'm holding her right now."

"I'm her favorite uncle."

"And I'm her only grandfather. I've got dibs."

"Please, people, you're giving me a headache," Aisling complained, sliding lower on the bed. "You're all going to get a chance to hold her ... and babysit ... and change diapers. No one will be left out."

"I don't think you'll have to convince us of that," Braden said as he drifted closer to the baby. "We'll gladly do all of it ... even the diapers."

"Of course we will." Cormack took me by surprise when he shifted the baby to Braden's arms, something unsaid passing between him and his son. "She's part of the clan. Once you're part of the clan, there's no shaking us."

"No," Braden agreed, slowly lifting his eyes to me. "I believe I was trying to tell someone something similar earlier today."

"I think she'll figure it out on her own," Cormack offered helpfully.

"Who are we talking about?" Jerry asked, confused. "Are we talking about the baby? I missed something."

"You did, but I'll fill you in later," Aisling said. "For now, I need a nap ... and some ice cream."

"I'll handle the ice cream." Cormack smoothed his shirt. "It's my job as spoiler-in-chief, after all."

Aisling's smile was sly. "And don't you forget it."

Printed in Great Britain
by Amazon